BULLET PROOF

WATERPROOF NAVY SEALS

JO CHAMBLISS

Bulletproof
By Jo Chambliss

Copyright 2022 by Hover Press
ISBN: 9781088105276

Edited by: Audrey Pitt

Cover Design by: CK Book Cover Designs

For Rose
Editor, teacher, friend

BULLETPROOF

JO CHAMBLISS

CHAPTER 1

TIMOTHY "STONE" O'REILLY

This is the last time I let that asshole, Bishop, set me up on a date.

It just so happens that this is also the first time I let the moron set me up on a date. I would rather sit at home plucking out my pubes one-by-one than spend another minute with the monster bitch I've been saddled with for the night.

"She's just your type, Stone. You have a ton in common. And she's hot," he'd said.

I swear to everything holy, the man may know God, but he doesn't have the first damned clue about women.

The night from hell started out fine. Nicole, my blind date, blew me away when she answered the door looking like a supermodel. Bishop had been right about that, at least. The way her emerald-green dress hugged her body from her tits down to the flare at her knees was enough to make a man drool. Long blond hair, pale skin, and plump red lips curled in a come-hither grin had my brain malfunctioning when it was time to introduce myself.

However, all my hopes for a fun evening were dashed against the rocks the moment the harpy opened her mouth. *"Um… how old are you? James said you were, like, thirty. You should shave or dye your beard to look younger."*

And that was just the start of it. Things just went downhill from there. Next came low-key insults about me being a naval officer driving a Ford Fusion.

I'm not the kind of guy that puts up with shit like that. The only reason I bit my tongue and stayed the course is that I agreed to the date with Nicole as a personal favor to Bishop's girlfriend, Lucy. Nicole is Lucy's cousin. She's in Virginia Beach, visiting her mother for a few days. Lucy, being as nice as she is, didn't want to leave Nicole out while the rest of us lived it up at the Navy's annual birthday celebration.

Being the only single guy in our group and ever the faithful friend, I was volun*told* for the job by Bishop. Loyalty like that is an admirable quality to have, but right now, I fucking hate myself for it. Still, a promise is a promise, so every thirty seconds at least, I remind myself that this is for Lucy, and I keep from driving my car into each building I see.

By the time we arrive at the DC venue hosting the ball, I've never been more thankful to end a car ride. Now, all I have to do is survive the night. At least Lucy will split Nicole's attention and offer me a reprieve. I hope.

It turns out that I have no such luck. Nicole barely glances at her cousin, keeping firmly to my side and in my ear throughout dinner. Over each course, I have to listen to Nicole talk about her dreams of becoming a famous influencer, complaining about the stuffy Navy traditions, joking about how bufty-whatever the hell that means– the enlisted sailors' uniforms look, how butch the female officers' uniforms are, and on and on and on.

During one such tirade, I notice Warden and Bishop trying their hardest not to laugh. They're enjoying this — *the bastards*. Although I wish like hell I had a way to make them join in my suffering, I remember why I'm doing this at all. *Stick it out for Lucy. Just a bit longer.*

Cousins. I swear to God, I don't know how these two women could be from the same family or the same species, really. And I kinda don't get what Lucy sees in that asshat, Bishop. If he's not a complete idiot, he'll do himself a favor and hang on to her.

Then I realize if he marries Lucy, he'll get to deal with Nicole at family functions for the rest of his life. That almost makes my misery worth it.

"Ermahgerd. How long is this speech going to last?" Nicole whines.

Okay, maybe not.

The single, happiest moment of my night is when the ball ends, and Warden's girlfriend, Trish, declares her feet to be done. Knowing those

3

two, that's code for *I'm ready to get laid,* but I'll take it — anything to get out of here.

Lucy is also ready to bow out, meaning no one will suggest an after-party. Everyone agrees to call it a night, thank God. As we walk out, Warden and Bishop bring up the rear, cackling about something. I imagine they're making bets on whether I bed the gorgeous troll I brought to the party. I would rather volunteer for an STD infection and treatment study.

The six of us leave the banquet hall, heading for the valet stand in front of the hotel. There's a bit of a line waiting, which means I'm stuck here with Nicole a while longer. I turn back to see if the group wants to go to the bar and wait out the crowd, but my friends aren't behind me. Lucy and Trish have Bishop and Warden pinned against the wall, and no one is getting felt up. Trish has her finger pointed at Warden's nose, and I watch in amusement as Lucy smacks Bishop on the shoulder.

Curious, I turn away and back up a few steps to eavesdrop, careful not to get too close. I can just pick out what Lucy says when she whisper-yells at the men, *"Stone hasn't said a word all night. I told you not to set him up with Nicole. Now, he's miserable, and I'll get to spend every day at work for the next two months listening to her complain about how he ghosted her."*

At work? So, that's it. My set up was a setup. If I hadn't been a breath away from stabbing myself in the eye all night, I might actually be impressed by how well they pulled this off. I'll still have to kill them, though.

Now, it's time to let them know hell's coming.

I circle behind my two best friends, position myself between them, and bring my hands up to rest on the backs of their necks. To those around us, we probably look like three guys posing for a group shot. If only they were that lucky.

With a painful grip on their delicate pressure points, I plant a smile on my face and gush, "You guys… You're just the best. I can't tell you how much I enjoyed the evening. I'm going to pay you both back real soon."

The pair try to appear unaffected, but Bishop's eyes are watering, giving him away. My date preens, assuming I'm pleased with her, making me squeeze tighter. The two pricks duck out of my death grip before the pressure can make them drop to their knees.

I wink at Lucy, who winks back. *Well damn. Overhearing her was no accident.* Bishop had better hang on to her. She's probably the only human capable of keeping his ass in line.

The valet line moves faster than I thought, and a driver soon arrives with my car. I swear, I've never been happier to escape a social gathering. By the time I've driven back to Nicole's hotel, she's made three suggestions to come to her room for a drink and numerous touches to my arm and leg. All of them went ignored. Unfortunately, she doesn't take the hint.

I'm not a man with a fragile ego, but she knocked my beard, my car, and my profession. I'd have to be one sorry asshole to want her after that.

Pulling under the portico at the hotel's entrance, I wave off the valet as Nicole grips my thigh tightly, shifting her hand just enough to brush up against my flaccid dick. *Nope. Un uh. Hell to the fucking no.*

I'm out of the car in a flash, running around the hood to her side. Steeling myself for Custer's last stand, I open Nicole's door and brace myself for her last bit of theatrics. She flashes a lot of leg getting out of the car, but I am not tempted. Not even a little. I deposit Nicole at the door and remove the hand wrapped tightly around my arm. "I hope you enjoyed your evening. Good night."

Nicole stands at the entrance with her mouth hanging open as I all but run back to my car, breathing a sigh of relief when I slip in behind the wheel— alone.

Instead of bedding down for the night at my hotel, I pack all my shit and head home. The four-hour drive back to Virginia Beach should be enough for me to cool off. If it isn't, I can always take an icy swim in the ocean.

During the long drive, I use the time to plot

the slow torture of my so-called friends, Dillan "Warden" Knot and James "Bishop" Stoddard. I won't get them back right away. They'll be expecting that and will be on guard. Nope. This level of payback deserves to marinate for a while. I'm going to take my time; let them sweat a little. Then, I'll strike when they least expect it.

I reach Virginia Beach around one a.m. and stop for gas and a candy bar. The anticipation of the chocolate splurge perks up my mood, underscoring just how shitty my night has been. *You know your date was a trainwreck when a Snickers bar is the highlight of your night.*

The night is warm for mid-October, and the new moon leaves the sky void of any light outside the manmade kind. Even the clouds are hiding the stars tonight. A strange night all around. At least it's quiet. I need a year's worth of silence to recover from Nicole's *stimulating* conversation.

There's only one car at the station when I turn in. I pull alongside the pump opposite of a black Passat and hop out to top off my tank.

About five bucks into my fill-up, a cute woman wearing scrubs and a lab coat more or less stumbles out of the convenience store carrying a Red Bull and a snack cake. Her dark hair is a sexy mess on her head, and her eyes are hidden behind barely open lids. In short, the woman looks dead on her feet.

I watch in amusement as she walks up to

my car and tugs on the driver-side door handle. When the door doesn't open, she tilts her head and squints her eyes tighter. Not once does she look up, meaning she doesn't notice me standing at the back, filling the tank with gas.

The breeze loosens strands of hair from her messy bun, and they stick to her face, adding to her frustration. She bats the rogue strands out of the way, but the wind blows the silky locks right back.

The woman gives up on taming her wild hair and lets her hand fall back to her side. The gas pump shuts off, indicating my tank is full, and I replace the handle in a hurry, not wanting to miss seeing what the woman does next. I turn back in time to watch her try the handle again and swear at the door for not opening. Next, she pulls out her keys.

A beep sounds from the black Passat as she presses a button on the fob. Then, the pretty lady tries the handle one more time. At her dirty curse, I can no longer hold back an amused chuckle. "Can I help you, ma'am?"

She jumps in surprise and stares blankly at me for several breaths. Her eyebrows knit together, and now she looks, really looks, at the car she's trying to get into. Her cheeks turn a charming shade of pink, and she lets her shoulders droop. "Shit. I'm sorry."

Her voice, made for candlelit bedrooms, caresses my skin and heats my body from the inside out. *Down, boy.* "No harm done, Miss, though I wonder if there might be if you get behind the wheel as tired as you are."

"Doctor," she says without lifting her head.

"Pardon?"

"It's Doctor, not Miss. And it's fine. I live just—"

"Whoa! Hey!" I throw up my hands to stop her from pointing and look around the otherwise empty gas station parking lot. Her eyes widen just before squeezing shut, and her face bunches up in embarrassment.

"Don't tell a stranger where you live, and certainly don't point people in that direction! Do you not have any sense of self-preservation?"

The woman is so beat that she doesn't even ruffle at my half-joking, half-scolding tone. She shoves a stray hair from her face and sighs. "I would like to say yes, but I did become a doctor, so I guess not."

That's when all my humor evaporates, replaced by genuine concern. I wouldn't stand by while any civilian was in danger, but this lady calls out to me in some primal way, bringing out all my protective instincts. "You should call someone to come get you. I know the owner of this place. He won't mind if you leave your car here until morning."

"Oh. There's no one at home…" She pauses, and her cheeks flash a deeper red when she realizes her mistake. "…and I just broke another safety rule, didn't I?"

My smile returns. "I'm beginning to think you're a lost cause."

My comment is rewarded with a bashful smile that even the harsh security lighting above can't spoil.

Through a yawn, she says, "Most people believe doctors have a God complex and think themselves invincible."

I lift my hand to my chin and give it a thoughtful squeeze. "Hmm. Not picking up that kind of vibe from you." Dropping the hand again, I turn serious and add, "I don't think it's wise for you to drive in this condition. Can I call you a cab?"

Her nose scrunches up at my suggestion. "I'm a doctor. I wouldn't get in a cab without a hazmat suit. I'm sure I'll be—" Another massive yawn interrupts her overconfident self-assessment. When the yawn is over, I wait expectantly for her to finish her statement, but she never does.

"Tell you what. I think I've got a plan to get you home safely that won't involve you catching some rare communal cab disease or ending up on the news."

"I'm listening," she mumbles.

"We go back inside, where I give the clerk my ID and keys. I'll drive you home in your car and catch a cab back here. I've had my communal cab disease vaccine. You call the clerk to report that you're home safe, but I still have to return in a certain amount of time, or he calls the police and informs them that I'm up to no good."

The brunette beauty rubs her eyes and chuckles at me, but then her sleepy smile morphs into bewilderment. "You're serious."

"As the oath I swore to the Navy."

Her eyes roam from my face for the first time, finally noticing the dress uniform. The exhausted doctor is frozen, trying to decide if I'm crazy, or if she is for not immediately turning me down. She sways on her feet and then looks at the clerk watching us through the window.

I'm genuinely shocked when the tired doctor answers with a whisper, "Okay."

Her bashful consent has me rushing to comply. Quick as a flash, I move my car, then pull out my license, military ID, and keys, jogging them inside to the clerk that I'm on a first-name basis. He's laughing his ass off, having figured out what's going on. I'm just trying to hurry so the lovely doctor doesn't talk herself out of the plan. For some reason, I'm not ready to leave her company.

As I guide the zombie doctor to her car, I shake my head in dismay because she never asked to see my ID. Hell, she only knows my name because I offered it.

I secure the doc in her passenger seat, and my smile fades when I think about what could have happened if I hadn't run across her. She could have ended up wrecking her car, or God forbid, someone with less than respectable intentions could have seen her and decided to take advantage of the situation.

In the next breath, I'm behind the wheel of the woman's Passat, following directions on my phone's GPS to her house. She wasn't kidding about living close. Her address is less than two miles from the gas station. The drive is super short but long enough for the weary woman to give in to her fatigue and pass out against the passenger window. She never would have made it home. I don't even know how she made it to the gas station.

Her house is a small cottage type with white brick and black shutters. It's petite, clean, and looks like it was made with her in mind. After parking in her driveway, I take a moment to study her profile. Thick lashes fan out over smooth cheeks. Though her hair is messy, her nose, lips, and neck give her a graceful appearance.

I reach for the hospital ID hanging from her rear-view mirror. Her picture sends a shock of desire through my middle. The image is vibrant and playful as if teasing the viewer with some private joke. *Hmm. Dr. Cassidy Emerson. You intrigue me.*

Deciding I've ogled enough, I lean over to nudge her awake. "Dr. Emerson, we're here."

She starts and sits up, rubbing her eyes and smearing day-old makeup. "Oh. Right."

It takes her a couple of tries, but she opens her car door and gets out, forgetting her drink and snack. As I exit on my side, I grab them both and drop a slip of paper onto the seat. The note contains my name and number on the off chance she'll remember me and reach out. Whether she does or not, I plan to have a case of Red Bull and Little Debbie cakes shipped to her with instructions to call me if she ever needs a late-night ride home again.

Dr. Emerson hasn't advanced any closer to the house when I reach her side of the car. She's leaning against the hood with her eyes half closed. I pick up her hand and gently place the keys in her palm. "You forgot your snack."

She stares at the junk food in my hand and admits, "That's not a snack. It's dinner."

My exaggerated frown makes her laugh. "You know, Doc, you might want to rethink a few of your life decisions, so I'm not reading your obituary in five years."

The woman smiles—a real show-stopper—making me stumble. I walk with her up the front steps to ensure she doesn't fall and hand over her dinner once the door opens. "Thank you for the lift home. Do you want to wait inside for a cab?"

"Thanks, but no. You don't need anything else coming between you and your pillow. Since it's not even two miles, I'll walk back."

The doc frowns and touches her fingers to my shoulder. "Are you really going to walk back to the station? At this time of night? This is a good area, but isn't that dangerous?"

I point to the trident pin on my chest. "See this? It means that I can handle anything I might run across tonight."

She tilts her head, and something flashes in her eyes. "Even crazy doctors without a sense of self-preservation?"

I lean forward just a little, a small smile playing at my lips. "Especially those."

Her beautiful smile returns, and I'm nearly a goner. "Good night, Mr. O'Reilly."

"Tim."

"Good night, Tim.

"Sleep well, Dr. Emerson."

"Cassidy."

"Sleep well, Cassidy."

I watch Cassidy walk inside, not moving from my spot until she's safely locked inside her home. Then I turn on my heels and start the long walk back, feeling much better about my night.

CHAPTER 2

TIM

The palest moonlight pours through our windows, pooling on the king-sized bed where my wife and I lie in the quiet. The soft glow falls on blue silk sheets that have slipped down, presenting a view that leaves me with no interest in going back to sleep.

I'm awake early, but I don't mind. I savor the moment, something I've done often since waking up in the hospital. Cass's beautiful body is fully exposed to the night and dressed in nothing more than the moonlight. Unable to resist touching her soft skin, I trail eager fingers over her shoulder, down the curve of her spine, and over her round ass. Cass doesn't stir, but I do, incited by memories of our shared passion last night.

My wife and I made love for the first time since I died.

One month ago, to the day I left my wife. A greedy bastard had decided to cut my life short, and a team of trauma doctors had done all they could to keep me alive. Cass and my men could only wait to see how I would respond. Despite the medical team's best efforts, my body gave out, and my heart stopped after three days in a coma.

Cass fought to bring me back to life. Every day since then, I've been working to get this body back to its full potential so I can be the man she deserves.

Recovery has been a battle. There was a lot of damage to overcome, and the progress has been slow. *Last night, though. Mmm.* Last night was our first time trying to bring *us* back. I've missed us.

We shouldn't have had any energy left after what had been an exhausting day for both of us. Yesterday was my last day of physical therapy. I pushed my limits the entire session so everyone taking notes would report to the admiral that I'm well on my way to a full recovery.

While I was being encouraged — yelled at — by my two best friends during the exercises, Cass and her team spent long hours delivering a set of twins from a mother who refused every manmade medical intervention. We arrived home at the same time, each of us looking worse for the wear.

Still stumping with my cane, I intercepted Cass in the garage, led her to the pool's edge, and stripped off her scrubs. She offered no protest and promptly shed her underwear before jumping in. I followed close behind, though I had to use the stairs. For the next hour, my wife was content to rest against me in the water, her back to my front, as I caressed and massaged up and down her body. My hands lingered on her soft breasts, having missed the way they fit in my hands.

A breathy moan slipped past her lips as Cass eased her head against my shoulder. *God, I'd missed that sound.* Bracing one arm across her chest, I trailed my hand past her breasts, circled her navel, and slipped between her legs. Cass opened up for me, inviting my touch, and braced her feet on the pool walls on either side of my legs.

As my lips teased along her jaw and down her graceful neck, I teased and strummed her clit with my fingers. The closer Cass came to climax, the more she writhed against me, ratcheting up my desire. I wanted, no, needed to make her come, and I didn't hold back. Cassidy came on a whimper, clamping down on my arm as her whole body wound tight as a bow string.

When her whimper turned into a sob, I turned her in my arms, worried that something was wrong. "Cass?"

A single tear tracked down her troubled face, and she dropped her eyes in shame. "That's not enough. I need more. I need you, Tim."

I understood the meaning behind her words because they expressed how I felt. It wasn't the touch or the orgasms we'd been missing, but the union, the magical connection that happens when I'm tucked inside her tight body.

Nothing else can replace that feeling. Being without it for as long as we had, something inside feels broken. Like a big part of us is missing. I told my wife exactly that, and then I took her hand and led her inside.

For the last month, my body has had too much healing to do for us to risk the exertion that comes with sex. Not having that connection has taken its toll. I can feel it in my chest, and I can see it in Cass's eyes, so filled with shame that the touch of my hand did not fill that empty spot inside.

Standing naked in our bedroom, Cass expressed her concern that I might not be ready. After seeing my wife at her breaking point, I knew it was worth the risk.

Cass's eyes were so full of worry as I pulled her toward the bed, but she couldn't hide the hunger burning inside their depths. My heart pounded as I tipped her head back and pressed my lips to hers. I felt every beat of it in my throbbing dick.

She took a step back, pulling her mouth from mine. I reached out with a shaking hand to touch her, but my fingers came up empty. Cass had dropped to her knees, not caring that she was still dripping wet, and took me into her mouth.

The shock of pleasure almost took my still-healing body to the floor, but I held on to the bedpost and my cane, determined not to miss out or take this away from her.

As I reached the danger point of either coming in her mouth or collapsing, Cas stood up and took my hand, leading me to lie back on the bed. She was almost frantic with need when she reached into her nightstand for lube and her favorite vibrating cock ring.

Cass applied a generous amount of the cool liquid to my dick before sliding on the ring. She turned the vibrator to its highest level, and I prayed that I could last long enough to give her what she needed.

The lamp illuminated my scarred chest, and Cass hesitated before lifting her eyes to mine. Not a word was spoken between us, but I reached down and spun the cock ring around to set her at ease.

Cass understood the message and turned around to mount me in reverse, thus protecting my chest. With one hand braced on the bed and the other on my uninjured thigh, Cass impaled herself on me with a long groan and just sat, unmoving, for a good while. For that, I was grateful. I needed time to come down from my near orgasm, or I wouldn't have lasted thirty seconds.

I may have missed watching her breasts and beautiful face when she came, but somehow, staring at her rolling back as she rode me was just as erotic. And god, did she feel good.

The tight squeeze of her hot body, paired with the vibrator, had me seeing stars. I had a death grip on the sheets, begging all things holy that I could hold off my climax and stretch out the moment as long as possible.

Cass came three times in rapid succession, her movements becoming more erratic with each release. I relished all of it, the sights, sounds, and each time her tight sheath choked my dick in response to her pleasure. It only took a few more strokes after her third orgasm to trigger mine.

I don't know if it was the length of time since we'd last made love or that my body is still jacked up, but that was the most powerful, most life-affirming sex I've ever had. And it completely knocked me out. Cass curled into my side, I wrapped an arm around her, and then I was gone.

Now, a new day is coming, and I'll miss her sexy morning-after smile, one of my favorite things in this world. Today, I return to the Navy. I wouldn't miss that any more than I would have skipped out on making love with Cass last night.

Leaning toward my wife, I press my nose to her hair and breathe deeply. This simple act and leaving her in the early morning darkness have always been a typical part of our lives. It hasn't been an easy life, but I wouldn't trade it for all the gold and diamonds in the world.

Though it's not time to get up yet, I slip from under the covers. The pull of the Navy life is too strong for me to lie here and enjoy the last hour before my alarm goes off.

After a quick shower, I limp naked to the closet and flip on the light. The sight of my working uniform brings a smile to my face. Damn, but it feels to be going back. Soon, I'm dressed in the digital camo, and contentment washes over me like greeting an old friend.

It's just past four when I bend down to kiss Cass's bare shoulder and thank my lucky stars that I'm still alive and have her with me. With a final, longing gaze at her body, I grab my cane and walk out of our bedroom, looking forward to having some time alone at headquarters before the typical day's activities begin.

Arriving at the main gate of Joint Expeditionary Base Little Creek-Fort Story, I can't stop a grin from forming. This feels like coming home.

The sailor manning the gate lights up when he realizes who the early morning visitor is. "Good to have you back, Commander."

"Thanks, Chief. It's good to be back," I respond and pull through the gate.

I take a few minutes to cruise around the base, first by the amphib launch area and then past the training beach. The stars are still out, and the massive military presence isn't on the move yet, but that will change in the coming hours. This place is never quiet or still for long.

The last leg of my exploration takes me to headquarters. The place has been a bittersweet second home to me over the years. From this building, I send men out to fight all over the world. Some come back as heroes, and some never come back at all.

The losses are hard, and I feel responsible for each father, mother, wife, and child left behind. Their sacrifices hold me to the high standard I set for myself and my men. Every day of my time as commander, I've striven to train, study, and learn as much as I can, and I push my men to do the same. I'm not perfect, but I've upheld my vow to give my men the best intel, sound decision-making, and physical training possible to have the best chance of coming back in one piece.

Though I've been absent for a few weeks, I've not had to worry about the ship running aground under substitute leadership. My men have been in good hands with Admiral Jameson, my SEAL commander, at the helm. Ultimately, though, these are my men. My responsibility. And it's about damn time I got back to work. Moreover, I've realized I need them as much as they need me.

I park in the empty lot and grab my cane, eager to start my first day back on the job. Stumping along the walkway, I pause momentarily and close my eyes, recalling a memory of an epic paint ball fight between the Wendigo men in front of this building.

The men were celebrating an exercise

victory and were covered in purple whelps and globs of hot pink goo as they played like kids just a few feet from where I'm standing.

A flashback from a later time features a cross-team challenge with men from SEAL Team Three to complete the Murph. A bet was made between their commander and me, which included the two of us anchoring for our respective teams. Our team won the bet, but the terms were almost as unpleasant for the winners as for the losers. Memories of that day still make me itch. I'll never look at an athletic supporter the same way again.

I resume my trek toward home base and take a deep, satisfying breath before opening the door. The place is like a ghost town. Save for a few security lights placed around the building, the hallways, conference rooms, and offices are dark and empty and will be for about another hour.

I step out of the elevator on the third floor into another long hallway lit by intermittent safety lights. The scalloped pattern they make on the checkerboard floor, paired with the hazy moonlight spilling in from the windows, is slightly disorienting and makes the place seem almost haunted.

If spirits inhabit SEAL Team Two headquarters, I assume they're of some of the greatest heroes this country has ever seen. And staring down this darkened hallway, I feel those spirits cheering me on, urging my return to the fight.

Step by step, supported by the cane, I navigate the hallways until I reach my office. Once inside, I flip on the light and adjust my eyes to the sudden brightness. From here, I can smell the leather of my chair and see the models of some of the Navy's most storied ships on the credenza, things I'd failed to fully appreciate until now.

Adorning my office walls are framed citations from my time in the field and photographs taken throughout my long career. The pictures feature me with men from my first team after graduation, men who have served under me, naval ships, and even two presidents. Mine is a career I've spent my life building and one I'm damned proud of.

The cane is placed against the door trim before I finally limp to my desk. Sliding into my office chair again is almost as satisfying as sliding into Cass's welcoming body last night. Though I may not be whole yet, I am back, and it's only a matter of time before I'm running the Murph with my men again. Anything less would be unacceptable.

I'm not a commander in the habit of tasking my men with things I'm unable or unwilling to do myself. My reasons for keeping pace with the men I send to the front lines are to never forget what it is to be in their boots. I don't ever want to lose my appreciation for what these men go through, the constant, demanding training regimen, and the stress of knowing that one little slipup can result in the death of your entire crew. I never want to forget what these men and their families go through for the sake of our country.

Spreading my hands over my desk, I turn to stare out the window at the dark meeting field where, soon, all eight SEAL platoons of Team Two will gather to see if I still have what it takes to lead them or if it's time for me to step aside and let someone else take over.

Today is not that day.

The closer it gets to sunrise, the more I detect ambient noise in the building as people file in for the workday. Just before five, my assistant, Ensign Dorne, raps on my open door frame. "Welcome back, Commander."

"Thank you, Ensign."

"Sir, the men are lined up early if you're ready."

I offer the younger man a chuckle. "Was the admiral that bad?"

Dorne grins proudly. "No, sir. I guess they're just stoked that you're back."

I push out of the leather seat and brace both hands on the blotter. "Well, let's not disappoint them."

Standing fully, I limp back to the door. The young ensign retrieves my cane from its perch. He hands me the walking aid and gestures for me to precede him out the door.

The trip toward the front entrance is made a little faster than the trip in, partly so the younger man won't pity me but mostly because I'm damned anxious to be with my men again.

Ensign Dorne breezes around me to open the door, and the sight outside has a lump forming in my throat. Bright lights flood the grassy field. All one hundred twenty-eight SEALs, plus the masters-at-arms and support personnel from Little Creek, are lined up in the yard. Only the SEALs are expected to fall in, but apparently, the entire base came to show their support.

The sight is as overwhelming as it is humbling.

Someone calls for attention, and the group salutes as I step out onto the concrete landing. Leaning heavily on the cane, I advance to the front edge and scan the gathered sailors before returning their salute.

Not trusting my voice, I clear my throat before attempting to address the group. "At ease."

As one, the men and women gathered drop their hands, shifting to brace their feet shoulder-width apart with their hands behind their backs.

"Don't let this cane fool you. I am still very much the ass-kicker you know me to be. The only change is that I'm giving you the once-in-alifetime chance to return the favor."

Laughter filters through the group, and I take a moment to soak it all in before continuing. I pause my inspection on one particular group of eight. Each is wearing a broad smile, their faces conveying loyalty and pride that I'm back in command.

"If any of you see me taking it easy, not pushing hard enough to lose this damn crutch, you have temporary license to give back a little of the medicine I've dished out over the years. Your... encouragement won't register as insubordination but as inspiration. A challenge. A word of warning, though. Be ungenerous with your challenges. Very soon, I'll be able to answer and will do so with my boot."

The group laughs again, and I can't help answering with a grin this time. With one last look out over these gathered warriors, I offer another salute and release them. "Platoon leaders, carry on."

On the way back upstairs, Ensign Dorne fills me in on what the Pentagon has been doing during my absence. Admiral Jameson has kept me informed of any significant news, but there are plenty of bulletins and updates to read through. And, of course, there's always paperwork to be done and reports to file.

Back in my office, I decide the Pentagon can wait five minutes and step up to the pictures, studying every image. Of all the photographs on display, I pause on one in particular. Nine men, one of them being me, stand at the edge of our amphibious launch pad dressed in our bright, white uniforms. I'm standing next to Lieutenant "Fish" Hill, along with all the men of his squad, the Wendigos.

The picture was taken the day Tyler "Hawk" Morgan was married. Except for Warden and Bishop, I've never been closer to a group of men than the ones pictured here. These men and their families mean everything to me and have become my reason for continuing this fight when most others would pack it in.

Over the last month, Fish and all his men have taken shifts with me while their women ensured Cass was cared for. These men and my two best friends showed up every day, in the hospital and out, escorting me to therapy and then proceeding to kick my ass right along with the therapists.

Even if I had wanted to quit, which I almost did a few times, those men wouldn't have allowed it. There were times I swore at and threatened them, but never once did they leave my side or lighten up. And I'll never be able to thank them enough.

While I was being ordered around by my men, Dallas, Iyla, Charli, and all the other men's women made sure Cass had everything she needed.

I honestly believe that without these men

and women's support, neither Cassidy nor I would have survived the last month.

BULLETPROOF

JO CHAMBLISS

CHAPTER 3

TIM

The next four weeks passed quickly. I regained strength every day, but the limitations were sometimes frustrating. Still, I kept working, kept pushing, and made tremendous strides. I'm not fully back yet, but at least I can see the light at the end of the tunnel.

As another week nears its end, I'm shutting down my office a day early. Despite the progress I've been making in my recovery, the one big check I've yet to mark on my list is making up a couple of missed date nights with my wife.

Exiting the office, I pick up my cover from the side of my desk and glance at where my cane used to rest. I'm happy to see it gone.

I tuck my cap under my arm and head out, hurrying to get home. Today is the second Thursday of the month and our regular date night.

Cass and I had only been dating a few short weeks before realizing that either of our careers would be challenging for a budding relationship. Combine our lines of work, and you could end up feeling like strangers passing in the night.

Because of her many weekends of being on call and many of mine being out of the country, we instituted a monthly date night. Scheduled around her regular on-call shifts, date night was our time to put off the rest of the world and just be Cass and Tim instead of Doctor and, at the time, Lieutenant Commander.

With my schedule still being somewhat inconsistent, I didn't always get to be with Cass on date night. Unless I was actively on a mission, though, I always managed a face-to-face call with her or, at the minimum, to send a long message for her to read in my absence.

After being promoted to Commander and given the full-time job of managing SEAL Team Two, missing date night has, thankfully, been an exceedingly rare occasion.

Even though Cass and I were together for them, our two most recent dates have been less than memorable. Last month's date was spent sharing dinner, lying on the sofa. Not ideal, but infinitely better than the one before, during which Cass spent the night in a chair, watching over me and wondering if I would live or die.

With that nightmare behind us, I'm determined to make up for lost time. I'm not saying that Cass and I haven't made love or that the experiences were less than amazing. I will say we both miss and need back the fire, the burning hot passion that's always existed between us.

I'm giving that fire back to my wife tonight, or I'll go to hell trying.

I make one stop on the way home to pick up an order of white roses from the florist. After that, I continue toward home beneath the darkening sky, bending a few traffic laws in my rush to prepare for the evening.

I plan to get showered and dressed in my best suit before Cass returns from the hospital. I'll be waiting at the door with flowers and lead her to our massive bathroom, stripping off all her clothes, pinning up her hair, and guiding her into the bath I'll have prepared for her.

Cass will soak and drink champagne and then slip into a sexy dress we both love. I've made late reservations at her favorite restaurant and have candles, oils, and some of our toys hidden around the house for when we get back home. Just thinking about how our night could go has me dialing up the air in my SUV to cool down my heated skin.

I turn onto our street and let off the gas when I notice something strange about our house. The exterior is lit up as usual, but no light is visible through the windows. It shouldn't be this dark inside, even with no one home.

The worrying thoughts rolling through my mind have me calling Cass's phone through my Bluetooth system. When she doesn't answer, the accelerator is pressed to the floor again in my rush to reach our house.

Adrenaline pumps through my system as I slam on the brakes in front of the garage. I jump out of the SUV, run to the garage side door, and punch in the code to gain entry.

Cass's Lexus is parked in its bay, though I wouldn't have thought she'd be home this early. Slipping inside the dark room, I approach the car to find that the hood is cool to the touch. Cass has either been home for a while or never left. *Then why the hell is the whole damn house dark?*

Keeping my hand where it is, I swivel to study the door into the mudroom where she would have entered the house. The door is slightly ajar, and no light is visible in the kitchen.

Easing my way inside, I note that everything in the mudroom appears as it should, except for the darkness. I'm generally not given over to paranoia, but my mind quickly goes to a dark place. *Cass is in danger.*

I force myself to stay calm and hold still to pick up on any foreign sounds or smells coming from the kitchen. Detecting none, I pull out a small flashlight and step through the door to search for signs of a struggle. Cass's purse and keys are carefully placed where they would typically be when she's at home.

If she was attacked, it wasn't here.

A fear the likes of which I've never experienced seizes my heart at the alarming thought. Realizing where my mind is going, I grip the counter and take a deep breath. *Stop it, asshole. Cass has a core of steel and has mastered the self-defense training you've shown her over the years. I actually pity the idiot that would try to lay a hand on her.*

My hand moves away from my sidearm where it had instinctively gone, and I push all the way through the kitchen door to find more darkness waiting beyond. This time, I don't hesitate to flip on the light as I continue the search for my wife.

The house is eerily quiet. We don't have kids to create a constant buzz, no pets begging for attention, and no music playing through the integrated speakers. Danger or no, this is strange.

My search takes me to our bedroom door, where I listen for sounds of Cass showering or dressing. Still, I only hear silence. Fearing that she's not well and in bed, I gently open the door. The room is dark except for my bedside lamp, which highlights a note on my pillow. I approach cautiously, my unease ratcheting back up to DEFCON 3.

The note reads, *Let's play a game, Commander.*

My breath rushes from my lungs as all the battle-ready tension drains from my body, and a wicked grin paints my face. *So… she wants to play.*

I back out of the room and turn for my office, slamming my hand on the light switch once I'm inside. My next steps take me to the movable wall panel beside my desk, where a section pops loose at the press of the right area. The panel slides to the side, exposing my gun safe, and I punch in the code to open the heavy door.

Pressing the release on my Sig, I expel the fifteen-round magazine and lock back the slide, catching the chambered round in the palm of my hand. I smile again at Cass's note. It would appear this evening's plans have changed.

The safe closes with my gun inside, and I turn to walk out of the office, stopping at the sight on the console table by the door. A bubbling glass of champagne sits waiting with a pair of dice soaking in the sparkling wine.

I smirk at the hint and reach for the flute, bringing it to my lips. Holding onto the bottom, I drink it all, tipping the glass high enough that the dice tumble onto my tongue.

Knowing where Cass is now, I walk out of my office, a host of dirty thoughts rolling around in my mind and the dice rolling around in my mouth.

My steps are slow and steady, taking me to the game room, where I find Cass perched on the side of the antique Brunswick pool table. Above her, the dimmed billiard light casts a warm glow on her face and silky robe.

Cass is a vision, and just one look at her has my body responding with enthusiasm. Her hands are braced behind her on the upholstered slate surface, and a glass of champagne sits next to her hip. Her legs are crossed at the knee, splitting the robe and showing off a tempting stretch of toned leg.

Forcing my brain from its stupor, I take a single step in her direction, completely transfixed. Cass's breathing quickens at my hungry expression, causing her baby blue robe to slip and expose the secret that she has nothing on underneath.

Neither of us has spoken, but the fire in our eyes says plenty. With the dice still in my mouth, I stalk forward and reach for the tie at her waist. Just as my fingers brush the silken rope, she finally speaks, her voice heavy with arousal. "I want to play a game first."

I raise an eyebrow, not needing words to encourage her to continue. Cass pushes off the ledge, sliding down my body until her bare feet touch the floor. My goddess saunters to the cue rack to select a stick and moves to the opposite side of the table.

We face off, her wearing a wicked grin because she knows I can't beat her and me with the dice in my mouth, not caring. Whatever happens here, we both win.

"Strip pool," Cass announces. "Each shot I make, you take something off. Whoever wins is in charge."

The rules would seem heavily weighted in my favor, given that I'm in full uniform and Cass is only in a slinky robe. We both know better, though. I may be good, but I'm absolute shit at pool compared to her. I don't stand a chance.

I nod my assent and approach Cass to select a cue stick. I don't speak since, for some unknown reason, I've yet to remove the dice from my mouth.

As Cass racks the balls, I roll the dice around with my tongue and pick up a chalk to prep my stick.

"You break," she orders.

Torn between being greedy to have her body in my hands and enjoying the build-up, I grab my stick and line up to break.

As I aim the shot, I make the mistake of looking at my wife. She trails a finger across her chest and dips inside the lapel of her robe to tease a tight nipple. *Oh fuck.*

Sufficiently distracted, I send the shot wide. It barely glances off the balls arranged in a perfect triangle. Cass chuckles, a deep, sexy sound, but I keep silent to avoid giving away my oral secret.

She moves around the table, studying the configuration of the balls, and bends over to line up her first shot. Time slows to a crawl, allowing me to fully appreciate her pinned-up, silky brown hair with little wisps escaping and brushing against her cheeks. Her robe gaped slightly, revealing a teasing view of her gorgeous breasts.

One thing has become abundantly clear. I

lost this game before it started.

Cass's expert strike explodes the balls outward, sinking three of them. The result is that she has her pick of solids or stripes. More importantly, I have to remove three things right off the bat.

The sexy woman stands upright again and quirks a brow in expectation. Laying my cue on the table side, I remove my belt first. While looking straight at her amused face, I unbutton my top and shed the fabric, tossing it on the back of a nearby chair. My eyes don't leave hers until I pull my t-shirt over my head.

Cass's eyes go to my chest, pausing on the massive scar there. I'm afraid she'll back down from her plans, but she quickly shakes her head and drags her eyes back to my face. Grinning once again, she says, "I think I'll go with stripes. By my calculations, that gives me the right number of shots to get you naked."

I wave a hand over the table to invite her to continue and step out of the way. Her eyes narrow momentarily at my lack of verbal responses, but she doesn't ask. She approaches the rail and studies the table again. Cass gets serious then.

Minutes later, I'm butt-ass naked. Only solids remain on the table, including the eight ball. I haven't made a single shot since fucking up the break. Cass cleared the field of stripes in one continuous turn.

With a lingering look over my body, Cass licks her lips and then lines up to sink the winning ball. To pay back her earlier tease, I step across the table from where she's getting ready to shoot. My erection stands tall, fully visible above the bumper. Taking the shaft in my hand, I pump it slowly and watch Cass instead of the eight.

Cass flinches as I reach the tip, just before I hear the crack of the cue ball making contact.

The eight sinks — right before the cue ball falls in behind it. *Scratch. I win.*

Determined strides take me around the table, where I toss my cue stick on the felt surface, sending it rolling into the remaining balls. After taking Cass's stick from her hand and disposing of it in a similar fashion, I grab her hips and lift her onto the bumper.

She doesn't look disappointed with her loss.

Fingers shaking with restraint, I untie the knot at her waist. The blue silk falls open and slides down her shoulders with a little help. I press my body between her legs and release the clip holding her long hair. The shiny strands cascade downward to fan out over her back as I lower my mouth to hers.

My kisses are shallow, not yet wanting to reveal my secret. So Cass doesn't become suspicious, I quickly move from her mouth to her neck before shoving her to the tabletop and dipping my head to her full breasts.

I spend a lot of time refamiliarizing myself with her taste, exploring every part of her on my way down to her center. Before reaching the manicured patch of curls, I lift my lips from her smooth skin to stare at her beautiful body.

Cass's breasts rise and fall in time with her excited breaths. Her hips are open wide to accommodate my size, and goose flesh blossoms across her body as my eyes rake over every sexy inch of her.

When I finally dip my head to lick her slit, Cass shivers and moans my name. I grip and lift her feet to the worn wood surface to open her wider, giving me better access.

Her knees fall open, and I add two fingers to the mix with my tongue, teasing Cass to a frenzy. I tease and flick her clit with my tongue while the two fingers work a come-hither motion inside her, aiming to trigger that magical spot.

Sooner than I would have expected, Cass calls out in ecstasy, arching her back off the pool table's surface. I slow my rhythm to ease her down from the high, watching contentedly as her body shudders from the powerful aftershocks.

I pull my fingers from inside her, grabbing my dick and transferring her slickness to the hard-as-stone shaft. Taking in her boneless state, I grip her left leg under the knee, pulling her closer to the edge and fitting the head of my cock at her entrance.

Cass holds her breath as I press into her

body, and I realize I've done the same. I draw in a breath only when I'm fully seated, but still, I don't move. Cass opens her eyes, which are blazing now, and I bend down to kiss her. This time, I open up to let my tongue duel with hers.

Her eyes widen at feeling the foreign objects in my mouth, and I know I've got her attention. Standing upright again, I remove the dice for her to see. I think I've just figured out what to do with them.

Cass watches, mesmerized, as I place the pair of dice right on her clit. Then, after grabbing and lifting her other leg behind the knee, I pull out almost entirely before leaning forward and slamming back home.

Cass's eyes roll back at the extra contact of the dice with her overstimulated bundle of nerves.

I set a furious pace, holding tightly to her legs so she doesn't slip away from me. Moments later, Cass hoarsely calls out her second orgasm and tries to pull away due to its intensity. I don't let her, and I don't slow down.

My beautiful wife mewls in pleasure or pain, then grabs my arms and pulls me down. Her legs wrap around my hips as I oblige, continuing my feverish claiming of her.

The dice are rolling and pressing even harder against her clit, and before long, Cass is climaxing again. With my mouth on hers, I swallow her desperate cries as her nails dig into my biceps. The intense contractions of her inner muscles squeeze me to near choking, and soon, I'm exploding within her.

Having been thrown off my rhythm by the powerful release, quivering muscles stiffen, and I brace my hands on either side of her head while lightning shoots through my body. My breath saws in and out, heavy from our fierce lovemaking. All I can do now is drop my head against her chest until my body stops shaking.

My breathing gradually slows, and I drop my lips to her glistening skin, kissing across her collarbone. The moment I'm fully upright again, the picture before me becomes one I'll forever have burned in my brain. Cass hasn't moved except to rest her arms beside her. On her face is a profound serenity that I know has to be mirrored in my own features.

"You are so beautiful."

I reach out to move a few damp strands from her forehead as Cass hums in delighted satisfaction, and a small smile plays at her lips. I could stand and stare at her all night, but I don't imagine that hard surface will be too comfortable once the sexual haze clears.

Reluctantly, I back out of her body and remove the dice from her slick folds. Cass opens her eyes at feeling contact with the sensitive area and watches as I plop the cubes right back into my mouth. She grins impishly and holds out her hand.

After sucking them clean, I pull the dice from my mouth again and place them in her palm. Then, I pick her up from the playing surface. Glad that my body is capable, I carry her to our room and lay her on the bed before joining her on the other side.

"Yours was better," I tell her as I slide between the sheets.

"What of mine was better?" she asks as she rolls toward me. Cass begins running her fingers over my chest and abs, the feeling like heaven.

"Your plan for tonight was better than mine, which was to surprise you with dinner at Orion's Roof, hoping to end up in a similar situation."

The musical sound of Cass's laugh fills my ears, my favorite sound in the world. She rolls me to my back and moves between my legs. "Your plan sounds just as good as mine."

Her eyes glance over my angry, purple scars, but she remains focused. "I've missed us, Tim."

She doesn't say anything more, having taken me into her mouth.

CHAPTER 4

CASS

Tim collapses onto my back, pressing my knees harder into the mattress. His chest is heaving from his fine efforts to utilize the erection my mouth coaxed out of him. I relax my hips, lowering us to the bed and relishing the comforting weight of his body on mine.

The move has Tim slipping out of me, smearing my backside with our combined arousal. My breath hitches, and a pang of longing hits me. A longing that I'd never had until two months ago. A baby. The sudden and alien desire has been so unexpected that it scares me a little.

For as long as Tim and I have been together, almost ten years, neither of us has ever wanted children. Since he flatlined in the hospital, I've been thinking differently. Tim could have died, and I would have nothing left of him.

The thought of having a family, some lasting part of my husband, has been on my mind since Tim woke up in the hospital. For a while, my thoughts were merely wonderings of what if. This deep longing is new and unsettling. I haven't mentioned this to Tim; more concerned with his healing. It's not that I'm afraid of what he'd say, but I want to be sure it isn't a fleeting or misguided and selfish desire.

After tonight's vigorous performances, the yearning is real and suddenly too powerful to ignore. We're not too old. Tim is forty-seven, and I'm thirty-five. I just have to find the right moment to ask and be ready to accept his answer, whatever that may be.

If Tim still doesn't want kids, I'll probably be disappointed, but I love my husband. I've loved our life together. It'll be no hardship to continue just being Cass and Tim. I hope.

Tim's sexy rumble vibrates my shoulder where his lips are currently pressed. "You're thinking rather hard, my love. What about?"

Another time, Cass. "For one thing, that I'm hungry."

Tim lifts his head to nuzzle my ear and chuckles. "I've rather enjoyed feasting on you."

He rolls away, stands, and reaches for my hand. "Come on. I'll whip up something for us."

"Well, actually…"

I let Tim pull me upright and smile when I notice the used pair of dice on the bedside table. "I've got that covered."

A quick trip into the closet produces another robe for me and some sweats for Tim. Then I'm taking his hand and leading him to the pool house. A table is set inside, a bottle of champagne sits in an ice bucket, and dinner is chilling and warming as needed, waiting for us.

"You little minx," he says, kissing my neck.

I pull my hand from his to retrieve plates from the fridge and warmer, and Tim helps me set out dinner from Orion's Roof. As I reach for the sauce bowls, big arms wrap around me from behind. "I love you, Cassidy O'Reilly. You're amazing. I owed you a make-up date, but you planned an even better one."

Leaning my head back against his shoulder, I say, "Hmm. You did the hard work. This was an easy job that I'll gladly see to for the rest of our lives."

"Hard work?"

I turn in his arms to look him in the eye. "You battled your way back to me."

Tim dips his head to place a reverent kiss on my lips. "I'll always come back to you."

We separate to enjoy the sushi dinner and, afterward, sit wrapped up in a blanket and each other on a lounger by the pool. Tim, again, unties my robe, slipping his hand beneath the smooth fabric to trail over my body.

He pauses at my middle more than once, drawing little shapes low on my belly, something he's never done before. I know this is not a now-or-never situation, but the moment feels right to ask. *Here goes...*

"Tim, have you ever wondered—"

"She would have blue eyes like you," he

interrupts, "…and my Irish temper."

At my sharp inhale, his hand splays out over my flat stomach. *He's thought about it as much as I have.* Tears well up in my eyes as I stare at the dark sky. My voice, unsteady with emotion, asks, "She?"

"A little girl who would own my heart, just like her mother."

"What about a boy?"

"Boy, girl, it doesn't matter as long as they have your eyes and spirit."

Have… "Are you saying…?"

Tim sits up and turns my face to his, wiping away my tears. "Cass, you are my everything, and you've always been enough. Lately, I want more of you, of what we can be. I dream of caressing your stomach, knowing it's holding my child. I can see the love in your eyes as you hold our son or daughter to your breast. I know we never wanted kids, but now, there's nothing that I wish for more."

Fighting out of Tim's hold, I roll over in his arms. On my knees, straddling his thighs, I reach for his face with both hands. "You mean it?"

"Have a baby with me, Cass."

My heart overflows, and I dive forward, knocking him back on the cushion, virtually attacking his mouth and sinking onto his quickly-growing erection.

I'm surprised to feel a warm body next to mine when I wake up the next morning. Without opening my eyes, I caress Tim's hard abs and ask, "Playing hooky today?"

"Day off," Tim answers in his sexy morning growl. "In case I got lucky last night, I didn't want to worry about rushing out this morning."

Strong hands grip my hips and pull me to lie on top of him before beginning a sensual massage of my ass cheeks. Opening my eyes finally, I lift my head to stare at the man I love more than anything in the world. "I should have thought of that. I guess it's my turn to leave you in bed. At least I'm only working half a day today and not on call this weekend."

Maybe I can... my eyes fall away from Tim's handsome face, and I worry for a moment if our conversation last night really means what I'm hoping it means.

"Hey, what's that look for?"

Tim hooks a finger under my chin and drags my gaze back to his. "I haven't changed my mind if that's what you're worried about."

Damn. He always was a mind reader. "I just was thinking that if Dr. Hosier isn't too busy today, I'll see if he has time to remove my IUD."

Before I know it, Tim is sitting up, making me straddle his lap. "How soon after it's removed will we have a chance?"

I tug on his beard playfully and consider giving him the same speech my patients hear, but I'm just too damned excited. "As little as two weeks."

A yelp is torn from my throat as I find myself being whirled through the air and tossed on my back. "That gives us two weeks to practice so we don't miss the opportunity."

Tim bends to take a nipple into his mouth. His excitement spills over to me, making me laugh at his insistence, but our happy moment is interrupted by my ringing phone. Tim groans, recognizing the ringtone from the hospital's labor and delivery.

I grab the device, popping my nipple from Tim's mouth as I stretch. "Dr. O'Reilly."

"Hey, Doll. Jessa Walters came in overnight. Her membrane ruptured on its own at about midnight. She hoped that meant she could deliver without the C-section she's scheduled for today, but she's made no progress in the six hours she's been here. I swear, I just checked her and had to go up to my elbow to reach her cervix."

"Ok. I'll be in by seven. How's the baby?"

"All vitals good so far. Mom's body just doesn't understand the human delivery process. I'll wait for you to get here before I leave. Maybe two doctors will convince her to take the safe route and get this baby out."

"Right. Just like her first baby. See you soon, Mabry."

"Bring coffee."

The phone is dropped next to me on the bed, and I grab Tim's face, guiding his mouth back to my breast. "As you were, Commander."

Tim chuckles as he ducks his head. "Yes, ma'am."

Three hours later, I've just placed the last staple on Mrs. Walters' C-section incision and lean over the curtain. "Congratulations. She's beautiful."

"Thank you, Dr. O'Reilly," she answers dreamily.

I leave the parents and newborn in the care of the labor and delivery staff and head back to my office. There, I deal with the myriad of things to be handled on a typical Friday until I can shut things down for the day, a little early, actually. My long-time personal GYN, Dr. Hosier, is waiting for me in his practice two floors up.

When I called earlier, his assistant said they were both willing to stick around for a few extra minutes after their last patient to remove my birth control device. It's about that time, so I shut down my computer and grab my purse before heading in their direction.

My hopeful grin catches the attention of mine and Mabry's staff on the way out, but I keep my secrets to myself. Fortunately, most of them know about mine and Tim's regular date night and probably think I've got a certain sexy Navy man on my mind.

Less than an hour later, I'm in my car, driving out of the parking deck, excitedly making plans for a new kind of future. Since leaving the older doctor's procedure room, my mind has been reeling with all the possibilities and realizing that I'm not on any sort of birth control for the first time since meeting Tim.

I know medically, I shouldn't feel any different, but I *feel* different. In fact, my giddy hopefulness has me distracted to the point that I nearly take out a parked car while leaving the hospital.

Giving myself a verbal reprimand for being preoccupied behind the wheel, I take a deep breath to reset my focus and check all my mirrors at the red light.

"*Always be aware of your surroundings,*" Tim would say. "*Never assume being in a car means one hundred percent safety.*"

Because of those warnings, I notice a black SUV getting off the same exit from the highway as me a few miles later. It's hard to tell with all the black Tahoes in the area, but this could be the same one that exited the parking deck behind me. I don't overthink it, though. I've gotten off this exit before and been the follower of a car all the way to my neighborhood.

Eh. It's probably not even the same one. Black SUVs are as numerous as birds around here.

TIM

My wife's fine ass sways toward the bathroom to get cleaned up, and I'm helpless to drag my eyes away. I want nothing more than to get up and join her, but if I move from this bed,

I'll take her sweet body in the shower and make her late for her shift at the hospital. As much as we'd both enjoy the experience, I'd never keep Dr. Cassidy O'Reilly from a laboring woman.

So, I laze in bed for a change, if only long enough to watch Cass dress for the day. She steps out of the bathroom, tossing her towel at me to walk nude to our closet. *My god, she's beautiful. Still as striking as the day we met.*

A short while later, Cass ties up her hair as a finishing touch and gives me a goodbye kiss while I give her ass a squeeze. After that, she leaves for work, and I'm on my own for the morning. Knowing she's safely out of my reach, I finally get up and pull on the gray sweats from last night.

Over a bowl of cereal, I daydream about last night and wonder what Cass plans to do with the dice. My dick likes this line of thinking, but I give it a pat. "Down, boy. She's not even here."

I take my bowl to the kitchen and have just opened the dishwasher to load it in when the doorbell rings. A quick check of the smart home screen next to the mudroom door shows Dillan "Warden" Knot, former SEAL and CEO, standing at my front door.

While the rest of the world calls him Mr. Knot or just plain Knot, he'll always be Warden to me. I dry my hands on a towel and go to answer, not even bothering to grab a shirt.

"War…," I begin when the door opens, but

the name dies on my lips at his tired eyes and clenched jaw. *Something's wrong.*

"Stone," he says gravely.

I step back to allow my friend in, but he doesn't move past the entry hall. The big man moves as though dragging the world's weight behind him. I don't press, knowing he'll speak when and only when he's ready. A long, silent moment passes before he squares off with me and lets his shoulders fall. "Bishop's dead."

The air rushes from my lungs, and I stumble back to lean against the heavy door. *No. Bishop.* His name conjures a memory of the three of us laughing over something stupid, and I feel as if I've been hit by a sledgehammer.

Being a SEAL, dealing with death is never easy, but Bishop was family. Losing him is like losing a brother.

"What the hell happened?" I ask.

Warden shakes his head as though he can't believe what he's about to report. "He wrecked his car last night around nine. Asleep at the wheel, I'm told."

His angry tone indicates that he believes the report is bullshit. Given that I've been with Bishop on many missions where there was no sleep to be had, I agree with Warden. "There's no way that's the end of it."

"I got the mayor to contact the chief of police. An autopsy is being done. If they find anything out of order, NCIS will investigate."

Without him saying so, I can tell Warden expects something to be found. Whatever is or isn't found, our friend is dead. James "Bishop" Stoddard was one of the best men I've ever known and one of the two best friends I've ever had. He was younger than me by three years, and he had a kid.

Bishop's dead. Pain from the loss spreads throughout my chest, threatening to cripple me. I stumble through the entry, and Warden follows me to the living room, where we both drop onto the sofa. My elbows lower to rest on my knees as I work to force air into and out of my lungs.

Bishop is gone. What the fuck? Bishop, Warden, and I went through a lot together. We trained together, fought together, saved each other's asses a time or two, and celebrated with one another at marriages and births. Bishop was one of the men who showed up to push me along with the physical therapists over the last several weeks.

And now he's dead.

The grief I'm feeling can only be surpassed by that of his son, Jackson, who's had a hell of a lot of it in his young life. Just five years ago, Warden and I held Bishop and his son after Bishop's wife, Lucy, lost her battle with cancer. And now, Jackson has been orphaned.

In this loss, there is no comfort to be had by any of us on earth, but if there is a heaven, that's where Bishop is. "At least he and Lucy are together again."

"Amen," Warden grunts while swiping at his eyes.

"Where's Jackson? I can't imagine the world of hurt he's occupying right now."

"Jackson is at my house until Lucy's parents arrive from Maryland. I'm assuming they'll take him back with them."

Warden and I spend some time in silence, gridlocked by the shared pain of losing a close friend.

I drag my bare arm across my eyes sometime later, and the two of us begin discussing plans. First and foremost, we'll help Bishop's son and in-laws navigate the military funeral process and follow through with the shared final wishes Bishop, Warden, and I all had: to have our ashes spread over the training waters off Little Creek.

Out of the blue, Warden snorts out a watery laugh. "We'll have to watch the weather to make sure there are a few asses in the sky that day."

I drop my head and chuckle at the memory of the blind date revenge prank I pulled on Bishop, even as big, fat tears plop onto the rug below. After the disaster of a date with Nicole, I had waited about three months until the perfect idea and opportunity came along to get Bishop back for setting me up with her. Just before Bishop was to give a presentation in a training class, I added a cloud-to-ass extension to Chrome on his laptop.

The extension takes the word cloud and changes it to ass on whatever website he views. Presenting his topic on the weather's effects on tactical strategy, the word cloud, and therefore ass, came up quite a bit. From that day forward, a cloud was never called a cloud again.

"I'm going to miss his crazy ass."

"You and me both, man. You and me, both."

Warden leaves to return home soon after, and I follow to visit Jackson. Walking to the front door of Warden's estate home, dread weighs down each step. Jackson is only fifteen years old and had his whole world turned upside down. Again. What the hell can I say to him? As much as I want to put on a brave face and project some strength for his sake, I don't think I can. Part of me wants to turn around, leave, and seek comfort in my wife.

I don't because Warden and I have been just as much a part of Jackson's life as his own family. I can't abandon him now just because I'm hurting. Forcing a deep breath into my tight chest, I reach forward to push the chime, but the door swings open before my finger touches the button.

BULLETPROOF

JO CHAMBLISS

CHAPTER 5

TIM

"I knew you were out here, but it looked like you could use a minute," Warden says.

At my nod, he backs up, and I walk inside the lavish home of Dillan and Trish Knot. The two of us pass the grand, sweeping staircase, and just beyond, in the living room, I see Jackson sitting on the sofa with his head in his hands.

My next steps are shuffled, still fighting the urge to run. When Lucy died, things were different. I could be there for Jackson and Bishop, lending them strength and holding them up. Not now. How can I help this kid when I'm drowning in my own pain?

Despite feeling wholly inadequate, I take one reluctant step into the living room and another. The sound drags Jackson's eyes upward, and seeing my face, the boy who looks so much like his father jumps up and runs over to me. Skinny arms wrap around my middle, and Jackson sobs into my chest.

I hold on tight to Bishop Stoddard's son, even as my heart is splitting in two. When Jackson takes a shuddering breath and steps back,

Warden leads us to sit down together.

From what Warden told me at my house, Jackson hasn't spoken much since he and Trish picked him up last night. Though Warden and I have doubts about Bishop's accident, now is not the time to ask questions of a grieving teenager.

Warden and I sit with Jackson, ready to be whatever he needs, whether it's a shoulder to cry on, an ear to listen to him vent, or even a punching bag so he can work out some anger over how unfair life can be. I'm prepared for any of that.

What I'm not prepared for are the first words that come from Jackson. "My dad didn't fall asleep driving."

I toss a look Warden's way, having expressed the same suspicions less than half an hour earlier. Jackson must take our silence to mean that we don't believe him and launches into a fiery defense of his father. "Look, I know that's what the police are saying, but that's not what happened. Somebody killed him."

Needing to be careful here, I take a second to figure out how to best proceed. "Jackson—"

"No, listen, Stone. My dad would no more fall asleep driving than you would. You know him. He was a night owl, and it wasn't even that late when he wrecked his car."

"Hey, I'm not saying I don't believe you, but there's a lot to unpack here. And I don't even have all the details. Why don't you walk us through what happened last night?"

Jackson's shoulders slump in relief, and he takes a deep breath. "I had soccer after school yesterday. Dad picked me up at five when practice was over, and we went for pizza. After we left Cogan's, he dropped me back by the school gym to watch the basketball game. Halfway there, he started looking in the mirrors. Like, a bunch of times. Then he started making wrong turns. Some of them had us squealing around corners in traffic. I asked what he was doing, and Dad told me he was checking the suspension. Then he dropped me at the gym like nothing ever happened.

"When the game was over, my best friend's dad brought me home where the police were waiting. I know what they told me, but I kept thinking about what happened earlier. My dad didn't say anything, but I think we were followed."

Now, he stops talking altogether. He's unsure of himself or how the two of us will receive what he suspects. I've known the kid since birth, and though he can act like an idiot teenager sometimes, he's got a sharp mind like his father.

"Did you tell any of this to the police last night?" I ask.

"I did, but they weren't listening. That's when I called you two."

His last words are like a knife to the chest.

The boy tried to reach me during the worst time in his life, but I was too busy getting my rocks off to take his call. I didn't even know he'd tried until I found my abandoned phone in my truck.

"You two know my dad. He never gets tired."

Jackson's head falls as he corrects himself, "Never *got* tired."

"We hear you, Jackson," Warden declares. "Stone and I are both having a hard time believing that your dad would go out like that. While I don't have any answers to what might have happened, I promise someone is looking into it."

Jackson perks up, wholeheartedly convinced we'll prove that his father was murdered, if not solve the case ourselves. As much as I should set him straight, I don't have the heart to shut him down completely.

Warden and I quiz the kid more about Bishop's recent behavior and habits, and after I give the kid another hug, Warden walks me out. "What do you think?" he asks.

"Even without hearing what Jackson said, I think NCIS will report that Bishop's death was no accident."

Warden looks out over his manicured front walk. "Yeah. I just don't know what fucking good that's gonna do anybody."

The two of us reach my SUV, and Warden leans his hands against the hood. "I know your hands are tied, but I fully intend to stick my nose where it doesn't belong."

I knew he would. "Keep me posted."

Back home, I walk through the house like a zombie looking for Cass. I need her.

From the doorway of our bedroom, I hear the shower running. A few steps deeper inside, I notice the steam billowing out of the open bathroom door. I cross the floor, pausing when I reach the threshold between the two rooms.

Cass is standing in the shower with her hair pinned up and suds running down her smooth skin. For a moment, I wonder how it would feel if I had been in Bishop's shoes when he lost Lucy, how it would feel to be in Jackson's situation.

The mere thought of losing Cassidy brings me to my knees. Desperate for her touch, I walk to the shower and open the glass door. My beautiful wife turns and smiles, but the pain on my face has her reaching for me. "Tim, what's wrong?"

Needing her more than air, I step inside the shower, still fully clothed, and take Cass into my arms. I don't care that my jeans, shoes, and everything else are soaked. All I notice is her hair's light, flowery scent when I press my nose against the top of her head.

Cass doesn't press me to talk. She wraps her slender body around me, offering the comfort that only she can provide.

Eventually, the screaming in my soul quietens, and my death grip on Cass loosens. The misery of today's news has depleted me, and I drop onto the shower's bench seat. Cass dashes out of the shower for a few towels and returns, stripping off my sopping wet clothes.

With me now naked and having a towel draped around my shoulders, Cass straddles my lap and takes my face in her hands. "Talk to me, Tim. What happened?"

I lift my face to stare into her red-rimmed eyes, eyes showing a heart that's breaking on my behalf. "Bishop's dead."

"Oh, god."

Cass pulls me to her chest as another wave of anguish squeezes more tears from my eyes. My wife weeps with me and whispers comforting words in my ear, but still, I feel like I'm unraveling. I need an anchor, something to keep me from sailing over the edge.

Cass's warmth surrounds and calls to me, and I stand, holding her by the hips and walking us to our bed. Her head doesn't move from where it's resting on my shoulder until I gently lay her down. Knowing what I need, Cass opens up to me, and I push inside her welcoming body.

I pour everything I am into this moment and focus solely on my connection with Cass, in the tight squeeze of her inner muscles, the subtle hint of vanilla left by her body wash, and the way her skin pebbles as I drag my lips across her chest.

Cass shivers at the slight touch of my mouth on her neck as I move within her. Much more quickly than I would have thought, my body pulls tight, and a powerful release shocks through me. I drop my head to Cass's shoulder, and her arms go around my neck, holding me tight.

Cass didn't finish. Not wanting to leave her unsatisfied, I shift to the side and slide my hand down her stomach until reaching her slit. Cass puts her hand over mine to stop me and nudges me to my back. Her head goes to my chest, an arm wraps around my waist, and a toned leg is draped over my thighs.

Her touch works wonders in setting me to right and making me feel less fractured. Though the pain in my chest is no less agonizing, my soul is able to bear it, shorn up by Cass's strength. Because I can lean on her, I'll be able to pull my shit together and help Jackson.

Little by little, the pain turns into planning. The hurt will never go away, but I'll use it to find and catch Bishop's killer.

Feeling centered again and sensing the questions swirling through my wife's mind, I take a breath and lift my hand to bury my fingers in her hair. "Warden came by a short time after you left. Bishop was in a car accident last night," I say, keeping my suspicions to myself.

"Please tell me Jackson's okay."

"He was with a friend. No one else was

hurt."

Cass's hand lifts to rest over my heart. "Tim, I'm so sorry. I know how much he meant to you. He and Jackson both. Where is Jackson?"

"He's at Warden's house. Lucy's parents are on their way to get him."

"What can I do?"

I lift my head enough to kiss the top of hers. "You're doing it, Cass. You're doing it."

Cass feathers little kisses all over my shoulders and throat while her body is wrapped around mine. With each brush of her lips, it's like she's removing the devil's spikes from my chest one by one.

Hell is still beating at the door, but as long as I'm locked in this woman's arms, the devil can kiss my ass.

The following five days pass in a whirlwind of visiting with Jackson and his grandparents, helping them with military funeral details, and impatiently waiting on an autopsy report on Bishop. Though Warden and I have both since returned to work, I can't exactly say that I've been focused.

The more time passes without a definitive answer about Bishop's death, the more anxious I become. Something about the whole situation has left me on edge, and I know Jackson is desperately looking for closure even though he doesn't understand the concept. I find myself hoping the accident will be confirmed just so the boy and the rest of us can grieve normally and start to heal.

It's Thursday morning — the day of Bishop's funeral. Today, I have to say goodbye to one of the best friends I've ever had. Cass, wearing a beautiful navy dress with ruffles, sits on the bed, watching me button the front of my white dress uniform.

At the last one, she rises and approaches, running her fingers over my ribbons. Her hand comes to rest over my trident pin, the most important decoration on my chest and the one that won't be there for much longer.

Cass runs her hand down my arm to take my hand. "Come on, Warden and Trish will be here soon."

Barely a minute later, a knock at our hotel room door means it's time to go. Cass grabs her purse, and we walk out to join our friends.

The fall color season has long since passed, leaving barren tree limbs stretching out over piles of dead leaves. The air carries a chill from a cold front that passed through yesterday.

I'm sure any other time of the year, Frederick, Maryland is beautiful, but today, it's cold and lifeless. Maybe in a few weeks, some snow will fall and restore some of the splendor to the area so that Jackson will be surrounded by something other than death.

A tap on my shoulder snaps me out of my distracted condition, and the four of us climb in my Tahoe. The ride to the funeral home is short, and despite being early, several hundred servicemen and women are already lined up to honor a true American hero.

The four of us walk to the entrance and are ushered past the honor guard and into the chapel by one of the attendants for a private family viewing. Surrounding Bishop's casket are dozens of flower arrangements, and a flag is draped over the bottom half of the finely crafted box.

Trish and Cass walk to where Jackson is sitting, staring toward his father's coffin, unseeing. Besides walking in, my only action was to remove my cover and tuck it under my arm. I simply cannot force my feet to move any closer. At my hesitation, Warden steps forward to pay his respects and say his goodbyes.

I watch, paralyzed, as Warden pulls a large rock from his pocket and places it in Bishop's hand.

Warden's pet rock. He's had that damned thing for more than ten years.

"*What the fuck, man? What the fuck?!*"

The three of us had just walked around the northeast corner of HQ toward the parking lot to see the ground around Warden's Raptor littered with glass and the truck missing its side windows. Next to the driver's door, on the ground among the bits of tempered glass, was a large stone.

Warden ran over and picked up the rock with a smiley face drawn on it in black marker. "Ima kill the sonofabitch."

"Who do you think did it?" Bishop asked.

"Ion know, but when I find his ass, Ima kill him."

Warden Knot was breathing fire as he surveyed the shattered glass all over the ground and inside his truck. I had wondered if the stone would give me away, but neither Warden nor Bishop caught on. Biting the inside of my mouth to keep a straight face, I offered a helping hand like a good friend should. "Bishop and I will help you get the glass out of the cab and follow you to the shop to drop off the truck."

"Aight," he said, drawing a hand across his clenched jaw.

The whole time spent picking glass off the seats, Warden mumbled dark curses under his breath. By the time all the glass was cleared away, smoke was coming out of his ears, and I was choking to death, trying not to laugh.

I retrieved the rock Warden had dropped on the ground and followed him to a local Ford dealership. Bishop didn't ask why I insisted he go with us, but he didn't protest either. I wasn't about to let him miss out on this, the second part of my flawless revenge. Watching Warden explain the situation to the service receptionist had been almost too much for me to maintain my sympathetic cover in front of Bishop.

The best part, the perfect crescendo, came as we were leaving. I was stalling until the moment when a technician would come to drive the truck around to the service bay. While standing around asking Warden what his next move would be, the technician started *yelling in our direction.*

Warden looked back, confused at what he was seeing. The technician had rolled up one of the windows Warden thought was broken and was doing the same with the other three. We marched up to the left side of his truck just in time to see the driver's window emerge with a message in white shoe polish. It read, "Nicole says Hi."

"Holy shit," Bishop whispered before getting down on his knees and bowing dramatically. Warden turned slowly in my direction with blank eyes as though the prank had short-circuited his brain. I handed him the stone and walked to my car, laughing my ass off the whole way.

Warden kept the damned rock, even giving it prominent display space on his desk at Knot Corp. Every time Bishop walked into that room, he would take a marker and refresh the stone's smile while snickering over the memory.

Warden squeezes Bishop's cold fingers around the stone and walks away.

It's then that I finally find the courage to step forward. Bishop is wearing his white dress uniform with all his ribbons and medals gleaming. It bothers me that I still haven't heard any news of his autopsy, but in my gut, I don't need some report to tell me that my friend was murdered. "Who did this to you?" I whisper.

A soft hand slips into mine, and Cass lays her head on my shoulder. "Goodbye, Bishop."

The service goes by in a blur of voices, with

me not really hearing any of it. The crowd swiftly disperses, leaving only family, close friends, and several men who served with Bishop in the SEALs.

The casket is closed, and before the flag is draped over the top, the SEALs line up, remove our trident pins, and take turns pounding them into the lid. Then, it's our job as pall bearers to transfer the casket to the hearse.

Outside, the rest of the honor guard waits to give Bishop a hero's sendoff. Men and women holding flags line our path as a seven-person team waits a distance away to fire a salute.

Everyone except Warden and I step away. It's our job to present the flag to Bishop's son. I fight back a wave of emotion as we ceremoniously fold, snap, and tuck Old Glory into her signature, star-facing triangle. Warden then takes the folded flag and walks over to Jackson, taking a knee before presenting it to the boy.

Taps is played, the salute fires, and the hearse drives away, taking Bishop's body to be prepared for burial at sea.

Mrs. Golden, Lucy's mother, squeezes Warden and me both in turn. "Thank you for looking after Jackson." She swipes at a tear and adds, "I never imagined he'd have to go through this again so young."

"Remind him for us that he's not alone. We're just a phone call away," I tell her.

She nods as her husband loads Jackson into a waiting car, and the four of us are soon alone. None of us speaks as we walk around the building, each too brittle for conversation.

Clearing the last corner, I notice a lone figure waiting patiently beside my SUV. Warden stiffens beside me, likely with the same thoughts running through his head as mine. *Fuck.*

CHAPTER 6

TIM

Admiral Jameson approaches our group carefully, a tightness weighing down his brow. "Ladies," Jameson says with the tip of his hat. "Could I borrow your men for a moment?"

"Of course, Admiral," Trish says with a solemn nod. *She knows what Warden and I suspect. I never told Cass.*

Trish and Cass continue toward my Tahoe while Warden and I wait to hear the bad news we both know is coming. "We have a problem," he says.

Not a murder, a problem. My gut sinks, and my eyes fly to my wife's back.

"Stoddard's death was no accident. The county medical examiner had a backlog of bodies to process, and we only got the word two days ago. During the autopsy, a coded note was found lodged in Stoddard's throat. I held back from telling you two, figuring there was no point until we knew what the note said. As of this morning, we know."

The look on his face tells me we're not going to learn what the note said standing here.

The admiral confirms it when he opens his mouth next. "I know the timing is shit, but I want you to report to the Navy Yard to meet with investigators."

Glancing toward our wives, Jameson asks, "How soon can you be there?"

"We'll be there in an hour," I answer.

Warden and I exchange salutes with the admiral, and he gestures for his aide waiting in a nearby car. The black sedan pulls up, and the admiral leaves Warden and me to digest the alarming development.

Warden doesn't move a muscle except to remove his cover and rub his shaved head. "A coded note means this isn't over. Stoddard was only the beginning."

Of what? I wonder, looking at the woman watching me through the Tahoe's passenger window.

"Stone?"

"I heard you, and you're probably right. Come on. Let's get this over with."

An hour later, on the dot, I roll to a stop in front of the NCIS building on the Navy Yard. The plan is for the ladies to take the car, have a late lunch, and maybe do some shopping while Warden and I check out this note. I haven't breathed a word about my fears to Cass, as she's been through enough in the last few months. After watching me die and fighting to bring me back, she doesn't need another reason to worry.

Before climbing down from the SUV, I kiss Cassidy's soft lips. "You guys have some fun. We'll call when we're done here."

"Tim," she says, her voice worried.

I reach up to cup her cheek while staring at her lips. "Everything's going to be all right, Doc."

I turn away then so she can't see the lie in my eyes. Without looking back, I follow Warden inside to find out about this new hell we're facing.

Security checks us in without batting an eye at Warden being in full dress whites. He earned his rank and has every right to appear in uniform for official military functions.

Immediately after being cleared by security, Warden and I are escorted to a conference room, where Admiral Jameson and a few others are already assembled. Two of the agents in attendance are men I've worked with before.

"Gentlemen, thanks for coming," Special Agent Swanson says. "First off, I want to say that I'm sorry for your loss. The admiral told me how close you all were with Stoddard, and I regret bringing you in on the same day of his memorial service. The admiral also assured me that you would welcome any meeting that will bring about justice for your friend."

Not wasting any more time, the competent agent sits and activates a screen, which displays an image of a creased piece of paper full of gibberish. "This code was found in a plastic bag lodged in James Stoddard's throat during his autopsy. The note, among other things, was the reason Stoddard's death was ruled a homicide and the case handed over to us.

"We put our best people on this note, but after twenty-four hours, no one was even close to cracking it. Since our people were unsuccessful, we pulled in some experts from the private sector."

Swanson looks directly at Warden and adds, "Including one of yours."

"You've had Birdie working on this code, and I'm just now hearing about it?" He asks.

His mouth draws downward in a disgusted frown from the perceived betrayal of one of his most faithful employees.

Birdie is a tech genius at Knot Corp who eats complicated ciphers for breakfast. Her skill is well known in the intelligence community, and she's often called upon to help out various agencies. Her reputation is such that it's not a stretch to assume that she was likely the first, if not the only person, called in.

"In short, yes. Miss Crenshaw was asked to attempt to break this code. As is always the case, she is not allowed to speak on the nature of intelligence requests with anyone outside this agency. In this case, she was given no information about the assignment's origins. Even upon deciphering the code, which she did two hours ago, she still had no idea it was related to

Stoddard's death. And still doesn't.

"We don't normally utilize such clandestine methods, but since you knew the victim... well, you see the dilemma. It turns out that we were right to keep her in the dark. Admiral Jameson says the deciphered note is still a code of some sort and that you have to crack the next level."

"Me?" Warden asks.

"Both of you."

Warden turns to me, and I get the feeling our day is about to get a whole lot worse. "Show us the note."

With the click of a button, the image on the screen changes to display a short, typed message.

Knight II takes Bishop

At seeing the words on the screen, my back goes ramrod straight, and my denial is instant. "That's not possible."

I lock eyes with Warden, and we both turn to the Admiral. He knows that Stoddard, Knot, and I served on the same SEAL team and would be familiar with our nicknames. He ought to know. He was our commanding officer.

Admiral Jameson offers a single nod in confirmation. "This is why I had to bring you in."

"The admiral told me about Bishop being Stoddard's nickname in the SEALs. We need your help figuring out the rest of this message. It's obviously chess-related."

"No, it's not," Warden counters, his

rejection as resolute as my denial.

"Explain," Swanson says.

Warden takes a deep breath as a memory from years ago plays in my head like it happened yesterday. *Stoddard's bowed head in the dining tent. His attitude, his Bible, and praying over food earned him the name Bishop sometime during the second day of basic training.* He was a Christian man, but one who didn't go around beating peoples' heads with a Bible. He respected all and had problems with none.

Warden leans his elbows on the table and breaks down what's in the note. "Yes, Bishop was Stoddard's nickname in the service, but not for the reason you think. The knight reference is also not chess-related. Our platoon had two guys in it with the last name Knight."

I jump in and add, "Quinn Knight, or Knight I, was solid— a good SEAL. He retired about twelve years ago and lives in Florida."

"What about Knight II?" Swanson asks.

Warden's eyes lock onto mine, and his voice is flat when he explains. "Killed in action seventeen years ago."

"Killed in action?" Swanson asks.

"Operation Altha. Beirut," I say in answer.

When I don't say anything else, Swanson prods, "I'm listening."

I turn to catch the admiral's eye and lift an eyebrow in question. This information is classified, meaning I can't share it without approval, not even to catch Bishop's killer. "Sir?"

"Go ahead, Commander."

Looking straight into the sharp investigator's eyes, I dive into the telling of the worst day of my career as a SEAL while Warden gets up to pace the floor.

"Operation Altha was a high-profile rescue mission. My squad was sent into a Hamas camp to locate and retrieve Dr. Milton Foster, whose captivity had been revealed to the world through the terrorists' mouthpiece, Al Jazeera."

Agent Swanson takes notes as he listens and says, "I remember the story and that it didn't end well. The details of his death were never made public."

"And for damned good reason," Warden pipes in.

After his outburst, the agitated CEO resumes pacing, and I continue reporting the events from that complete clusterfuck of a day. "My team arrived in Beirut without any fanfare, having been sent in secret. Despite that, the high-profile nature of the doctor's captivity meant that the airport and US embassy were crawling with press, including an American journalist and cameraman who had eyes on the military base. Like everyone else, these two anticipated a military intervention and hoped to video the extraction.

"And, like everyone else, they had a good idea of where the Hamas camp was and planned to watch for us to make a move and follow us in. Well, it worked. The two assholes spotted my team at some point during our arrival or transport off base. They must have had a staging point planned far enough away from our target zone that they didn't show up on thermal scans.

"In the days leading up to the mission, we'd surveilled the area via satellite, giving us movement patterns for those in the camp. At our planned go time, new images confirmed occupants were following their regular pattern. We moved in, not knowing until we'd reached the camp boundary that we had someone behind us. Our scout sniper picked up the heat signatures during a perimeter scan and reported that someone was coming up on our six.

"We repositioned some guys to take the sniper's place so he could track this new threat. The secondary target was just two slow-moving guys, so the mission wasn't deemed to be compromised. Even if it had, it wouldn't have mattered. We wouldn't get another chance at the doctor, so we had no choice but to proceed. The two shadows continued their advance, but the lack of activity in the camp indicated that they weren't in contact with the newcomers.

"Stoddard, Knot, and I reached the tent where the doctor was being held without incident. Before we could breach, the sniper reported that our followers appeared to be a Caucasian news crew and had also reached the camp.

"So now, we were in a race to get the doctor out before the reporters could blow our cover. Attempting to detain them would have been a risk and taken time we didn't have.

"We almost made it. As Knot and I breached the doctor's holding place, the idiot cameraman turned on his filming light, which was visible through the tent fabric. The guy guarding the doctor panicked and started firing. I killed the terrorist, but not before he'd killed the doctor and shot Steven Knight, Knight II."

Swanson leans back in his seat, contemplating the story he just heard. I know the look. I've thought over that night and what we could have done differently about a thousand times.

"And you're sure Knight was dead."

It's just by the slimmest of miracles that I keep from jumping out of my chair and wrapping my hands around the man's throat. He's insinuating that I would leave an injured man behind.

I'm dying to do just that, to risk my career and tell him to kiss my ass, but I don't have to. Warden does. Slamming his fists on the table surface, he leans over and seethes, "We're damned, fucking sure. We took turns carrying him and the doctor the five miles back to our evac point. Knight was missing the back of his head and the doctor the left side of his face."

Warden uprights himself again, snatches his cover off the table, and stomps toward the door, apparently not feeling very forgiving. Fortunately for him, he no longer answers to the Navy and doesn't have to play nice. He chooses this moment to remind everyone in the room of that fact. "Now, unless you have something useful to discuss to help us find Bishop's killer, you can kiss my ass." To the admiral, he adds a little more calmly, "You know where to find me."

Though Warden can get away with storming out, I have to be more careful, not to mention diplomatic. Addressing the senior agent, I say, "Knight's identity and death were confirmed by a base doctor. You are more than welcome to check into it if you like."

Agent Swanson lets Warden's outburst go, as well as my comment. He's either used to angry outbursts or was squeezing us intentionally to see what oozed out. Satisfied with what he got for his efforts, he moves on from the subject, instead asking something that surprises me. "What happened to the reporter and camera man?"

"Once the camp was secure, they were… detained."

Agent Swanson scoffs. "Meaning someone beat the shit out of them."

"They were detained," I repeat flatly.

"Ok, Commander. Who *detained* them?"

"Stoddard and Knot, and I helped."

CHAPTER 7

CASS

"I'm worried about him," I confess quietly.

I watch Tim walk with Dillan toward the NCIS building. He wouldn't meet my eyes, not since leaving the funeral. Something's wrong.

"I know what you mean," Trish, my friend and Dillan's wife, says. "Dillan took Bishop's death hard. Thinking he was murdered has made it so much worse on him."

My jaw drops. "What did you just say?"

Trish's eyes widen like a deer caught in headlights. "Oh, I um... Dillan doesn't..." She sighs. "Shit, Cass. I shouldn't have said anything about it."

"What shouldn't you have said anything about?"

"Dammit. Okay, first of all, no one is hiding anything from you. The police ruled Bishop's death an accident. It's just that Dillan doesn't believe Bishop would fall asleep driving. I know he and Tim have talked about it, but that's it. Dillan was, is, upset. He could be wrong, though."

"Look at where we are, Trish. This isn't the

Pentagon. We're at NCIS headquarters. Tim O'Reilly and Dillan Knot don't believe in coincidences, do you?"

She turns and looks out the window where our men have just disappeared inside. "I guess I don't."

A security guard taps on the hood, pulling me out of my worried daze. I put the car in drive and pull forward to leave the Navy Yard. *Oh, Tim, why did you keep this from me?*

Trish reaches over and places her hand on my arm, knowing what I'm thinking. Her slender fingers give me a reassuring squeeze, the dark skin from her Caribbean heritage starkly contrasting my honeyed coloring. "Don't be upset with him. Maybe he just didn't see the point of bringing it up unless there was proof."

Trish and I go quiet, both lost in our own thoughts over what's happening inside and what happens next if our men learn that Bishop was murdered. Selfishly, I wonder what it means for mine and Tim's plans to start a family.

"That has to be it."

"What?" Trish asks, suddenly concerned.

"Trish, I know why Tim didn't talk to me about his suspicions. We're… ah… trying to get pregnant. It's a recent development. We want to start a family. I'm guessing that Tim was worried that I'd suggest putting our plans on hold if he said something."

With my eyes on the road ahead, I don't

see my friend's reaction, and she doesn't comment. When she's still silent ten seconds later, I start to worry. The light at the next intersection turns red, and I finally risk a glance in her direction. The regal woman is dancing in her seat like a toddler needing to potty. "Trish, are you okay?"

Like a stopper has just been pulled, Trish erupts in screeches and giggles while grinning and slapping the dash. "First of all, you have the worst timing ever. I want to scream like a kid on Christmas but would feel like shit for celebrating an hour after Bishop's funeral. How am I supposed to handle this? I'm going to be squealing for the rest of the day."

More in control of her excitement, she adds, "And yes, I think this would be reason enough for Tim to keep quiet about Bishop's possible murder. Oh my god! This is so great! May I ask what ended the embargo? Shit, I kind of hate you for waiting until today to tell me or not waiting until tomorrow to tell me."

She squeals again, and I understand her conflicting emotions, as they're the same ones I'm feeling. "Okay. So, I'm sorry I told you like this. The timing sucks. It does feel good to tell someone, though. As for the embargo ending, I think it happened when Tim flatlined in that hospital. I can't explain it, but even as we fought to bring him back, I was grieving not having a piece of him to hold on to. And I regretted never giving him another part of myself. I finally got the nerve to bring it up to him a week ago, but he beat me to it. He'd been feeling the same way."

Trish gives me puppy dog eyes. "Cass, that's so sad but beautiful at the same time."

Though Tim is alive and well, the memory of watching him die is still potent and brings such anguish and fear. Sensing my change in mood, Trish pats my knee and turns to face forward again. "Now, let's go eat. I'm feeling practice sympathy hunger."

At her announcement, I laugh hard enough for tears to leak out, and wipe my eyes as the light turns green. Trish directs me to Wisconsin Avenue, where we find lots of boutique shops and specialty cafes.

It's almost two on a Thursday afternoon, meaning parking is plentiful, and the shops are mostly empty. Our first stop is at a deli for a late lunch. Trish suggests visiting some shops when we've finished and haven't heard from the men yet.

I'm not terribly motivated to go shopping, still too worried about Tim. *Precisely what he was trying to avoid by not telling me about Bishop.* Knowing that, I let Trish pull me around the various boutiques, even perking up a little when I'm shoved inside a maternity store.

"It's a little early for this, isn't it?" I ask as I pick up a cute wrap dress. "I won't even ovulate for another seven days or so."

"Nah. Anyway, you can wear a lot of this stuff before and after the baby."

Trish squeals again in anticipation. "Oh, I just love pregnant bellies, as long as they're not mine!"

Not wanting to burst her happy auntie fantasy, I browse the colorful maternity tops. Pulling out one that's my style, I say, "I thought you liked being pregnant."

"Yeah, but that was ten years ago. And the maternity clothes weren't even this cute then."

I move to another rack and pick up a tunic shirt I wouldn't have guessed was made to cover a growing baby. Spotting a mirror close by, I step over and hold the top against me. *Ok, Trish's enthusiasm is starting to rub off on me.*

A sales associate notices me modeling the top and walks over to offer help. "We have bellies you can strap on to see how the top will look on you later."

I barely suppress the urge to roll my eyes at her polite suggestion. "Oh. Thank you, but no."

Having worked my way to the back corner, I scan the store for Trish just as a woman walks in ahead of a scruffy-looking man with a hat pulled low on his head. The guy is staring at the floor, obviously not thrilled about being here.

Truthfully, I'm starting to feel a little weird about being in a maternity store when I'm not pregnant. I turn away from the rack to find and force Trish to move on to the next store when she comes barreling toward me with a grin. "You have to try this on."

It's a long sleeve, bodycon wrap dress with a deep vee in front. The color is navy blue, so dark it's almost black, and the bottom would nearly reach the floor. Maternity or not, I like the dress, so I give in. "Ok, but just this one," I tell her in a voice as stern as I can manage.

I take the dress from her wagging fingers and leave to try it on. "I'm not putting on the fake belly, though," I yell back at her as I go.

A sign for the fitting rooms points me toward a short hallway in the back of the store. At the end is a rear access door, I assume, for loading stock. The door has a large metal bar stretched across the door frame to prevent it from being opened from the outside. Two fitting rooms are in a shorter hall on the left, and a single bathroom is on the right.

The dress fits perfectly. The style is such that adjusting for a growing belly only requires loosening the tie around the waist. I spin around in front of the small room's mirror before removing the dress and putting my own clothes back on. *Trish wins. I'm buying the dress.*

I've taken one step out of the fitting room when a large hand clamps over my mouth. "Not a sound," a gruff voice whispers in my ear.

The hand covering the bottom half of my face is calloused and rough on my skin. The man's other hand has a painful grip on my left arm. A moment of blind panic seizes me, and I struggle to remember the self-defense training Tim has drilled into my head over the years.

In theory, I know how to get out of a situation like this, but reality is much more terrifying than practice. Unlike in practice, it won't be enough to just break out of a hold. I must devise a good exit strategy before my attacker can recover and strike again.

Even as Tim's voice sounds in my head, telling me to stay calm and think clearly, I'm having difficulty shaking the paralyzing fear. *This can't be happening in broad daylight in a maternity shop.*

My instinct is to scratch and claw like a demon to get away, but Tim has always preached to me that cat fighting isn't a reliable plan. I'll need to use my head to have even the slimmest chance of getting out of this unharmed.

I focus on breathing slowly and deeply, even as the guy starts dragging me away from the changing rooms. *Get his hand off your mouth and scream.*

His fingers won't budge, so I begin working things out in my mind, matching up escape scenarios to the hold this asshole has on me. I know the moves, but with all the hundreds of times we've been at the gym and practiced evasive maneuvers, I still hesitate to execute any of them. In practice, I knew Tim wouldn't hurt me just as surely as I know this guy would.

Think, Cassidy! Don't be a victim!

This could be a simple robbery. In case this guy only wants money, I drop my purse and kick it across the floor. The guy notices but doesn't seem to care. *Shit. The only other possibility is kidnapping.* Panic wells inside again, but I hang onto Tim's training and fight for control over my mind and body.

What is this guy doing, Cass? What is his plan? He won't take me through the front entrance. There would be no way to get past Trish, the clerk, and any other patrons in the store. *We're going through the back door.* Since I threw away my purse, I don't have my phone or pepper gel. I have Tim's keys in my pocket, which means I have a small knife and paracord. All I need is an opening and for me to keep my wits.

Since the guy will have to let me go to move the gigantic steel tube from across the rear door, I'll have at least a slight chance to launch an attack and get away.

As predicted, the man spins me toward the barred exit upon reaching the main hall in the back. Only he must have removed the security bar before grabbing me. Feeling like it's now or never, I turn my head, drop my weight, and attempt to grab his leading leg from between mine. Instead of dropping him to his ass, I'm promptly spun around, ending up in a modified guillotine hold that cuts off my ability to scream or even breathe. *This guy is well-trained.*

I'm now worse off than before I made a move and still unable to signal help. Scarier still, my kidnapper doesn't seem to have any reservations about roughing me up, which doesn't bode well for my immediate future.

To open the back door, he practically throws me against the heavy steel hardware stretching the width of the panel. The contact with the panic bar unlatches the door, which swings open freely. Now, there's nothing stopping him.

Operating in pure panic now, I grab the door frame as we pass through it, just getting my fingers around one of the brackets for the security bar. My desperate grip stops our momentum, and the guy doesn't waste time trying to pry my hands loose. He raises his free arm and slams his elbow down across my forearms repeatedly until I have no choice but to let go or suffer four broken bones.

While his one arm had to let go of me to strip my fingers from the metal grip, his other relocated to my mouth again. I scream into his hand anyway, but his tight grip ensures that barely a muffled moan can be heard.

As he controls the door's closing, tears stream down my face, blurring my vision. I blink away the wetness to try and get some idea of where this asshole plans to take me. I'm also scanning for anything that might help me get free. The alley is lined by the rear entrances of the shops on one side, and on the other is a short block wall with a thick row of cypress trees behind it.

The man's body blocks my view to the right along the alley, and there's only empty alley to the left. Before I can figure out what's happening, the guy vaults over the wall between two of the decorative trees. My face and arms are scratched by the pointy foliage on the way through, and my right leg slams into the rough concrete cap of the wall.

The jarring blow steals my breath, and the abrasive concrete bites into my shin as it's dragged over the rough surface.

On this side of the wall is a small parking lot with no people visible. I'm half carried, half dragged between the empty cars toward a white utility van parked about halfway down the block. *He was ready to run no matter what store he took his victim from.*

The man releases one arm to reach for his pocket, and I know I have only seconds before being trapped inside the van. If that happens, I'm as good as dead.

My arms throb from the blows by his elbow, but I have to try something. Deep down, I know this will be my last chance. With plenty of room to move my sore arms, I reach into the right-side pocket of my dress. Tim's keys are thankfully still there, and I pull them out carefully to keep from jingling the metal.

I flick open the knife kept hidden by the key-shaped hilt. With the man's left hand still having an unbreakable hold on my mouth, I expect him to open the van door with his right. *You're running out of time! Plan your strike, Cass.*

My blade is small, and a strike to his jean-clad legs will just piss him off. I'm held against his front, so I have no visible targets.

It seems I've only got one shot, and it's not a good one. I'll have to make a blind strike and pray I score more than a glancing blow. Six feet from the van, I'm out of time and options. Bad target or not, I have to try now. The attack has to surprise the guy and buy me at least half a second, or I'm screwed. I grip the knife in my right hand and ready myself to run, hoping my injured leg holds up.

As soon as he turns to open the door, I'm granted just enough distance to attack. I plant my feet like Tim taught me and turn my upper body with the swing. I strike over my left shoulder, and the knife makes contact.

My satisfaction is short-lived, as the blow glances off as I feared it might. Fortunately, the wound and subsequent pain seem debilitating enough that the guy lets go of me and howls.

Still holding on to the knife, I take off, running as fast as my damaged leg will let me, not once looking back at my attacker. Whatever he wanted before is probably long forgotten. If he catches me now, he'll kill me. Getting away and staying alive is all that matters at this point.

I don't feel the scratchy limbs of the cypress trees when I shove back through them during my escape. The block wall slows me down just a little, but then I'm quickly, if unsteadily, on my feet again. Limp-running from the scene, I scan the nearby structures and landscaping, looking for the best escape route. A steady stream of cars rolls by the mouth of the alley that I couldn't see earlier. Unfortunately, that's a hell of a long way to limp in high heels, knowing that guy won't be down for long.

What I see of the building and alley doesn't provide me with any better options. Looking again at the rear of the building, it's a safe assumption that all these rear shop doors have security bars and that those inside won't answer panicked banging.

The maternity shop door might still be accessible, but all of the rear doors of the shops are the same and blank except to display suite numbers. I have no way of knowing which door is the right one. Even if I did, none of these doors have handles on the outside.

My only option seems to be the worst possible one. I'll have to run for it and hope I bought myself enough time to reach the end of the block.

I've made it about fifty feet when the sound of squealing tires is heard coming from the other side of the block wall. This could mean the attacker cut his losses or is driving around to catch me in the alley. Not wanting to wait around to find out, I keep moving as fast as I can, though each step sends lightning up my leg.

Two loading docks ahead, I notice that one of the shops' rear doors is barely open, whereas the others look to be sealed tight. That has to be the door to the maternity shop. Banking everything on that assumption, I head straight for it, clawing my nails at the edge of the heavy metal to pull it open. Just as my fingers get purchase, the van enters the alley on the right, speeding in my direction.

I pull hard and slip inside when the opening is big enough. A split second later, I'm yanking the thing closed again, then lifting and setting the heavy bar across the security latches.

I sink to the floor, heart pounding and breathing hard, not quite believing what just happened. I don't even know how long the attack lasted. Seconds? Minutes? It felt like an eternity.

Trish. I need to get to Trish, but my body refuses to do anything besides quiver. Unable to move, I call out in a shaky voice, "TRISH!"

My right hand still clutches the bloody knife, and I notice blood spatters on my left shoulder and chest.

My friend's frantic footsteps barrel around the corner, followed closely by the sales lady. "Oh my god! What happened?" the frantic clerk asks.

Ignoring her question, Trish turns to the

woman, yells for her to call the police, and then drops to her knees beside me. "Cass, what happened to you?"

I can't stop shaking long enough to speak. No matter, Trish knows what to do. Closing my eyes, I try to lie on the floor, but Trish catches me and rests me on her lap. Her voice is little more than an echo in my mind as she calls her husband's name.

CHAPTER 8

TIM

"I'll accept that Steven Knight is not Stoddard's Killer," Swanson concedes, "but that doesn't leave us anything to go on. No other physical evidence recovered from the body or Stoddard's truck could identify his killer."

"Sir, I wish I—"

Before I can finish, the door is thrown open with enough force to bounce off the wall. Warden thunders in, holding a phone to his ear, looking like someone set his world on fire. I clock his expression and don't like what I see in his eyes. "Stone, it's Cass."

The worry fueling this monster of a man petrifies me, and my heart drops into my stomach. Ignoring the questions from the other men in the room, Warden hands me the phone, and I see Trish's name on the screen. "Trish, what's going on?"

The ordinarily unflappable woman is hysterical. "He tried to take Cass!"

Now, I stop breathing. I'm on my feet at the next heartbeat, yelling into the phone. "Take Cass?! Who?! Wait, tried?"

Warden grabs my hand holding the phone and places the call on speaker.

"Some man tried to kidnap Cass. She fought him and made it back inside to safety. I don't know who he was."

"Trish, how is my wife? Is Cassidy okay?"

"She's pretty scraped up and bruised, but she'll be okay."

I look around at the men in charge, needing to get out of here and get to my wife.

"Go," Agent Swanson urges.

Needing no further encouragement, I rush out the door behind Warden. "Dammit!" he yells. "We're on foot!"

"I'll get you there," the agent volunteers.

Warden takes the phone from me and starts working the screen as we rush from the room. "We're coming, Wildcat. Just hang on."

The surprisingly spry old admiral keeps up as Agent Swanson leads the way through the building to his unmarked SUV.

"I hear sirens. The police are almost here," I hear over Warden's phone speaker.

"You stay with me. We'll be there in ten minutes," he tells his wife.

"Five," Swanson calls out.

The whole ride, I listen to the occasional reports from Trish, though nothing about the attack makes sense. I've always been a cool-headed thinker on deployments, but not now. This isn't a mission. This is my wife, and some crazy fuck tried to take her from me.

I know we've reached the scene when the area is surrounded by flashing lights, police tape, and media crews setting up to capture all the scintillating details. Swanson's badge grants us entry beyond the police tape, and I take off running toward the area of Wisconsin Avenue with the highest concentration of first responders.

Shoving my way through the crowd, I don't even look at what type of store it is before rushing inside. Then, all the rest of the world fades away when my eyes land on my disheveled wife.

The room goes quiet, and she notices me a second later. Seeing her awake, alert, and mostly unharmed nearly shifts my heart out of overdrive... until I see her bottom lip quiver.

I hit my knees in front of her, not caring the slightest bit about the fate of my crisp, white uniform. Cass chokes on a sob and launches from the chair to throw her arms around my neck.

We nearly topple over, but I manage to spin us around, so I end up sitting with her across my lap instead. Cass presses against me, and I hold on to her just as tight, resting my cheek on the top of her head.

The split in her dress has opened to expose the bottom half of her right leg, showing me a nasty, eight-inch stretch of bruised and scraped skin. Her shoes are all scuffed, and the fabric of her dress is damaged.

No one in the room speaks; the only sounds heard come from the radios attached to the uniformed officers. I sense someone approaching but hear the admiral's murmured request, "Give them a minute."

As much as I wish I could take her someplace private, the SEAL in me knows better. We can't. The faster we can move on this attacker, the better our chances of catching him.

Reluctantly, I loosen my arms around Cass and lift her chin to look into her eyes. Slight bruising mars the soft skin around her mouth and chin, and I swallow my rage for her sake. "Cass, did he hurt you?"

She shifts to sit upright on my lap. That's when I note the angry purple bruises on her arms. Cass shakes her head absently. "Nothing that requires medical attention."

A DC detective squats down next to us and asks Cassidy something, but I don't hear it. Spotting his badge, I have a flashback. I'm in that car again. *Bullets fly, metal crunches, and the smell of blood and smoke fills my lungs.*

The next thing I know, Cass has both my cheeks in her hands and is pressing her forehead to mine. "Tim?"

Her voice pulls me out of my nightmare, and I take a deep, shuddering breath. Needing a minute to shake off the memory, I shift to stand us up. A couple of chairs are brought over for Cass and me, and we sit down with Cass never letting go of my hand.

The detective that's now standing nearby tries again, "Mrs. O'Reilly, I'm Detective Jemison Quill. I know you've had a hell of a scare. I first want to say that I'm glad you're safe and that I'm tremendously impressed that you were able to escape."

Cass looks from the detective to me. "You did that, Tim. I beat him because you taught me how."

I bend forward to kiss her forehead and lean back again. "I'm so proud of you. Who was he?"

"I don't know. I never saw his face. When I had the opportunity, I stabbed him and ran."

The detective holds up a plastic evidence bag containing my key knife. A wound from that little blade would hurt but not stop a determined assailant.

Trish speaks up from next to Cass, held in the arms of her mountain of a husband. "I told the detective about a man in a ballcap. They're looking through the security footage now."

As if on cue, another man with a badge, askew tie, and shoulder holster walks up. I don't bother standing to greet the man, and he doesn't seem to be offended. "Sir, we just checked the footage. It's grainy, and the guy wore the cap low on his head. We never got a shot at his face. We can only confirm that he's above average height and seems fit."

Quill doesn't react one way or another to the disappointing news. Instead, he focuses on Cass once again. "Mrs. O'Reilly, I'd like you to walk me through what happened, beginning when you arrived in the area."

Slipping her left hand into both of mine, Cass recounts the story while her other hand picks at the frayed fabric of her dress. The further she goes into her account, the tighter her fingers squeeze mine.

Cass digs her nails into my skin as she reaches the part about holding onto the door frame and taking blows from the guy's elbow. Her words have me studying her arms and hands, and my blood boils at what I see. Several of her fingernails are ripped and bloody from her desperate attempt to hold on to safety. The red marks and bruises forming up and down her forearms are a testament to the abuse she took.

Once Cass finishes her statement, I pull her into my lap again. Quill directs Trish to sit next to us and asks her to relay her view of the events.

She soon finishes, and the detective stands when there's nothing more to be learned from the two women. "We're going to do everything we can to find this man," he says as he passes out business cards. "Call me if you remember anything else about the attack."

The detective gestures to the paramedics and back to Cass. "I'd feel better if you would reconsider getting checked out at the hospital."

Cass shakes her head. "There's no need. I'm a doctor. Some ibuprofen and an ice pack will be enough."

Our time here appears to be ending, but Admiral Jameson steps to the center of the group and faces the detective. "Sir, was this a crime of chance, or was Mrs. O'Reilly targeted specifically?"

I stiffen beside my wife and frown at the admiral. I'd been so preoccupied with Cass's wellbeing that I hadn't even considered her being an intended victim.

"I'm afraid that's impossible to know at this point. Unless we catch the guy or find video footage of him stalking her, we may never know. It is doubtful. Mrs. Knot indicated this was a spur-of-the-moment shopping trip. Since you live four hours from here, I feel it's safe to assume we're looking at a crime of opportunity."

Warden passes me a look. He isn't so quick to dismiss the potential danger, and since this concerns my wife, I'm not either. "What do you think, Cass? Was anyone following you?"

Her eyes close, and her forehead creases in thought. "I changed lanes periodically and never noticed a white van behind me. However, Trish and I were talking pretty intently. I could have missed something. I don't know."

Detective Quinn looks surprised and a little suspicious that someone would actively watch for surveillance in their daily lives. I see no reason to explain, and he doesn't ask. Nevertheless, Cass's explanation doesn't change anything for the detective. "I'll be in touch with any developments." He turns to go, then pauses and looks at Cass again. "I really think—"

Cass interrupts his second attempt to get her to the hospital with a dismissive wave. "I have only superficial injuries. I want to go home."

Detective Quill nods and leaves to confer with his colleagues.

I stand and pull Cass with me, turning to face Warden as I do. My unspoken question is answered with a nod, and he says, "You guys go on. Trish and I will stay in Alexandria tonight and head back tomorrow. You call if you need me."

"Thanks, man."

Warden squeezes Cass's shoulder, and I lean down to kiss Trish on the cheek. "Thanks for being with her."

Trish hands over Cass's purse, and I lead my wife outside. Agent Swanson is waiting with the other officers and steps forward when we walk out. Cass is tucked under my arm, so he addresses me directly. "She's okay?"

I nod. "A little banged up, but she managed to free herself. The police are looking, but the asshole was careful. There isn't much to go on."

"Regrettably, that is an all-too-often reality."

"Does that go for Stoddard's murder too?"

Swanson doesn't react to my criticism, instead suggesting, "Go home, Commander. Take care of your wife. I'm glad she's alright."

I turn away from Swanson and navigate through the assembly of cops to find my car. When we clear the mass of bodies, reporters outside the police barricade start yelling questions and taking pictures. "I hate reporters. Fucking vultures."

Thankfully, my Tahoe is parked within the police boundary so that I can get Cass loaded in without being mobbed. One of the DC uniforms moves a barricade so we can leave, and I finally breathe a sigh of relief when the circus is behind us.

My hand doesn't leave Cass's thigh the entire trip, just as her arm remains wrapped around mine. A thousand times, I look over to her, and a thousand times, I'm thankful that she wasn't taken.

Losing her would have done what four bullets couldn't. It would have killed me.

CHAPTER 9

CASS

My eyes are wide open and focused on the shoulder boards of Tim's uniform. His warm hand rests possessively on my thigh. The security of his presence, the Ativan the paramedic gave me, and the white noise of the road pull me toward sleep, but I'm fighting their effects. I've seen Tim suffer nightmares from the horrors of his job, and I'm afraid that if I close my eyes, I'll be fighting for my life again in my sleep.

Eventually, despite my fears, the medication and adrenaline crash win out, and I lose the battle somewhere along the way home. Mercifully, the nightmare doesn't come. I don't dream at all.

I awaken when the warmth of Tim's hand leaves me. That's when I notice the engine is quiet. Heavy lids open to seek out my husband, and I recognize the inside of our garage. Tim is out of the car, walking around to my door, and then reaching inside to pick me up.

With a hand on his cheek, I say, "You don't have to carry me. I'm okay."

Tim presses his forehead to mine. "But I'm

not. What could have happened keeps playing in my mind over and over again. Cass, for all I've seen in my military career, I never understood what it meant to truly be afraid until I got that call today. And no matter how many times Trish or Warden told me that you were safe, my heart wouldn't beat right until I saw you with my own eyes. So, please. Let me hold you for just a minute. I need this."

Being in his arms feels too good to refuse, so I lay my head against his chest, close my eyes, and breathe in the crisp, masculine scent of his cologne. Tim touches his lips to my temple, keeping them there, and carries me into the house like a bride on her wedding day. None of the lights are turned on, but Tim doesn't seem to mind. He doesn't stop until we reach our room, where he finally sets me on my feet.

Standing in the darkness, I take his face in my hands. After a moment spent letting my eyes adjust to the darkness, I bend him down to touch his forehead to mine. "I want you to know you saved me. Every lesson you ever taught me over the years went into saving myself. I'm standing here because of you."

Tim's vexed smile and matching pinched brow suggest that he's both impressed and unconvinced. The tightness in his voice bears this out. "I'm as proud of you as I've ever been of any of my men, but I'm not equipped to handle the thought of you being in danger."

I want to promise him that he won't lose me, but I've been a SEAL's wife and a doctor long enough to know how fleeting and fragile life can be. Tim kisses me tenderly, silently accepting what he already knows to be true. All either of us can promise is that as long as we're both breathing, we'll do it together.

A long moment passes with his lips on mine, and then Tim pulls away. I'm led to the bathroom, where my ruined dress is removed, and Tim inspects my collection of scrapes and bruises.

I'm not sure, but I think I hear him murmur, "I hope the fucker dies from the stab wound."

Seeing nothing needing further first aid, he turns on the shower and washes us both. He leaves me in a towel just long enough to step to the closet, pull on some sweats, and bring back a chemise.

Tim pulls the soft cotton gown over my head and gently wraps my damp hair. The brief touch of his fingers to my scalp has me tipping my head back and moaning.

"God, I love that sound," he says as he takes my hand and leads me to the kitchen. Once there, he deposits me on a stool to be a spectator as he pulls some chicken from the fridge and covers it with blackening seasoning. While the breasts sizzle on the stove, he prepares a salad to go with them.

Tim pours each of us a glass of wine and serves up the meal at the bar. He slides his stool close to mine and, once again, wraps his fingers around my thigh.

Half-way through the salad, I've had enough and lean my head against his shoulder. My fork clatters to the surface, and Tim turns to gather me onto his lap. "Cass," he begins, but his voice trails off.

"I know, Tim."

Without another word, Tim stands and walks us back to our room, where he positions me under the covers, strips off his sweats, and joins me, pulling me into his arms. Nothing more is said. Nothing more is needed.

Tim is still with me when I wake in the morning. I remember hearing Admiral Jameson ordering him to stay home today, just as I know Tim has already contacted Mabry to tell her I won't be at work. Though she won't expect me to make an appearance at the hospital today, I give myself zero chance of making it to dinner without at least a call from her.

Having an unexpected day off, Tim and I plan to laze around the house, and I'm glad for it. My arms and right leg protest at even the slightest movement. A shower helps to loosen my stiff muscles, even if the soap stings a little.

Trish calls while I'm sitting at my vanity towel-drying my hair. I answer the call on speaker and start working my damp hair into a braid. "How are you holding up, Sweets?"

"As long as I don't sit still for too long, I don't stiffen up too much."

"Honey, I'm not asking about your skinned leg. You had to stab a man that was trying to kidnap you yesterday. It's okay to say, 'I'm fucking scared,' or 'Mad as hell.' I won't judge."

"Fine. I had a moment in the shower when a muscle in my neck spasmed, and I had to remind myself that I was alone in my bathroom. Then I reminded myself that I beat the asshole that tried to kidnap me, not the other way around."

"Damn right, you kicked his ass. And stabbed it, too. Too bad you didn't castrate him while you were at it."

"Sorry, there just wasn't the time."

Trish laughs but then goes quiet. "Are you really okay, Cass?"

"I really am, and I'm going to keep going okay. I'm going to have fun and deliver babies and start a family and travel the world."

"Ha. Hopefully, not all at once."

"Well, in three and a half weeks, I'll be able to do at least three of those things all at the same time."

"Wait, you're not still planning to go to Africa, are you?"

"Why wouldn't I? I haven't missed a Doctors without Borders trip since my first year out of residency.

"I… I don't know. I just thought with you trying to start a family, and after what happened yesterday," her voice falls away.

"I'm preferring to think about what *didn't* happen yesterday. And if I am going to start a family, this is likely the last charity trip I'll be able to make for a long time. Besides, it's too late to get a replacement."

Tim walks into the room, bare from the waist up and carrying two cups of coffee. I can't help but stare at the sexy man, even as his face tightens in worry. Recognizing that look and what's likely coming, I sign off the call, with Trish still asking questions. *I'll get back to her later.*

My eyes never leave my husband's as he approaches and sits on the bench at the foot of the bed. He doesn't have to say what he's thinking. It's written all over his face. He wishes I weren't going to Africa, but he knows me well enough and respects me enough not to ask. Still, I feel the need to reassure him and maybe myself. "I've been on a dozen of these trips since we met."

He nods. "True."

"I always call you, every night, using the satellite phone with a GPS locator that you can track."

"You do."

For all my effort, I'm only getting his blank face, which makes me sigh. "Tim, I know these one-and-two-word responses mean you're not sold on the idea. If I were honest, I'd say that I'm not either. To be *brutally* honest, I'm even having trouble with the thought of driving myself to work on Monday. But I can't allow fear over what almost happened to take control of my life."

I reach out and take his hand, bringing his fingers to my lips. "I'll make this trip to prove to myself that I can, and then you and I are making a baby."

The tension in Tim's shoulders relaxes a fraction, but he only continues to stare. I stare right back, and then it's Tim's turn to sigh. "All right. You make this trip and come back safely so I can knock you up."

With that settled, I expect to resume life as I've known it for the last ten years. I realize soon enough the kidnapping incident affected me more than I could have imagined. I'm afraid of people. A doctor who's afraid of people.

My first trip out of the house—post-kidnapping-attempt—happened over the weekend. I remained glued to Tim's side the whole time. When I went out alone, I was jumpy, always looking over my shoulder. I don't venture far, either, refusing to go anywhere except straight to and from work for the whole next week.

Eventually, I'm confident enough to visit the grocery store and salon and meet Trish for lunch. The constant awareness hasn't waned, though. In the back of my mind, I still wonder if the asshole from DC will find me again, irrational as it is.

No good news comes from the DC detective, which isn't helping my paranoia. I've not been afforded the closure of an arrest that would allow me to relax fully. The last update disclosed that the white van used in my attempted kidnapping was stolen, and no ID has been made on the kidnapper. During the update, Tim had the foresight to ask about similar attacks to mine happening. He still worries that mine might have been an isolated event, indicating I was targeted after all. Detective Quill explained that due to the high crime rate in DC, kidnappings for ransom or rape aren't exactly rare. The problem is there are too many snatch-and-grab cases of a similar nature to identify a single signature.

That means the investigation is well on its way to the cold case files, and I worry that I'll spend the rest of my life looking over my shoulder.

It's now been nearly a month since the attack in DC, and we've come to the night before my trip. I hate to admit it, but I'm struggling to psych myself up for the mercy trip. I don't let on to Tim, though. He's still not thrilled about me leaving, but I think it has more to do with his need to have me close than a fear of what might happen.

I feel a little guilty about what my absence

will do to him, but I believe Tim needs this as much as I do. He can't let his fear rule him, either.

I watch Tim turn kebabs on the grill from the kitchen window as the sun fades in the distance. As usual, we've already packed my gear in the truck, so tonight and tomorrow morning will be stress-free. This time around, it seems even more important. Tim and I will need every second we can get to soak in each other's company before I leave.

Feeling suddenly inspired, I set down the tray of dishes and salad I'm holding and strip off my clothes. Then, acting as if everything is normal, I take the tray outside and set the outdoor dining table.

Tim hasn't noticed me yet, too busy working on our dinner at the grill. I move around to his side of the patio, stretching to set out the salad bowls and cutlery.

The grill lid closes behind me, and I hear, "Damn me to hell."

I bite my tongue to keep from giggling and continue my task. The tray of kebabs is dropped onto the granite top next to me just before voracious hands grasp my hips. Tim draws my ass against his growing erection. He bends over me then, nibbling on my neck. "Mmm. Maybe I'll have you for dinner instead."

Tim grinds against my ass until I'm eagerly pressing right back. Without warning, he steps away. He dumps the kebabs into the salad, grabs the bottle of wine and the bowl, and shoves me toward the oversized lounger by the pool.

Dinner is laid on one side of the lounger, and the sexiest man I've ever seen strips naked right where he stands. As he kicks free of his pants, he yanks me to his chest.

We're pressed together lip to hip, but that's not enough. Tim grabs at my thighs, positioning my legs around his waist as his tongue pushes past my lips. My hands go to his ass and then to his head to run my fingers through his hair.

Tim sits down on the lounger and leans back with me straddling his lap, not once breaking the kiss. Using only his upper body strength, Tim lifts and lines me up with the head of his cock. He then proceeds to let me down slowly. "Mmmph. Fuck, Cass."

I hiss at the exquisite intrusion and lean forward, pressing my breasts against his chest. Tim's grip on my hips keeps me from riding him, so I tease him with my lips and tongue.

Tim still doesn't move, and my body begins fidgeting, begging to be taken. I plant one last sensual kiss on his neck and sit up to study his face. Tim reaches into the bowl of kebabs and salad, pulling a roasted tomato off one of the sticks.

A gush of heat rushes to my core when I realize what he's planning. Tim wants to feed me while filling me.

He brings the seared vegetable to my lips and lifts me a couple of inches off him. He thrusts his hips upward as I bite into the juicy tomato, and the unexpected move has me chomping down hard enough to spill some of the juice onto my chin.

Tim leans up and licks it off, relaxing his hips at the same time. Several times, he thrusts and withdraws slowly, driving me crazy. *Turnabout is fair play.* Following his lead, I lift off him slightly to reach into the bowl, pulling a shrimp from one of the skewers and wrapping it in a piece of the lettuce. I lower back down, squeezing my inner muscles tightly as I do. Tim groans, and I offer him a bite of the shrimp, staring at his mouth the whole time.

I ride him for a few strides, and he reaches back in the bowl for another bite, jerking his hips upward as he does. After this bite, I grab the bottle of wine and bring it to his lips. He takes a sip and returns the favor, and then I feed him a chunk of pineapple.

We keep this up for several minutes, the pace slow enough to keep us from climaxing but hot enough to keep us turned on.

When we've both had our fill of dinner, I push the bowl away. "I'm finished," I say breathlessly.

Tim chuckles darkly. "No, you're not."

He rises from the seat, still inside me. Tim pulls me off his rock-hard shaft and positions me on my knees on the cushion. Leaning over me, he growls into my ear, "You're nowhere near done. Hold on, baby. This is going to be rough."

I shiver at his words and barely get my hands wrapped around the top of the lounger before Tim rams into me from behind. No more slow pace now. Tim pounds into me savagely, hell-bent on driving me crazy.

I'm not worried about neighbors seeing. There's an eight-foot fence around the backyard. It is not, however, out of the realm of possibility that I can be heard. Tim pulls out of me and thrusts forward again, sending his cock right up my slit. The ridges run back and forth over my clit until I think I might lose my mind.

Wanting to muffle my out-of-control moans, I bury my face in the cushion. Tim wraps my hair around his fist and pulls hard, forcing my head back up. "No, you don't. I want everyone in this whole neighborhood to hear you scream."

He's not hurting me, but he's never done something like this before. His dirty demand excites me, bringing me even closer to the orgasm I'm now trying to suppress. *I can't believe it. After all these years together, Tim can still get me as excited as a horny teenager.*

The harder I try not to think of our neighbors hearing us having sex, the more turned on I become. I bite my lip to stay quiet as the pleasure builds, but Tim figures out what I'm doing and is having none of it. He releases my hair and shoves his fingers into my mouth, freeing my lip. "You fucking scream for me, dammit."

Oh shit. Who is this monster? Tim's newfound dominance makes my blood sing, and I push against the lounger to meet Tim's every violent thrust. My core clenches, and I start to shake. I'm close.

Tim wraps a hand around my throat, pulling me upright. His punishing pace never falters. "Give it to me, Cassidy."

My body responds on command and implodes with an orgasm powerful enough to scramble my brain. Unable to stop myself, I cry out from the sheer intensity of my climax and again because Tim's not allowing me any time to recover.

I'm experiencing full-on sensory overload, and Tim keeps thrusting. The hand not holding my throat creeps around to finger my clit and doesn't budge when I try to pull his hand away.

A second orgasm hits seconds later, and I'm screaming again and clawing at the cushion. Tim's grip on my hips is stronger than mine on the lounger. My fingerhold is quickly lost when Tim yanks me back again.

I give up my fight to escape. I'm spent. The only reason I'm still upright is because Tim is holding me. Using the little energy I have left, I squeeze my inner muscles as tightly as I can.

Within seconds, Tim's rhythm becomes

erratic, his movements spasmodic. Whispered curses and moans announce that he's close. He thrusts once more and groans loudly, collapsing forward.

It's a long time before I recover and stare out over the pool, but even then, Tim is still at my back. His only change in positioning was to drop his head to rest between my shoulder blades. Something's off here, and suddenly, Tim's uncharacteristic, violent claiming makes sense. He's scared.

Tim's never been afraid of anything... except losing me.

CHAPTER 10

CASS

"Tim, talk to me."

I push back against him, encouraging him to let me up. He does, and I turn around to find him resting on his haunches.

"I can't." Tim looks away from my face and sighs. "I can't say what I really want to."

"You don't want me to go to Africa."

His eyes squeeze shut, giving me all the answer I need. "But I would never ask you to give it up. Please understand. I've never meant to take you for granted, but four weeks ago, I learned that with your safety, I have. Knowing you had to fight for your life while I was just across town has shaken me.

"You're getting on a plane in the morning, and I'll be a nervous wreck. That's my hell and a normal part of surviving what happened. You're smart, though, and I trust you. That's the only reason I haven't tried talking you out of going or packed a bag to go with you. I won't ask you to promise me that you'll be careful. I don't need to because I know you will be. Even with that confidence, I'm terrified. I need you to come back to me."

I rise to my knees and crawl to him until we're touching again. My hand works between us to rest against his chest, right over his beating heart. "Tim, you are my home. I have to come back to you. Now, take me to bed and do that again so I'm sure I won't forget."

The next morning sees the typical chaotic rush of a Doctors Without Borders travel day, though, for my part, things run pretty smoothly. My alarm goes off at four, and I take a luxuriously long, hot shower, knowing it'll be the last real one I'll get for a while. Tim joins me halfway through and washes himself, pulling me to him once we're both clean.

For a long while, he just holds me as the hot spray envelops us in a cloud of steam. Eventually, time threatens to get away from us, and we must get going or risk being late to the airport.

As he does most of the time now, Tim keeps his hand on my thigh during the entire drive to Norfolk International, his thumb tracing lazy circles on my knee. The ride is made in silence, with neither of us feeling much like talking. Tim, for all the reasons he stated yesterday. Me, because for the first time in my career, I'm not looking forward to making the mercy trip to Africa. Once we land and begin seeing patients, I'll perk right up. For now, I'm still feeling a little nervous and clingy from my ordeal in DC.

The big charter plane is already loaded with equipment and medicines when Tim and I arrive at the airport. By the time my gear is added to the cargo hold, all that's left before takeoff is for the team of doctors, nurses, techs, and security contractors to board.

Tim greets Rachel, the team leader, and a few others he remembers from trips past. After surveying the rest of the volunteers, he places a hand on the small of my back and guides me behind an empty forklift.

"Only three guards?" Tim asks when we're out of view of the others.

"Looks that way."

Tim draws a hand down over his face as he groans. "I wish this organization would use Warden's company for security."

I chuckle at the old argument and press in close, touching my lips to his cheek above his beard. Then I remind him, "The security guys are paid volunteers, just like everyone else. I doubt the organization could afford Knot-level security."

Tim's arms go around my back, squeezing me tight. He captures my lips, and my fingers fist in his uniform as his hot tongue dips into my mouth.

"Get a room," Beth Meridian, our longtime anesthesiologist, teases as she walks by our not-so-private spot.

Tim lets me go with a grin, but then his smile devolves into a grimace. "Be safe, Cassidy O'Reilly. I love you, and I need…"

My husband shakes his head against overwhelming emotions and brushes a wisp of hair from my face. Then, without another word, he turns and walks away. It's on the tip of my tongue to say *I love you too,* but I don't trust my voice. If I show any fear or hesitation, he'll turn around and carry me back home.

With the unspoken words clogging my throat, I turn to board the plane, pulling on my noise-canceling headphones as soon as my ass hits the seat. I'm in no mood to be good company. Honestly, I'm skirting the edge here and don't want someone on my team to see me cry.

The DWB plane lands in Nairobi at eight A.M. local time after a miserable, boring flight, made longer by the lack of conversation, thanks to my aloofness. The interpreters arranged by the organization meet us on the ground, and we start unloading our equipment into the provided trucks.

Before heading out, we'll take a couple of hours in the city to gather enough perishable supplies for eight days in the bush. This is in addition to the non-perishable food stores we brought with us. Once various fruits and vegetables are collected, we'll set off on the five-hour drive to Baringo and set up camp in Orus. The site was chosen due to its central location between the three remote villages we're helping on this trip.

As usual for these medical mercy trips, our mission includes malaria prevention and treatment education, as well as general and emergency medical services. My job will primarily be educating the women of the villages on maternity care and birthing procedures, and the other doctors will be performing minor surgeries, addressing dental care, and overall health assessments.

It's normal for me to attend two or three deliveries while in camp. Most of the time, the deliveries are pretty typical, and I use the opportunity to watch the midwives in action and instruct as needed. In the non-typical deliveries I've dealt with, the village matriarchs always observe and assist, further preparing them to handle most situations that can arise during childbirth. Sadly, there's no way to teach them to save a mother or child that won't make it without surgical intervention. Those are the deliveries that I'm most thankful to be here for and why my assistance has never been refused. Each time I perform a c-section in the bush, I'm humbled by the trust these people place in me to care for their loved ones.

Before too long, the cook and assistant return from the market, and it's time to start the last leg of our journey. Halfway to our destination, we stop to stretch our legs and pick up an additional interpreter. During the respite, I put in a call to home. It's three P.M. here, which puts it at seven A.M. in Virginia.

Tim answers right away, his handsome face filling the smartphone's screen. He's freshly showered after morning physical training and sitting behind his desk. "Good morning, Handsome."

"Good afternoon, Beautiful. How's the trip so far?"

"The transfer in Nairobi went smoothly. We stocked up on local produce and stopped to pick up another interpreter who will stay in camp with us. I expect we'll reach Orus in about two hours."

A knock sounds at Tim's door, cutting our call short. He glances at the screen and winks at me.

"I'll call you when we're in place and set up."

"I love you. Watch your six," he tells me.

"Always."

I put the phone away, and Dr. Adams, the senior physician on this trip, takes the empty spot beside me. "Ready to get to work?" she asks.

"Can't wait," I answer. Thinking it over, I can honestly say that I mean it. All my pre-travel jitters have passed, leaving the excitement I usually have building up to our work helping the villages.

One thing that isn't normal is the number

of people we have with us, and I ask Rachel about it. "Hey, what's with the small numbers? I noticed on the plane that there were a lot of empty seats. That seems unusual for one of our trips."

"You noticed that too, huh? I don't know. We usually have some last-minute cancellations and a no-show or two, but never to this level. Still, we have enough to get by. It might actually be a good test to see if we can shave our personnel numbers a bit and use that money to bring more medicine."

I snort inelegantly. "We've had a few over the years that I would have gladly traded for a tongue depressor and an aspirin."

Rachel howls in laughter. "Right?"

The sun is just beginning to set when we arrive on location to make camp. We're all hands on deck to unload and set up tents before dark, but the work is completed quickly with well-practiced hands. By the time we're finished and dinner is served, I'm surprised to learn I have a tent to myself.

A naughty thought crosses my mind, and I have just the thing to liven up my after-dinner calls to Tim.

TIM

The training beach is a flurry of commotion as I watch from high off the ground. The men grapple with one another, throwing around sand and each other to win the day. I've taken a break from the four walls of my office to observe this week's Monster Mash, our regular Friday training competition among the platoons of SEAL Team Two. Though the exercise is grueling, the men enjoy these games and the bragging rights that come with winning.

The thirty-foot tower from which I'm watching the competition allows me to see the green training field, the amphib launch area, and the stretch of shoreline the men are using now.

I came out here under the guise of watching the mash, but my true purpose was to have a minute to myself. I've been on edge all day long, unsettled by a sense of foreboding. My sixth sense has always been a big part of my career, but this is different. Storms seem to be brewing all around me, figuratively, literally, professionally, and personally.

To date, NCIS has made no progress in identifying Bishop's killer. That means we have no idea what the bastard's next move is. And we know he's planning something, or he wouldn't have left us a note.

The detectives in DC have failed to close the case of Cass's attempted kidnapping. I imagine there may be too many open cases where they have a lead to follow after a ghost that didn't leave a trace except for some blood on a knife. Since his DNA isn't on file, we have nothing.

These personal situations, though disturbing, are only half of the equation. The sudden, numerous reports of activity abroad are added to the weight resting on my shoulders. In the past four hours alone, I've received twelve bulletins concerning security for various European embassies. That number in such a short span is something I've never seen in my career. Stranger still is that the alerts represent each country in our assigned territory. My suspicion of a hoax led me to check in with Admiral Jameson, who confirmed that the chatter was real.

The geopolitical geniuses at the Pentagon are stumped, and even our resident expert, Chief Hagan "Ink" Fischer, is clueless, given the European countries' lack of overt terror activity.

I lean down on the tower's safety railing and take a deep breath, letting it out slowly. My whole adult life, I've dealt with danger and uncertainty. However, since dying and coming back to life, my world has seen so much upheaval that I'd swear I woke up in a shitty alternate universe.

My head is still bowed when I feel the tower supports vibrate, indicating someone's coming up the ladder. I don't even have to guess who it probably is.

The visitor crests the top and casts a shadow on my left. "Dorne said I'd find you here," Warden announces.

I turn my head and note the tactical pants and Knot PMC polo shirt. "What are you doing here?"

"I was just in Norfolk for a meeting and

thought I'd check in on a friend. He's a guy we both know that recently lost a close friend, whose wife was nearly kidnapped, and who is worried about said wife because she's currently in Africa."

I look out at the ocean so Warden won't see how unsettled I am. "Cass is smart. Scrappy. And she's with good people."

Not fooled by my dodge, Warden joins me at the railing and leans forward so I can't avoid looking at him. "And yet?"

I allow my head to drop. "I don't know. There's too much shit happening to get a handle on any of it. That note on Stoddard was only the beginning. What that means, I have no clue. Besides scaring the shit out of me, DC made me understand why Basset left the force there. There's too much crime and not enough cops to sort things out, and that's when they have decent leads to follow. Cass's case is on ice. They aren't even looking for our guy anymore."

Remembering who I'm talking to and that he can almost read my mind, I stop trying to hide what's really going on inside my head. I turn to face my friend again, letting the mask fall away. "And, yes, Cass is on the other side of the world, but Africa isn't a problem. She's with a solid group of people and has armed security in her camp. Her safety *should be* the least of my concerns right now."

Warden's voice softens even as he rolls his shoulders. "You know, Stone, this is the first time in twenty years I've ever seen you rattled. And I know it's not over the sudden influx of alerts for your men I just heard about or even a psycho killer. You that worried about Cass?"

I drop my head again, looking down through the gaps in the floor. "Cass and I have decided to start a family. All I can think about is wanting her home, safe with me."

"Shit," Knot says in a rush of air, sounding relieved. With a clap on my shoulder, he laughs at me. "Damn, man. You had me worried there. Just wait. You have a kid, and you'll learn what being scared means."

I shrug his hand off me. "Not helping, asshole."

His chuckle becomes a full-on belly laugh, and he pulls me in for a rare hug. "You'll be a great dad, my man."

Warden hangs around a bit longer, watching some of the monster mash with me, but eventually has to return to his role as CEO of the country's most highly respected private military firm. Shortly after, I make my way back down the ladder and to my office, where, once again, chaos ensues.

Just before two, I duck out for a late lunch, knowing this should be about when Cass settles in for the night and calls. At the base clubhouse, I walk back and stand on the deck, waiting for her to Facetime me on her satellite phone.

As I wait, I stare out over the water

churning under an angry sky filled with dark clouds. The waves are high thanks to the late-season hurricane tracking just offshore.

If it's predicted to get any closer, all the ships docked along this stretch of coast will get underway to avoid being beaten against the docks. *The Navy and the Coast Guard are better at running out to meet the storm head-on instead of waiting around to take a beating.*

Then why am I struggling to do the same?

Cass's call comes in while I'm locked in my turbulent thoughts, and I rush to answer, anxious to see her face. The call connects, and it takes a half-second delay for the picture to come in.

I know a brief moment of stunned paralysis as it isn't just her face I see on the screen, but her whole body, naked as the day she was born. My wife is stretched out on her cot and must have her phone propped up on a table at her feet. "Holy mother of god."

Her answering laugh at my reaction reaches into my soul, loosening some of the tension that's had me tied up in knots since I left her at the airport four days ago.

"I sincerely hope you're somewhere private," she giggles.

"Standing on the back deck of the Eagle's Nest."

Her voice lowers to become sultry and teasing. "I feel sorry for you, then."

Cass tells me about her day, how busy

she's been, and what the rest of her schedule looks like. The whole time she talks, wicked little fingers drag across her collarbone, up and down her middle, and trace around hardened nipples. "After discovering that I had my own tent, I couldn't resist trying this out. I was going to do it before now, but this is the first time I didn't crawl into my tent at the end of the day."

"I'm not complaining," I lie. My dick is certainly complaining.

In case anyone walks out onto the deck, I turn my back to the rail to ensure no one can walk up behind me and see the screen. I also pop in my Bluetooth earbuds so no one can hear. This moment is for me and me alone.

Cass asks about my day as her knees fall open, and a single, slender digit slips into her glistening slit. Mesmerized by the erotic show Cass is performing, I glaze over the typical goings-on here, leaving out the cluster of alerts that have come in.

Now glistening with arousal, the finger is lifted to spread the wetness over a taught nipple before Cass repeats the act on the other side. "I don't know why we've never tried this before."

My voice is strained when I say, "Because when I was deployed, I was always in camp with a bunch of horny bastards that didn't need the extra stimulation."

Her laugh is a beautiful sound. "I guess you're right. Though, we've not exactly been short on erotic adventures, have we?"

Her middle finger has returned to her clit and is now strumming the bundle of nerves. "No, we haven't."

Cass's sexy voice drops to a whisper, and she begins an erotic walk down memory lane, recalling her favorite and most risky places we've had sex over the years. Her hands never stop moving, switching from kneading her breasts back to teasing her clit.

My dick has long since grown hard in my pants, and despite the discomfort of a raging hard-on in this public place, I'm thanking god for the hi-def phone camera that allows me to see her pussy in such detail.

Before long, Cass's words fade away before long, and her slow breathing gives way to short pants. Her fingers continue to play over her clit, making me wish even more that I was with her. "Those are my hands on you, Cass. While my fingers tease that sweet little spot, I'm using my tongue on your nipples. When you can no longer lie still because of all the sensations, I'll kiss my way down that body, and it'll be my tongue on that pretty pussy that sends you over the edge."

Cass's pants become moans as she pleasures herself for me, my dirty narrative adding to her desire. Her fingers speed up, and her body draws tight, so very close to orgasm.

The sounds she's making have me hard as brass, and I hope to god no one in her camp can hear. I don't dare ask how close her neighbors are, as Cass is smart enough not to do this with an audience.

Her clit swells with each caress of her fingers, and I swear, I can smell her scent and taste her on my tongue. The phantom senses are so real that I have to clench my fists to keep from touching myself.

I've had nearly all the torture I can take when Cass's body shivers and she bites her lip to keep from calling out through her orgasm. She's magnificent, lost in ecstasy, and I'm holding my breath as I watch her shatter.

Cass relaxes and smiles languidly as heavy-lidded eyes open and find mine.

"You are the most beautiful thing in my world, Cassidy O'Reilly. I can't wait till you're back home and I can touch you again."

"Soon, my love. This trip will be over before we know it, and I'll be on my way back to you."

"I'll be waiting."

Knowing it's late where she is, I have her sign off to get some sleep, and I turn back toward the water until my erection settles down enough that I can walk into the restaurant.

BULLETPROOF

JO CHAMBLISS

CHAPTER 11

CASS

"You look mighty chipper this morning."

Rachel's comment draws the attention and grumbles of several others in the dining tent of our camp. I sit beside her with my tray and try to hide my smile.

The zombies dining on breakfast return to their coffee, thankfully ignoring me. Normally, I'd be in the same condition, but my digital rendezvous with Tim last night pepped me up quite a bit.

Since I'm no longer in my twenties, I'm certainly glad for the more energetic start to another long day. I'll need it. Since we still have four days and a lot of work left to do, there's no time to waste.

The whole camp hits the ground running after breakfast. We've visited all the villages and gotten an idea of what types of medical services are needed. We'll schedule each remaining day's focus, clinic configuration, and patient schedule based on these needs to ensure we get to everyone.

Those of us in special practices will have

our own schedules from here on out. For instance, I'll teach birthing classes each day in the village. The other doctors will be performing various procedures back in camp. I'll schedule return visits based on need, and for my off times, I'll be assisting in camp with surgeries and general medical treatments.

Of course, if any patients are too sick or immobile to make it to our camp for scheduled treatments, we'll carve out time to care for them in their village.

The week continues to progress pretty much the same as my previous trips have. Though the scenery is different, the way villagers welcome us is the same. The main difference between this trip and my many earlier ones has been my nightly Facetime with Tim due to me having private quarters. My satisfied smile returns each day after our phone sex, but thankfully, no one has caught on to the reason why.

On day six of our mercy mission, I'm in the surgery tent working with Dr. Adams to remove a growth on a three-year-old's eyelid that's hindering her vision. Rachel is just finishing when Angela, one of the nurses, sticks her head in the tent. "Dr. O'Reilly, it looks like you have another customer."

I don't look away from the instrument I'm holding when I ask, "What have we got?"

"A boy walked all the way from the Pokot

village. An elder woman sent him to tell you that a first-time mother has been pushing since sundown. The baby is stuck."

My heart falls at what sounds like a hopeless situation. "Dammit. Sixteen hours. It's probably too late to save the infant."

"I know, but maybe you can save the mother. Go. I'm good here," Rachel says.

I rip off my gloves and grab my equipment bag off the storage shelf. Letting Angela lead me outside, I follow her to where the boy waits. The competent nurse has already appropriated the land cruiser and an interpreter and is requesting a security volunteer.

The one named Bill quickly jogs over and jumps in behind the wheel. Angela, the boy, and I climb in the back, and we rely on the interpreter to work with the child to get us to the right place.

The drive is a rough and slow one out of necessity. Uneven roads that rarely see vehicle travel have roots encroaching the dirt path barely wide enough for our truck to fit. Tree limbs as big as the boy's arm reach for us as we rumble by, branches that would smash a window if we were going any faster.

The security guy driving understands the urgency and pushes the safari truck as fast as is safe in this area. It still takes two hours to reach the village. Several people run out to greet us when we arrive, but I leave the pleasantries for the interpreter. Meanwhile, Angela and I jump out of the truck and grab the medical equipment bags from the rear cargo area.

We're then led straight to the midwife's hut and find the laboring mother in bad shape. She's barely conscious until she calls out in pain during a contraction, only to collapse again afterward. Angela and I scrub with alcohol and shove into some gloves to see what we're dealing with.

Thankfully, the interpreter finally rushes in at this point. I'm going to need him. Kneeling between the mother's knees, I start firing off questions, trusting the interpreter to keep up while the nurse checks the mother's vitals. As I listen to the various responses, I reach a gloved hand inside the woman's cervix to get a clearer picture of what's happening in case the village midwives made an incorrect diagnosis.

The infant is turned in the right direction but isn't engaged. *There's a chance it's still alive.* The problem is that we've got an obstructed birth and still risk losing mother and baby. Even if we get the baby delivered, there's a high probability of uterine rupture. "Angela, see if you can get a beat on the infant."

I continue my exam, prodding the woman's abdomen, and Angela nearly shouts. "Cass, I've got a steady beat. I don't believe it, but I've got a beat holding at one-fifty. It's still alive."

"We have to perform a cesarean, and we have to do it right now."

I throw off my gloves and reach for my bag. Angela does the same and lays out a surgical mat, carefully positioning sterile instruments for the procedure while I set up to put the woman under general anesthesia. Not ideal, but I'm not waiting for Beth.

When we're ready to get started, I bark at the interpreter to clear the room of everyone except for the midwife to receive the newborn.

Angela gives the midwife a mask when the hut empties and gets ready to intubate as soon as I inject the sedative.

"Fetal heartbeat?" I ask.

"One-sixty, dropping to one-thirty during contractions."

"Beautiful."

A drop of sweat crawls down my forehead as I pour disinfectant over the mother's belly. I wipe my face on my sleeve and scrub the woman's abdomen for all I'm worth to reduce the chance of her developing a post-operative infection. Meanwhile, Angela finishes intubating and announces, "Okay. We're good here."

She secures a mask over my face and her own and then helps me to re-scrub and don new gloves. She goes through the same process on herself, and then I finally lift the scalpel.

Several tense moments later, Angela holds the incision open so I can reorient the infant. It's a snug fit, but the head delivers, and I pull the infant from the uterus—a boy. Beckoning the midwife over, I pass the baby off without checking for life signs. At this point, whether he's alive or not, my priority has to be making sure his mother lives. The last thing I do before returning to mom is tying off then cutting the umbilical cord so the infant doesn't bleed out.

Returning to my inspection of the mother's open womb, I'm shocked and glad not to see signs of a uterine rupture. I deliver the placenta without complication, and just as I begin closing the cesarean incision, I hear a weak first cry of the newborn. Despite myself, I feel a tear leak out and track down my face into my mask.

The child makes another feeble sound and then begins crying in earnest. "You did it, Cass."

I lift my eyes to Angela's and see the same emotion mirrored on her face. "No, *we* did it."

The smile under my mask is vast as I staple the incision closed, serenaded by the beautiful sound of the healthy baby's cries. Angela takes over once I'm done, removing the breathing tube and gently bringing the mother out from under the anesthesia.

Filled with wonder and humbled by the miracle of life, I stand, remove my gloves, and step over to the midwife holding the newborn. The sage woman seems to know what I want and offers the child to me. The beautiful little boy is swaddled tightly in a handmade blanket, possibly woven by the woman who attempted to deliver him.

"He's perfect. A little miracle."

She must have understood as she smiles and says, "Wewe, mponyaji, ni muujiza."

A knock at the hut's opening has me turning around to find the interpreter grinning. In his thick accent, he translates, "She says, 'You, healer, are the miracle.'"

My attention returns to the child, and I brush a bare finger against his soft cheek. Lost in the moment, I hold and rock the infant a while longer before handing him back to the midwife. I need to go over post-operative care with her now that all the excitement is over.

Spotting a basket of fruit on a stool near the door, I pick up a pawpaw fruit. I retrieve the stapler from the surgical mat and get the caregiver's attention. I press the stapler to the fruit to demonstrate and explain the care necessary for the wound.

The interpreter passes along my bandaging and cleaning instructions as I return to my bag for a staple remover. Returning to the midwife, I take the tool and show her how to remove the metal closer. Just so she's comfortable, I place another staple in the fruit and trade the instrument for the baby. The interpreter explains that I mean for her to practice removing the staples, which she does successfully.

The staple remover is placed in the midwife's bag, and the mother awakens enough to be given her infant a short time later. That means it's time to leave her in the care of her family.

Angela and I pack up our gear and have the interpreter tell the family I'll be back in two days to check on mother and baby. Grateful goodbyes are shared, hand-made blankets are presented to Angela and me, and I virtually float on my way to stow our bags in the land cruiser. Feeling gratified, I climb in the front passenger seat with the security guy while Angela and the interpreter take the back.

We set off back toward camp, with me riding a giddy high over what we accomplished today. To hide my constant, dreamy grin, I stare out over the treacherous yet beautiful terrain until the safari truck's engine dies. The vehicle lurches to a stop, and I turn to the guard for his assessment of the situation. We're at the crossroads that goes either left to the camp or right, deeper into the wild.

Before I can process what's happening, Bill pulls a gun from his hip and turns in his seat, shooting Angela and then the interpreter. A scream rips from my throat as my ears ring from the deafening blast. I grapple for the door handle, desperately trying to jump from the seat.

Bill grabs my hair, jerking my head, and pulls me back in. "I don't think so, sweetheart."

"Let me go!"

My demand is ignored, and he grabs my hands, squeezing my wrists together and securing them to the dash handle with zip ties.

"Who are you? What do you want from me?"

"Aww, you don't recognize me? I'm hurt."

I study the man's face for the first time since getting on that plane. There's nothing familiar about him. However, on his left side, under his short beard, I notice recently gnarled skin that could be from... a knife attack.

TIM

It's around seven in the morning, and I've just finished meeting with all my platoon leaders and sat down behind my desk when my phone rings. Glancing at the device, I'm a little surprised to see Admiral Jameson's name appear. This can't be good.

I pick up the phone and answer, "O'Reilly here."

"Get to Norfolk. There's been a development in the Stoddard case."

"What kind of development?"

"We've got another note. Knot's people are already working on it, and Knot's on his way in."

The man hangs up without waiting for a response, and I'm in my truck racing toward Naval Station Norfolk four minutes later.

Warden's already occupying a guest chair in the admiral's office when I walk through the door. Notably missing from the meeting is Agent Swanson. It occurs to me to wonder why, but I don't waste my breath asking.

"You made good time, Commander."

Something about the tone of his voice sets my hackles to rising. Warden stands and moves across the room, staring out the window. He hasn't even looked at me. In answer to the admiral's comment, I say, "Your order indicated speed was prudent."

The admiral and Warden exchange a look, and the old man continues. "A note was delivered by courier to Knot's building in DC an hour ago."

"Okay. How long before Birdie cracks it? Is Swanson on his way?"

"Commander, we didn't need Birdie to crack it," the admiral says but doesn't continue.

Now, Warden looks my way, and at his horrified expression, I feel like the floor has been pulled out from under me. "Tim, the note said, *Knight II takes the Stone Queen.*"

My phone is out immediately, and I'm shaking my head, refusing to believe what they're trying to tell me. I dial the number to Cass's sat phone in the next instant. *No service.*

Without explanation or any idea of what I plan to do, I spin on my heels and reach for the door.

"Where are you going?" the admiral yells out.

"I'm going after Cass."

"You can't do that!" the admiral says.

I turn around slowly and, with fire in my eyes, dare him to stop me. "You knew they had my wife before bringing me here. I've already wasted too much time, time Cass may not have. Are you now ordering me to stand down?"

The admiral is silent, knowing what will happen if he says yes.

"Dammit!" he yells instead.

He scrubs a hand over his face and slams his fist down on his desk. After what appears to be a violent internal debate, he says, "I'm authorizing you to identify, locate, and neutralize a direct threat against active and retired Navy personnel and their dependents."

That's good enough for me. I pull the door open, but then the admiral calls out again. "Wait, O'Reilly. That authorization may have kept you from quitting on me, but it isn't going to help you either. This could easily go sideways, and the way I see it, you're fucked already. All your men are on alert due to the noise in Europe, meaning you don't have a team, and there's no way you're going up against just one man."

My men.

Only the uncertainty of their imminent deployment gives me pause. Turning back to the admiral again, I ask, "Will you see to my men personally?"

My mentor nods solemnly. "I will safeguard your team, but you're still rushing out that door without the support of one."

"He has a team," Warden declares as he crosses the room. "And I don't need authorization from anyone to back him up."

Admiral Jameson shakes his head but looks relieved. "I'll give you two days before informing Agent Swanson. Then he'll be the one calling the shots. Godspeed and good luck. You're going to need it."

Outside the building, I take off running for my Tahoe but stop at Warden's sharp yell. "I can get us there faster!"

I don't argue. A quick redirect has me gunning for his Escalade. Warden tosses me his keys and jumps in the passenger seat to get things moving. "Airport," is all he says before pulling out his phone and barking orders to whoever answers.

The Escalade screeches to a stop fifteen minutes later. We've arrived at the Knot Corp hanger and jog over to a man standing next to the jet already rolled out onto the tarmac. "Brock Lawson," the man says as he offers his hand. "I've got gear for both of you on board."

He's dressed for action and is the only operative here. I guess that means he's going with us. Warden secures the hatch once we're inside and bangs on the cockpit door. "Let's move!"

The plane is rolling before my ass lands in a seat.

"Lawson," Warden growls. "Have you gotten in touch with anyone on the ground in Nairobi?"

"Not yet. I've sent a message to area teams

through the main office. I'll check back when we're at cruising altitude."

I'll do better than that. Two minutes later, my phone is out, and I'm pulling up the contact for Dr. Adams. Though I've never needed it before, I'm damned glad to have it now.

Thank god, the salty doctor answers. "Rachel, this is Tim O'Reilly. Where is Cass?"

Her voice carries the kind of panic that confirms my worst fear. Cass has been taken. "Tim! God, I don't know. She was called out for an emergency at about nine this morning. She went to a village about two hours from here and hasn't come back. She's not answering her phone either."

"Was she alone?"

"No. A nurse, an interpreter, and an armed security guy went with her. That was eight hours ago."

"Has anyone gone to the village to find her?"

"We can't. It's close to nightfall here, and they took the only truck that can make it over those trails. We'll have to wait till morning and head out on foot."

"Shit. I want you to call this number if you hear anything. I'll be there in eighteen hours."

Eighteen fucking hours.

The next few hours are spent going back and forth with the trip organizers. I want to know the name and history of every person who made that trip, but I'm getting stonewalled. It isn't until Knot's lawyers get involved that they agree to discuss the identities of the group's participants with us.

So we're not wasting time waiting for information to be relayed, Warden's got his team on a video chat, which has the organizer on a conference call at home base.

"Start with anyone on that trip that hasn't traveled with the team before."

The answer comes quickly. "All the medical personnel on this trip have volunteered at least once before, and the interpreters are the same ones that worked with us last year."

"What about your security team?"

The sound of keyboard clicks is heard over the relayed call. "They're both volunteers from area firms. They were thoroughly checked out."

"I still want Knot's people... wait a minute. You said both. There were three at the airport when I dropped Cass off."

"That's impossible. We only hired two men to act as security on this trip."

"I don't care what you did. I'm telling you, three security operatives boarded that plane!"

Warden covers the mike and whispers to me. "Hey, this helps us. We'll rule out the two legit men, and we should be able to get surveillance photos of the third."

I deflate instantly and drop my head in my hands. I stood next to the bastard that could be hurting my wife.

Warden must signal the lawyers to cut the organizer loose as I hear them thanking her for her time. When she's gone, he orders, "Call the number for Dr. Adams. Ask if anyone has a picture of the three security guys' faces. When you get something, run it. I want to know who this bastard is."

A hand lands on my shoulder. "We'll get her back."

I drop into the nearest seat and close my eyes, shutting out all the chaos and noise. All I can think about is Cass.

The first time we made love, I felt like the luckiest man alive. She was so beautiful, her skin so soft. I'll never forget the sounds she made when I first slipped inside her body. She felt so right like she was made only for me. We were magic together. I wanted to ask her to marry me right then.

I only made it two more months before I did ask. And she said yes. Cassidy took my breath away again on our wedding day. She looked like an angel walking down the aisle in her white gown. Her smile was brighter than the sun. During our first dance as husband and wife, she lifted on her toes to whisper in my ear, "*I promise always to be your safe harbor.*"

Cass is every dream I've had come true, and now that someone's taken her, I'm living my worst nightmare.

BULLETPROOF

JO CHAMBLISS

CHAPTER 12

CASS

A scream catches in my throat, unreleased because I can't seem to breathe. *He killed them! Bill just shot Angela and Kasim!*

Even with my hands bound to the dash handle, I turn as much as I can to see if there's any chance either of them could still be alive. Angela is slumped over, staring sightlessly. A single rivulet of blood oozes from the hole in her forehead.

Knowing I'll find Kasim in a similar condition, I turn away quickly to stave off the sudden and overwhelming nausea. That's when I notice the blood spatter all over my arm. My empty stomach churns violently, and I spin back toward the dash, putting my head between my knees and retching.

By the time the dry heaving stops, I'm completely drained. There's no bravado, no calm, collected planning, and no hope to get out of this alive.

It's obvious now that my attack in DC was anything but random. That this guy had the means and patience to stage my capture in Africa points to a much larger and darker force at work here.

My thoughts turn to Bishop's death, and somehow, I know they're related. Everything that's happened points to Tim being the ultimate target in the deadly game being played. *And I let them do it. I made it easy.*

I should have made an effort to identify the man in DC; should have at least gotten a good look at his face instead of running as soon as I got loose. If I had, he probably would have made a move again anyway, but not here. Then Angela and Kasim would still be alive.

The fake security guy cranks the safari truck's engine and turns the heavy vehicle to the right, away from camp, with the bodies still in the back seat.

He drives for several miles, long enough for my senses to numb completely and my sobs to reduce to occasional sniffs. The truck lurches to a sudden stop again, and I brace myself for certain death.

I don't get a bullet to the head, but Bill — I'm sure a fake name — takes advantage of my bound hands and searches through my pockets. He stops when he locates the satellite phone that everyone knows I carry. I'm divested of the device, and it's carelessly tossed on the ground outside. As if losing my phone isn't enough, the asshole pulls out his gun, and with one shot, he's disabled it permanently.

Now that my phone is out of commission, he gets out of the truck, opens the back doors, and pulls Kasim and Angela's bodies out, dropping them to the ground with as much care as he showed the sat phone. "You bastard. You can't just leave them here!"

"Watch me." Behind the wheel again, Bill starts up the land cruiser's engine and drives away, leaving the bodies for the scavengers to find.

Though I'm still in shock at the horror of my situation, a deep, burning rage begins to take root. I channel all my fear and hatred for this bastard into a steadfast determination to beat him again. To think that he would so carelessly discard two people who dedicated their lives to helping others. This man doesn't even deserve to breathe the same air as them. I don't know how, but I will make him pay. Hippocratic Oath be damned.

For the remainder of the ride, I keep my head down and my mouth shut. It's a fight to stay focused and keep my wits. My thoughts keep straying to the bodies unceremoniously tossed on the ground and to my husband, who I might never see again.

Focus, Cass. You can't go back and change the past. You're here and will just have to battle through this like Tim would want you to.

Fake Bill is thankfully ignoring me as he manages the rough terrain and a couple of phone calls. From what I gather through his side of the conversation, he's to continue east to the flats, some twenty miles away, and wait for a helicopter to arrive sometime in the morning.

Based on my study of area maps, the flats they're talking about are next to a water source that's bound to see plenty of animal traffic. At night, that means predators. There's no way he's prepared for such a dangerous excursion. The chances are good that we'll both be dead by the time transport arrives.

I bite my tongue against bringing this up, deciding my time is much better spent observing and planning like I did in Washington.

My main disadvantage is that I have zero weapons this time. And this time, the man has a gun. Not to mention, my hands are bound to a sturdy safari vehicle. This thing is equipped with emergency rations, shelter, first aid, and other supplies necessary for survival, but it has no weapons. That is to say, nothing designed to be used as a weapon.

There are plenty of medicines that I could use to incapacitate the asshole. I just have to get free to utilize them. That's not going to be easy. I surprised him once already in DC. I don't expect he'll lower his guard this time.

It's nearly dark when we reach the grazing flats. We're the only two humans for a dozen miles at least. And with our lack of equipment, we're not at the top of the food chain.

At least Bill has only the animals to fear. On the other hand, I am a captive of a psycho killer with unknown intentions. The more I think about my vulnerability, the more my fear intensifies. Absolutely anything could happen, and I'd be powerless to stop it.

About fifteen feet from the water's edge, Bill stops the truck and kills the engine. He reaches over to lift my veil of hair that worked out of its ponytail. A shiver works down my spine, making him laugh, but he releases my hair and opens his door. I draw in a shaky breath, and Tim's voice sounds in my head, reminding me to stay focused and not panic.

Leaving me bound, Bill steps out of the truck and opens his pants to relieve himself just a few feet away. *With any luck, he'll get bitten by one of the venomous snakes native to this area and die where he stands.*

In case that doesn't happen, I'll keep my eyes and my options open. Through the open door, I hear the hiss of a zipper closing, and the murdering asshole walks to the truck's passenger side. My door opens, and the guy rests his arms on the roof, caging me in. "Looks like it's just you and me tonight, sweetheart."

I keep my eyes on the floorboard, refusing to meet his gaze. "You don't talk much, do you?"

He reaches in and cuts the zip tie anchoring me to the dash. The one holding my wrists together is left in place. "I have to use the bathroom," I blurt out.

"Be my guest," he says with a wave of his hand.

"Could you free my hands? I mean, where am I going to go? I'd be dead in five minutes if I walked more than thirty feet."

The man grabs my neck and shoves me into the side of the truck, pressing his body hard against mine. With a sick gleam in his eyes, he says, "If you run, it won't be the lions and tigers you have to worry about."

After his warning is delivered, my bindings are cut, but it's quickly made evident that I'll get no privacy. Untucking my shirt, I pull it down to cover me before loosening my belt, lowering my pants, and squatting next to the truck. My bladder, full to aching, is relieved, and I do up my clothes as fast as I can, all under this psycho's watchful eye.

A new zip tie is placed around my wrists, and I'm dragged to the back of the vehicle. "I know there's provisions in here. Let's see what all we've got."

He pulls the fire starter and fuel out of one of the life safety boxes in the cargo area and loads my arms with the food and water. Bill secures the hatch again, and I'm dragged and dropped on a spot about six feet from the vehicle. "Who are you?" I ask as he lays the foundation for a fire.

"I don't think that's any of your concern at the moment."

Fearing I know the answer but asking anyway, I ask, "Then who am I to you?"

"Bait."

Tim. I was right. I'm too afraid to ask anything else.

I'm given canned peaches and beef jerky for dinner, and then my hands are freed, and I'm offered the chance to relieve myself once more before being tied up in the truck's back seat. Because of the excitement in his eyes, I refuse, wanting to keep as many layers of protection between him and me as possible. "I'd rather risk pissing my pants."

I yelp as the guy leaps forward and crushes me to the side of the car like he did before. "I should get something for my trouble. You did carve up my face pretty good."

I shudder and turn away, but the man roughly grabs my hair, yanking my head back around. The pain in my scalp elicits a helpless whimper just before Bill's mouth crashes down on mine, and his other hand reaches for my belt. On impulse, I bite his tongue hard enough to draw blood, shove his hand away, and focus all my strength, fear, and revulsion into a heel stomp on his foot. Too late, I realize the man has on steel-toe boots, and my effort is wasted.

The man punches me in the face and slams his fist into my stomach. The first blow stuns. The second knocks the wind out of me and lands me on the ground. My mouth opens and closes like a fish while my lungs try to restart. This is my worst fear and biggest mistake. I've let myself become vulnerable.

With no other ideas coming to me, I reach down to the ground and grab a fistful of dirt and rocks. I'll likely only have one shot to blind him and attack before Bill touches me again temporarily.

A truck door opens, the bottom brushing over me before I'm picked up and tossed on the seat covered in dried blood. I finally suck in a much-needed breath when my hands are roughly yanked together again and fastened with a zip tie. Bill pulls them down toward the floorboard, and another zip tie is removed from his pocket. This one, he uses to secure my wrist binding to the leg of the seat that's bolted to the floor.

The door is slammed shut again, and hot tears of relief flood my eyes. I rest my stinging cheek against the seat cushion, not even caring that the tears are causing the bloody seat to smear red on my face.

I'm still holding onto my fistful of rocks and dirt while Bill stomps around outside. His occasional curse sounds stilted because of his injured tongue. I don't dare laugh, not just because he might lose his temper and kill me, but I'm afraid that once I start, in my delirium, I might not be able to stop.

Several hours pass with me lying completely still, bunched up and tied to the back bench. Bill has long since taken up his post in the driver's seat, chased from the open air by the sounds of the jungle waking up. Luckily, he's chosen to ignore me entirely in favor of passing the time by playing a game on his phone and communicating with his contacts.

He's wisely left the windows up in the truck, which means the air inside is uncomfortably warm and ripe with the smell of sweaty bodies and blood. Despite the less-than-ideal conditions, Bill puts his phone away and is soon snoring, giving me the best, and likely only, chance I'm going to get to escape.

I'm still tied down and have no weapons other than the pebbles and dirt gripped in my left hand. That fist has been held tight for so long that I have to pry it open with my other fingers, careful not to drop anything. The moon shining through the windows provides just enough light to search my hidden cache for anything useful.

Of the bits of earth and stone that I intended to throw in the man's eyes, there's only one stone in the small collection with a surface that is abrasive enough to be useful. Being as quiet as I can and moving as little as possible, I shift on the seat and pull the plastic binding around my wrists tight against the metal bar anchoring it. Now, I position the rock in my hand to start sawing through the plastic restraint.

My fingers are already tingling with the lack of blood flow, but I'm determined to free myself and ignore the growing numbness. Only a few strokes in, the rock I thought was hard enough for the job crumbles into dust. It turns out that it was little more than petrified dirt or manure. I bite my lip to hold in a frustrated sob, but I'm ready to give up and drop my hands in defeat.

On the way down, my left hand lights upon a jagged edge of the seat frame. It's in a spot where the leather seat has worn away from years of use. Feeling hopeful again, I roll over enough that both hands can get a grip on the zip tie binding me to the seat. Pulling a section of the band tight, I work the plastic back and forth, slowly across the rough metal, to test how much sound it makes. *Not any louder than his snoring.*

Considering the alternative, I decide it's worth the risk. For the next few minutes, I continue working the strap over the metal barb until a satisfying snap brings a smile to my face. Now, I focus on cutting the tie around my wrists. Since I'm no longer tethered to the seat, maneuvering for this cut is much less taxing.

Faster than with the first cut, my hands are free, but I'm still not out of the woods. Even more carefully now, I rise to my knees to figure out the next part of my plan. Simply getting out of the car won't help. There's nowhere to hide and no safety from the large predators that roam the area.

I'll have to see about reaching his gun or, at the very least, his phone. The gun would be my first choice for obvious reasons, but if I can't remove it from the holster without waking him, there's no point in trying. If I could get his phone, which has to be a sat phone since it works out here, I should be able to call Rachel and have help sent my way.

The problem is assuming I can even get out of the truck undetected. If I could get to the medical supplies, I'd be able to mix up something that could render Bill unconscious or kill him outright. Unfortunately, a wire separator blocks access to the cargo area from inside the vehicle. And there's no way I can get out and open the back hatch without waking my captor. Especially since I'd have to get the keys from his pocket since I watched him lock the door earlier.

As wrong as it feels, I have to go against my training that says to get away from danger. In this case, there's just as much danger out there as in here.

Okay, Cass, it's time to find out what we're dealing with.

My heart thunders in my chest as I lean forward, testing the back seat for squeaky spots that might give me away. When I'm in a good position, I draw in a deep breath and hold it for my reconnoiter of the front seat.

Calls from monkeys, bullfrogs, and other animals blend together to help mask the small sounds I'm making as I lean over the creaking leather upholstery. The good news I gather from my vantage point is that the asshole's phone isn't in his pocket. The bad news is that the device is perched on his right thigh under his hand. *Damn.*

The gun is also a wash because it's in its holster on the man's right hip... which his right arm is currently resting on. *What the hell do I do now? I've got to get one or the other.* If I can't get the gun or the phone, I'm screwed.

I could take off my belt and choke the guy, but with his strength, he'd probably be able to pull the strap out of my grip easily, freeing himself before killing me.

Back to the gun and phone. Even if Bill's arm weren't covering the holster, I would expect some sort of closure over the stock for me to release to draw the weapon. That leaves the phone as my least bad option. I take another deep breath and let it out slowly before drawing in one more and holding it.

Reaching carefully over the seat, I grip the phone with two fingers and gently tug it.

Beads of sweat form on my forehead, and my heart is racing. When the man doesn't stir, I pull harder to dislodge the device from under his hand. My seat creaks at the same time his last finger slides off the phone's screen, and my breath chuffs out in alarm. I freeze and remain completely still for several heartbeats to be sure I haven't woken him up.

Bill doesn't move, and I'm nearly dizzy with relief as I slowly pull my arm back upward.

As I'm drawing the rest of myself back over the seat, an amused voice whispers in my ear. "Going somewhere?"

I scream, drop the phone, and go straight into attack mode. My hands attach to Bill's face, clawing everything I can reach. Going against the oath I swore to do no harm, I dig a thumb into one of Bill's eyes. The man starts howling and reaching for the gun at his hip.

Because of my position, I can't use either of my hands to stop him. The gun is pulled free from its holster and then lifted toward me. In Bill's thrashing panic, he knocks the weapon into the steering wheel before finally disentangling it. I have no choice but to let go of his face with my right hand and use it to deflect his aim.

I chop down, somehow shoving his arm enough that he's aiming at the floorboard. A shot goes off, its trajectory taking it through the vehicle's footwell. Bill grapples me with his left arm as his right hand lifts the gun again. A second strike to his arm sends the next bullet forward, though I can't see where it went.

As I strike his gun hand again, my left hand seeks to gouge his other eye. I'm just not doing enough damage. I'm fighting a losing battle here, and we both know it.

Bill reaches up with his left hand and grabs a handful of my hair, yanking me to the side. This frees him from my grabby hands, giving him enough space to finally turn the gun, aiming it over his left shoulder in my direction.

Jerking my head away from his grip, a large patch of hair rips from my scalp, but I have enough momentum to grab his right elbow and pull.

When the third shot goes off, Bill stops fighting.

Fire rakes across my left bicep, making me scream, but the loud ringing in my ears keeps me from hearing it. More importantly, Bill is no longer waving the gun around. Reaching for the handle beside me, I force the door open and stumble out of the safari truck. My frenzied escape lands me on the ground on all fours, and the potent cocktail of adrenaline, fear, and relief has me losing the meager contents of my stomach.

My insides eventually settle, and I lift the hem of my shirt to wipe off my mouth. *Get up, girl. You're not out of the woods yet.* Though my kidnapper hasn't come for me yet, I can't just assume he's dead. If Bill *is* dead, I've got work to do.

Shaking legs push me up from my knees, and I turn slowly toward the truck. The dome light shows that Fake Bill hasn't moved, but I hesitate to approach. Eventually, and on unsteady legs, I reach for the driver door handle as my breath saws in and out.

Slow and easy, I ease the handle up and swing the door open. Bill's chest is moving, but only just. There's a lot of blood. If Bill isn't already dead, he's close to it, and a check of his carotid confirms the prognosis.

His pulse is weak. The call to action tenses my muscles, but I won't be working to save this man. I would have no success anyway. What I will do is get the hell out of here.

Though my arm is stinging like a bitch, I grab his left hand and shoulder and pull his lifeless body from the seat as gently as he did with Kasim and Angela. His phone falls with him, landing just a few inches from his bloody face.

I bend down to retrieve it and notice a dripping sound coming from the engine area of the truck. There's no point in looking under the hood. I know bodies, not cars.

It is probably safe to assume this bastard's bullet must have hit something in the engine when he was firing blindly in the cab. With it leaking, there's no way this rig will make it back to camp. I'm still spending the night out here, where there are more dangerous things than asshole kidnappers to worry about.

I finally grab the phone, which appears to be similar to mine. I push the button on the side to activate the screen, but the only response I get is a flashing battery sign.

Searching the dead man's pockets, I hope to find a charger. My search turns up nil, so I try the cab of the cruiser—nothing there either. Utterly defeated, I drop the device and allow myself to crumple to the sandy African soil.

Fighting off sobs, I yell, "Is it too much to ask for a little fucking help here?!"

My loud outburst silences the monkeys and birds in the bordering trees for a brief moment before they all respond at the same time.

"Very helpful, yes."

I've got to get away from this bloody body that is likely already attracting predators. Though the truck is literally and figuratively shot, I figure whatever distance this thing can get me is better than nothing. I bend over and search the dying man's pockets.

Finding his wallet, I open it up and locate his ID. *I figured Bill Smith wasn't his real name.* Finally, I have a name to go with the face, though the name is unfamiliar to me. *Robert Gilley.* I shove the wallet in my pocket and get back to my search.

I'm looking for the keys to the truck, and as soon as I find them, I get my ass moving. Without sparing another second, I jump in the driver's seat and crank the engine. I don't even bother adjusting the seat before kicking up dust on my way out of there.

I think I've made it about two hundred yards when the engine begins sputtering. With all my shouting, cursing, and begging, the damned thing still only makes it another fifty yards or so before it dies completely. The truck made it far enough into the tree line to block the jungle road but not deep enough to be safely hidden from whatever group of criminals will be coming by helicopter in the morning.

Regardless of the risk tomorrow brings, I have to deal with the situation right now, and that's the big cats. I have no choice but to shelter in the disabled truck until daybreak.

When the sun rises, I'll take the gun and start the long hike back to camp so I'm not here when the bad guys show up. For now, all I need to worry about is dealing with this wound in my arm and getting some rest.

So that nothing can sneak up on me, I turn on all the safari vehicle's lights and go to the back for the first aid supplies. The bleeding from the gunshot graze has slowed, so I cut away my shirt to see what I'm dealing with. The wound isn't deep, but it also isn't pretty.

It needs stitches, but I wouldn't close it without ensuring it was clean. Since I'm limited in supplies and working with one hand, I have to settle for pouring a disinfectant over the wound and applying some clotting agent. I'll cover it loosely for now and properly close it when I can get a shot of antibiotics. *If I make it back to camp.*

"Stop it, Cassidy. You didn't escape being kidnapped twice just to die in the jungle. You're going to make it back to Tim, and then the two of you are going to make beautiful babies."

Grabbing all the first aid supplies I need, plus some water and protein bars, I shut the hatch and climb back in behind the wheel. The animals

I disturbed have all returned to their nighttime serenade, not caring that a human sits among them, scared to death and bleeding.

A loud noise jolts me out of a deep sleep hours later, and I scream, thinking I've just met my end. When my eyes open, I'm face to face with a monkey sitting on the truck's hood. Nervous laughter bubbles forth until I notice the sun's position high in the sky. I look at my watch to see that I've slept till noon, and my panic returns.

Lucky that I have yet to be discovered, I jump out of the truck and open the back, sifting through all the supplies. I dump out my medical bag and throw in the rest of the water bottles, protein bars, fresh bandages, and ibuprofen.

From the survival box, I grab bug repellant and cover myself. I realize this hike could go into the night, so I toss extras of everything inside, including a flashlight and matches, not that they'll keep me safe.

I'm as prepared as possible and start the long hike back to camp.

CHAPTER 13

TIM

Thirteen hours after learning of Cass's abduction, Warden's helo races across the African sky to Orus. With my heart in my throat the whole time, the long hours of travel have been the worst I've ever experienced, and that's saying a lot.

Cass has now been missing for twenty-three hours. I know from my earlier conversation with Dr. Adams that a search team wouldn't have mobilized until sunrise about two hours ago. They would have been on foot and carefully searching the surrounding jungle. Despite what we told them, the medical team is holding out hope that Cass's crew just ran into trouble and is stuck somewhere along the road.

They should be reaching the village Cass visited yesterday right about now, but it doesn't matter. They won't be any closer to finding her.

Those who took her would have to be organized and well-funded to have been able to pull off this level of kidnap mission. Thankfully, Warden also has those qualities because I'm in no shape to lay out and execute carefully constructed plans.

Almost the entire trip, he's been pulling strings and doing everything he can from the air. I've been fucking useless, spending more time pacing the floor than anything. The admiral was right about me not having a team, or in this case, even any connections I could exploit.

What I do have is a fucking rich best friend who all but rules this world. And I plan to use every resource he has to get my wife back and stop these assholes.

One such resource is an unending supply of airplanes. At our first and only fuel stop, Warden had no intention of waiting for the requisite cool down, refueling, and start-up procedures generally included in such a long flight. No, the bastard had another jet waiting to leave the second we touched down in Doha, Qatar.

We grabbed our bags and ran down one flight of steps and up another. We were in the air again in less than ten minutes.

In Nairobi, things moved just as fast. When we deplaned, Warden had a Bell 412 waiting to fly us to the medical camp in Orus. Not only was the Bell waiting, but a black monster crawler was also hitched up to the helicopter to go with us. The roll cage and polycarbonate panels don't exactly fit in with other safari rigs, but I only care about speed and stability traversing the jungle.

The three of us are soon loaded and lift off

carefully, dangling the crawler below us on a cable.

Once the bird is in the air, I contact Dr. Adams again, patching the call into the helo's radio for Warden to monitor. "Rachel, this is Tim. I'm about fifty minutes from your location. What can you tell me?"

"The search team has just reached the village where Cass had to attend a birthing emergency. The midwife there reports that Cass performed surgery to deliver a baby and left afterward. The group wants to start looking in the opposite direction of the camp."

"Don't. Call them back."

"What?! Why?"

"Rachel, Cass was taken by dangerous people. I know this because they sent me a message. If your people go after them, they'll all be killed. Just have them start back toward camp. I'll handle finding Cass."

Minutes feel like hours as we cover the remaining miles to the camp in Baringo. Upon reaching the camp's coordinates, the helo flies a circle pattern above the installation. The pilot radios that we will not be landing here. The tents take up enough of the clearing that there's no room for the helo's rotors.

The pilot lowers the craft to just over the tops of the trees, floating the crawler about three feet above the ground. He releases the cable holding the monster machine, which lands with a big bounce. The pilot then shifts to hover a few feet to the left, Lawson tosses pairs of gloves to Warden and me, and the co-pilot drops a rope out of the side door. It's been a long time since Warden or I have had to fast-rope down from a helo, but I don't see either of us balking at the jump.

All three of us strap on our equipment packs, and the pilot gives us the thumbs up to go. Lawson goes down first, followed by me and then Warden. As soon as we're clear, Warden signals to the co-pilot, who pulls up the rope as the bird flies away. He turns to me then. "Well, this is your show, man. I'm just here to back you up."

"Let's check in with Rachel first." Pointing at the crawler, I gesture to the crawler. "Lawson, check this thing out and make sure nothing broke loose in the landing."

"Yes, sir."

Warden and I hand our bags to the operative and leave him to stow them in the ATV while we approach the camp. On our way in, Warden and I are met by one of the security contractors. Michaels, if the manifest is to be believed. He takes in my navy uniform with wide eyes.

Not caring that we have an audience drawn out by all the noise, the first words out of my mouth are, "Nice job, asshole!"

"Hey! Whoa!" Warden yells and jumps between us just as the security man lunges for me.

"Knock it off, Stone! This won't help Cass."

The camp that hadn't come out for the arriving helo notices the yelling, and several people come running to find the source of the commotion. The angry security guy asks, "Why are you jumping on me? It's not like we let Dr. O'Reilly leave without a security detail."

"He wasn't fucking security!" I yell at the man. "I checked with your organizers. This trip only had two security men signed on. The guy you're missing, the man that took my wife, no one has a damned clue who he is! I would think that's something you might have checked."

The guy pales and stammers. "That... that was taken care of by the organization. I was just glad to get some last-minute help."

I storm past the guy looking for Dr. Adams and feel a tug on my left arm. "Easy, Stone. These guys are first-time volunteers and had no reason to doubt one another."

Warden's right, but dammit, I don't care. As we near the hospital tent, a graying man steps out of the tent and, with wide eyes, spots us and sticks his head back in. "Rachel!"

Dr. Adams rushes from the tent to meet me, pulling off a pair of medical gloves as she approaches. "Tim. God, I'm so sorry. I don't know how something like this could happen. What do you need from me?"

"I need coordinates for the village and a map of all roads in this area."

Warden opens up a big-ass tablet displaying a satellite view of Baringo. Rachel points to a village peeking out from under the trees. "The Pokot village is here, and this is the road."

Her finger trails from our location to the remote community, though the "road" she indicates is barely visible by a thinning of the tree canopy along the way. Michaels joins the conversation and points to a crossroads a few miles from the village. "I walked to this point at sunup. There was no sign of them. The search team hasn't reported anything unusual from this point to the village."

I bite my tongue to keep from tearing into the man again. He may be shit at security for not checking up on his counterparts, but that's not my problem right now. Finding Cass is.

Doing what I should be doing, Warden studies the image and calls my attention back to the screen. "This village has water around a third of it and a steep hill on the north side. This road to the west looks to be the only other way in or out."

"That's right," Rachel confirms.

"Where does this road go?" I ask.

She leans close as if looking for some landmark and pointing when she finds it. "Hmm. Somewhere around here, I think, there's a fork. The left road leads to a big hunting field. The other goes around to the back side of this lake."

I lift my eyes from the screen to Knot. "We know they didn't come back this way because there's no way to get past the camp without being seen. But that would mean whoever we're dealing with wasn't planning to leave the area on a truck. If they had a bird waiting in this field, we're already too late."

Warden shakes his head after thinking about what I said for a second. "The medical emergency wasn't planned, meaning the guy was capitalizing on a lucky situation. He would have had to call someone, and no one can mobilize as fast as I can. I say there's a good chance we beat them here."

"Not if he already had someone in Africa," Michaels says.

"You, shut up," I say with a finger in his face.

Jogging steps approach from behind me, and I turn to see Lawson joining the group, which gives me an idea. *Michaels was right. This guy wouldn't have followed Cass to Africa without a plan to get her out.* "Lawson, I want you in the guy's sleeping quarters. He wasn't working alone. Find out what his exit strategy is."

Lawson grabs Michaels and runs in the direction of the group of tents.

I turn my attention back to the doctor. "We're going after Cass. Get a treatment area ready. She might need your help when we find her."

"You two be careful," she says as I turn to join Warden.

The big crawler's engine is rumbling when I climb up and strap in. Not even a second later, we're tearing down the jungle lane to find my wife.

We move fast toward the wooded crossing, the powerful crawler traversing the rough terrain with ease. We also aren't wasting precious time looking where we know Cass isn't. Finding the intersection Rachel described, Warden slows down to look for signs that Cass was taken this way in case Michaels or the search team missed anything.

About twenty minutes after we pass the turn to the village, we come upon a gruesome scene. Two scavenged bodies lie across the road near a phone sporting a bullet hole. I recognize the blond hair with purple streaks as belonging to one of the nurses Cass has worked with multiple times over the years. Climbing out of the crawler, I pull out the sat phone and call Lawson. "Camp."

"We found two of the missing. Go get Dr. Adams."

"On my way."

Heavy footfalls sound through the speaker, and then Rachel's voice, "Tim, did you find her?"

"No. We found bodies. They're about three kilometers past the fork headed toward the lake. The nurse with purple hair streaks and a young man. Doc, we can't stay here and deal with them."

"I know, Tim. You go find Cass."

"Thanks, Doc," I say before disconnecting.

Warden and I move the two volunteer workers with as much care as possible and start down the road again. Two hours later, we come face to face with a land cruiser blocking the road. We can't get around it, and the damned thing's too heavy for the crawler to push out of the way.

Warden kills the ATV's engine, and the two of us get out to investigate. While Warden goes straight for the safari truck, I'm scanning the jungle, looking for signs of an ambush. Or maybe a terrified doctor.

"Holy fucking hell. Stone, you need to see this."

Based on the fury in his voice, I almost don't want to. The only reason I'm able to move in his direction at all is because I know Cass isn't in that truck. Warden's summons would have sounded a lot different if she was.

With one last scan of the tree line, I walk the few yards to the cruiser's door that Warden holds open. My heart sinks at the carnage. "What the hell happened here?"

There's blood fucking everywhere.

"I'd guess the two we found on the road were shot in the back seat," he says as he points to the spatter patterns. "At some point, there was a struggle over the gun."

Following the point of his finger, I spot the bullet holes in the floorboard and firewall. "That could explain the abandoned truck."

To confirm my theory, I back up and drop down on all fours. Sure enough, there's a small puddle of fluid under the engine. I lean back on my haunches, and my brow furrows.

A glance at my friend shows that Warden's face is tight with the effort to avoid saying something, but I don't need him sparing my feelings. "Just say it, man. I'm struggling here and need your insight. Coddling me isn't going to help Cass."

He gives me a pained nod and takes a deep breath. "With the two dead, only Cass and the poser would have been left to fight over the gun. With as much blood as I'm seeing... I'm just wondering when the fight happened and where the loser's body is."

Swallowing the lead weight in my throat, I say, "Just keep looking."

Beyond the copious amount of blood, we find other signs of struggle around the truck's interior. I'm walking around to the other side when Warden points to something in the back floorboard: a pair of chewed-up zip ties.

I'm beginning to get an idea of possible explanations when something in the front passenger seat catches my eye. "Warden, look at this."

He joins me at the front passenger door to

see what I've found. Trash from various medical supplies and food wrappers are scattered around the front seat and floor. A moment passes while the expert strategist analyzes the debris left on and below the seat. Next, he lifts his head and scans the road from the direction we arrived and then to the opposite direction.

"The truck is aimed away from where this guy was headed. Someone performed first aid after the others were killed. Cass was bound but escaped. So, who was doing the doctoring, and are doctor and patient the same person? And where did the gunfight happen if not here?"

As one, we turn back toward the open field and watering hole. Using my field glasses, I scan the flat area near the water's edge. "I see something over there."

Abandoning our recon of the safari truck, we run more than two hundred yards toward the small lake and come upon a grizzly sight: badly mauled and scavenged remains of a man's body and a recent campfire.

The fire indicates the guy held Cass here for a while, likely waiting for extraction. With the dead man on the ground and the truck blocking the road, I can think of two possible scenarios. One, Cass killed him. Two, their ride showed up, decided our guy was dead weight, and took him out.

Option two doesn't seem plausible because there would have been no need to move the truck. Warden kicks out at the dead man's leg and voices the theory that has his vote. "Guess we know who won the fight."

"If Cass killed him, then where the hell is she?"

Warden's eyes are up and scanning the area around the abandoned cruiser. "This asshole had to be coming out here to meet someone," he muses. "Judging by the terrain and the doc's maps, the only way out besides that road is by air. I still think we beat them here, but I'll get my people looking just in case."

I don't feel like waiting that long. Turning away from the mutilated body, I begin a frantic grid search of the dusty ground. I'm looking for helo skid imprints. If I find any, I'll take measurements. With skid dimensions, Warden's people should be able to identify the bird that took Cass out of here.

After searching a radius of twenty-five yards from the campfire, I become encouraged by what I don't find. I increase the search radius another twenty-five yards to be thorough, but still see no signs that a helicopter landed here. Any farther out and a landing helo would be risking its rotors in the reaching jungle canopy or landing on the sloped bank of the small lake.

Bolstered by the real possibility that Cass made it out of the area on her own, I jog back to Warden to get us moving again. He's photographing the scene and collecting prints and DNA from our dead guy.

He looks up at my running approach. "Find something?"

With a shake of my head, I answer, "No skid prints. No tire tracks other than the cruiser. You were right. Whatever extraction this asshole was waiting for, we beat them here."

Warden shoves two tissue sample vials in his pockets and picks up a phone from the ground near the body. "That confirms she was the one to move the truck. Come on. She's on foot, and based on the medical debris we saw in the truck, she's injured."

The dead man's phone gets shoved into another of Warden's pockets for his team to crack into. Though this guy is no longer a threat, that won't end it. Dillan Knot will find out who the dead man was and bring down every person he's ever associated with. Fine by me.

The two of us run back to the abandoned cruiser, where I sift through the first aid box in the back for extra supplies in case Cass needs them. Bloody prints on several empty slots show exactly what supplies Cass used to treat herself. The labels tell me what had been there, giving me an idea of how badly she's hurt. Besides basic wound care products, there's an empty slot for a clotting agent, a suture kit, and a tourniquet.

"I think she was shot," Warden says over my shoulder.

My head snaps up as if I could sense her

just by looking around. "We've got to find her. She'll never make it back to camp before nightfall, and bloody bandages will be a dinner bell for larger predators."

Shoving supplies in the cargo pockets of my pants, I back away from the busted truck and look down the dirt lane. "Cass wouldn't walk the road in case that guy's partner showed up. She'll be deep enough in the jungle to keep from being seen but not deep enough to get lost. She also wouldn't have been able to make it too far. I'll start back on foot about ten yards inside the tree line. You get the crawler turned around and set a slow pace. I'll update you every fifty yards or so."

The two of us return to the all-terrain vehicle, where I shoulder on my small pack containing water and protein bars while Warden straps back in. Two extra magazines for my Sig go in my back pockets, and I grab the rifle loaded with tranq darts in case I should run across any predators.

Before I set out, Warden lays a hand on my arm to stop me. "This goes back to Bishop's murder. You understand this was never a one-man show. Be careful. We don't know how many we're up against. I'll contact the Admiral and update him on what we did and didn't find."

With a nod, I climb the bank on the right and push into the dense foliage. I'm close enough to the edge to follow the curve of the road but deep enough that Warden or anyone else down there can't see me.

"Where are you, Cass?" I whisper as I start tracking back toward camp.

It doesn't take long to confirm that Cass did precisely what I would have expected. *Good girl.* I'm on her trail and pick up the pace to find her. A trained SEAL wouldn't leave a trace of their existence, but Cass wasn't trying to hide her path. Her only concern was getting back to safety, and I'm glad for the signs she left behind.

With every overturned leaf or broken twig I find, I know I'm getting closer to finding her. Half an hour into tracking her progress, I come to a section of the hill face somewhat blocked by an outcropping of rocks. Here, she would have had to either try to climb it or risk exposure by using the dirt road to go around it.

A climb like that would have been challenging with an injury. Still, Cassidy wouldn't have wanted to risk being seen. I run up to the rock face and notice muddy scuff marks on one of the small ledges and wet blood on a vertical section. She did climb the face, and it was recent. She has to be close. "Cassidy!" I call out.

Hearing no reply, I step back a few yards, get a running start, and scale the rocks. From the top, I look around the jungle for signs pointing toward her. "Cassidy!"

Seeing more blood on a broad-leafed plant, I jump down the other side of the rocks and take off running. "Cass!"

She went this way; I can feel it. I push myself to the limit to cover more ground. My chest is heaving with the effort, but I don't care. I've got to find her.

Three hundred yards past the rock face, I pass a broad Meru Oak and call her name again. A slight shuffle of ground cover behind me halts my steps, and I skid to a stop in case I've attracted the attention of a hungry lion.

With my hand on my rifle, I turn around just in time to see Cass step out from behind that giant tree trunk. She shakes her head as though she's hallucinating. "Tim?"

Cass. My gut clenches at the sight of her. She's bloody, filthy, and looks exhausted, but she's my light and still the most beautiful thing in my world. Dropping everything in my hands, I run back to her, squeezing her to my chest and burying my face in her hair. "God, Cass. I was afraid that I was going to be too late."

I lean back and kiss her forehead before bending to look into her wide, disbelieving eyes. From her face, I scan the rest of her to find dried and fresh blood all over her. "Are you okay? Tell me where you're hurt."

Cass doesn't speak. She only stares as though she doesn't believe I'm here. Like I'm an illusion. Tears stream down her cheeks as she looks over my face and reaches up to touch my beard. "Tim."

My head turns to brush my lips over her

fingertips. "I'm here. You're safe."

I lightly trace my own fingers over her tear-stained and bruised cheek, and then I release her to check her bloody left arm.

"I heard your voice and thought I was going crazy," she says, still staring at me with wonder. Cass pulls out of my grip, halting my examination, and wraps her arms around my middle.

Then she collapses.

BULLETPROOF

JO CHAMBLISS

CHAPTER 14

TIM

The most courageous woman I've ever known cries in my arms. Her mind and body are in this turbulent cycle of coping with exhaustion, physical trauma, fear, grief, and relief all at once. That brutal cocktail is tough enough for even a trained SEAL to work through. Cass should never have had to shoulder such a heavy load.

I sweep her feet off the jungle floor and cradle her in my arms. My cheek rests on the top of her dirty and mussed hair as she fists my shirt in her hand and buries her face in my chest.

I should be attempting to raise Warden and get us out of here, but I can't seem to do anything more than stand here holding my wife. The tremble in my body is only partly due to her shivering. I came too damned close to losing her today, and I'm not ready to let her go yet.

When I'm feeling stable again, I take slow, careful steps back toward my discarded tranq gun. Like it or not, we're still at risk from natural predators as much as the human variety. The only difference is that I wouldn't *want* to kill an attacking animal.

Gradually, Cass emerges from her shocked stupor and lifts her head to look directly at me. "I can't believe you're here. For a while, I was sure that I'd never see you again. How did you find me? How did you even know to come?"

I pause a moment and meet her tired gaze. "Woman, you literally fought death itself in that hospital to bring me back to you. There is nowhere on this earth that I wouldn't find you, and I'll have to be dead before I let someone take you from me. As to the how, let's get you checked out first, and then I'll explain everything."

We reach my gun, and I gently set Cass on her feet to retrieve the weapon. With the rifle now in hand, I signal Warden to track my location. It's time to get the hell out of here. Cass puts her hand in mine and starts with me toward the road. Her steps are a little unsteady, so I support her as we walk over the uneven terrain to reach the dirt path.

Cass stiffens at the sound of the approaching crawler's engine, but I tighten my grip on her. "You're all right. It's just Warden."

"Dillan's here?"

I nod. "He's the only reason I could get to you so fast."

"Fast? I don't even understand how you knew to come at all."

I duck a low branch and hold it back so it doesn't hit Cass. "Warden and I were… informed and immediately took his jet."

Cass and I step out onto the jungle road just as the crawler comes into view. Cass is about to ask about me being informed when Warden jumps out and runs toward us.

The big man wraps his arms around Cass, carefully missing her bloody arm. "Damn, girl. It's good to see you alive. Was it you or lions that fucked that guy up?"

Cass's eyes go wide as saucers, and she wrestles to get out of Warden's arms. "The guy! He was the same one who attacked me in DC. I didn't recognize him from before because I never saw his face. He had recent knife wounds on his jaw hidden by his dark beard. He even admitted to being my attacker."

She pulls away and reaches a scratched-up hand into one of her cargo pockets to produce a wallet. She hands it to me, and I open it up, taking one good look at the guy's face before passing it to Warden.

"I swiped this off his body," Cass says. "What is going on here? Gilley wasn't working alone. He was expecting a helicopter to meet us on the savannah. Why would these people be after me?"

Warden pockets the wallet and says, "We don't know yet."

"I think these guys had something to do with Bishop's murder," Cass says.

"They did," Warden confirms.

Cass sways a little on her feet, likely

realizing how lucky she is to have escaped twice from an entity that took down a trained SEAL. She's damned lucky.

A long while later, the crawler breaks through the clearing at the back of the medical camp, and a host of people rush out of the tents in response to the noise.

Rachel Adams takes front and center, racing to meet us when she spots Cass climbing out of the ATV. The woman zeroes in on the blood staining Cass's clothes. After wrapping Cas in a huge hug, Rachel starts dragging her to the largest tent.

I follow them, not quite ready to let Cass out of my sight. At the same time, protecting Cass means checking in with the admiral. Since we beat Gilley's extraction helo, Admiral Jameson will need to put naval intelligence on tracking whatever craft flies anywhere near the location of the dead bastard that took my wife.

For the first time in my career, I'm torn between my wife and my job. When Cass reaches for my hand again, I decide the Navy can wait a few minutes.

Warden falls in step with the medical crew herding Cass into the treatment tent. Once inside, medical personnel move about in a flurry of activity. My beloved is torn from my grip as doctors and nurses fly around, readying everything they could possibly need to care for any wounds that Cass presents.

I realize beyond my own need for constant reassurance that Cass is alright, I'm of no use here. However, that's proven wrong when Cass shoves someone out of the way so she can see me again.

Pressing my way over to her uninjured side, I gently stroke my fingers over her battered face as Rachel cuts away the rest of Cass's sleeve. The doctor removes a large, bloody bandage, and Cass reports on her condition.

What concerns me most are wounds I can't see. Turning Cass's face to look back at me, I ask quietly, "Did he... hurt you?"

There's a brief flash of anger in her eyes before she answers. "He tried, but I convinced him it was a bad idea. That's how I earned this eye and split lip."

Stepping closer, I hold still as she rests her face against my middle. I'm furious she was ever in such a position, but my pride swells in her ability to adapt and overcome this recent attempt to kidnap her. "You're amazing, Cassidy O'Reilly."

I rub circles over the tense muscles in her back, and Cass sighs into my shirt. We remain locked in that position, not caring that everyone in the room can see. Meanwhile, Rachel continues cleaning around and probing Cass's gunshot wound.

"Well, young lady, it would appear that you've been mighty lucky. I wish all humans were as good at dodging bullets as you are."

Cass flinches and looks up, her troubled eyes landing on my face. The pain from her memories of watching me flatline further weighs down her tired eyes. "Yeah, me too.

The doctor injects Cass with a local anesthetic and gets to work closing the wound. As Rachel retracts the syringe, she asks, "So, does anybody know who was behind this? We're set to leave here in thirty-six hours, and I'm wondering if we have to worry about someone else in our group being targeted."

"I'm working on it," I answer in a stilted voice. *Except that I'm not working on anything right now.*

Cass looks up at my off-kilter response and seems to read my train of thought. She reaches up to place a hand on my cheek. "Go, Tim. You have a job to do, and you can't do it if you're here with me."

I cover her hand with my own and turn my face to kiss her palm. "I don't want to leave, but I need to end this threat to you."

I look over to where Warden is keeping an eagle eye on things. He nods, understanding what I expect of him, and I walk from the tent.

It's early in Norfolk, I think as I pull out my satellite phone. I'm not concerned about waking Admiral Jameson, though. He will be expecting to hear from me no matter the time. The phone rings once before I hear his voice. "O'Reilly. Give me good news."

"We found Cass alive. The asshole that took her is dead. She bested him... again."

"Again?" he asks.

"It was the same assailant from DC. Cass got the drop on him during the night. He fought back, and she managed to kill him with his own gun."

The awe in the admiral's voice comes through loud and clear when he says, "Hell of a tough woman you've got there. How is she?"

"She's got a graze getting cleaned and stitched up now. Otherwise, just some bruising and scratches. She's physically okay. She's just been through a hell of a scare. Despite everything that happened, she had the presence of mind to nab the man's wallet. I'm sending you images of everything inside. Also, Warden's man that came with us was sent to check out the man's tent. I haven't had the chance to check in with him yet. We've only been back for about ten minutes."

Admiral Jameson silently absorbs the reported information before speaking again. "So, some asshole in DC had the resources to follow your wife to Africa for the sole purpose of attempting to abduct her a second time. This level of operating would have required major legwork and decent ground support."

"More than that, sir. Based on where this guy took Cass after killing her associates, his only out would have been via helo extraction."

"So, *major* ground support then. I don't like what this is turning into," Admiral Jameson mutters before quieting again, contemplating something. "I think this is much bigger than just Stoddard and your wife. I think…"

His voice fades, and I know I still haven't heard the worst of it. "What is it?"

"Commander, your men were deployed shortly after you left."

"My men? Which ones?"

"All of them."

What the fuck?

"The noise coming from Europe is no longer chatter. We've received credible threats to US embassies in several European countries. Based on the sheer number of targets identified, I had to thin your guys out to cover them all. Navy Intel has everyone working round the clock to sift through the bullshit, but I get the feeling it's just that. Bullshit."

"You think this is a diversion and somehow related to Stoddard and the attempts on Cass."

"I don't just think they're related. The threats follow the same theme and were all physically delivered. That takes a lot of boots on the ground. As for the why, I believe this is a diversionary tactic. As soon as I deployed your men, intel was flooded with new information. Each team has had to be relocated at least once. Some more than once."

"What are we talking about here? What kind of threats have been made?"

"We don't have anything beyond the specific named targets. In some cases, it's the embassy itself. In others, it's a particular ambassador. All I know for sure is that everyone with a computer and half a brain is trying to find out who's behind it all and what their endgame is. The top brass in defense agrees that these threats must be a diversion, but because they're specific in nature, we can't just stand down and take a watch position. The Pentagon is scrambling because we're not dealing with a clash of ideologies or a people proclaiming a deep-seated hatred for the US."

Admiral Jameson goes quiet again, and I fear what's coming next. "Commander, I believe whoever is behind all this is after you. The problem is that I can't take my fears to the Pentagon because all I have to go on is a gut feeling."

"I'm sorry, I'm not following you. If it were just the attempts at Cass, I could see it, but Bishop? My men? Add in all of Europe, and we either have the mother of all coincidences or a fuck-ton of hell-if-I-know."

"You're right. It doesn't make any sense. I just can't help but think that Stoddard was on *your* team. Cassidy is *your* wife. The only SEALs affected by this cluster are *yours*. I'm not wrong on this, Stone."

Now, I'm the silent one. The notes I've seen mention Steven Knight. Could this be as simple as revenge for his death? I wouldn't have thought it possible. Even now, I'm skeptical. If someone out there blames me and is looking to avenge him, they'd have to have a hell of a lot of people willing to help. Too many factors are in play for one man or even a handful of them to manage.

I let my chin drop, and I sigh into the phone. *Time for devil's advocate.* "Say you're right, Admiral. The notes I've seen reference a man who died nearly two decades ago. Seventeen years is a hell of a long time to wait to come after me."

"I've considered that angle and don't have an answer for it, nor do I have any other ideas of who the culprit could be. What I *do* have is one-hundred-twenty-eight men plus your wife that are caught in the crossfire.

"Until we figure this shit out, I don't want the two of you to be anywhere a civilian can get to you. I prefer to have your asses on a plane back to Virginia tonight, but I'm at a severe disadvantage trying to do your job. This chaos in Europe is changing with the wind. That's an open invitation for screwups and getting good men killed. For that reason, I'm sending the three of you to Germany.

"I want you close to your men. We're in about as fucked up a situation as I could imagine, and clear communication is the only way everyone makes it back home. Your men will do their jobs for anyone issuing orders, but they'll do it with their heads on straight if they get their orders from you. And being at Ramstein, Cass will have access to any medical treatment she needs."

"I'm always ready to stand with my men, but I'm surprised that the Pentagon is allowing this."

The admiral scoffs. "Believe me. They weren't exactly supportive, but I rallied for it. Some wanted you to be benched completely until this is over, but enough of the top brass recognized there's too much worldwide publicity and too much that could go wrong if the men are out of sync. Ultimately, I convinced them that if I'm right and we hide you away, these assholes could react by taking out eight platoons of men just because they're pissed off. To put it bluntly, they'd rather risk losing you than all of your men."

"Which means my wife is also expendable."

"I'm not ready to sacrifice any of you, so I've already signed a contract with Knot's firm. A team is on its way to join you in Germany. Their job is to sniff around and watch your backs, leaving you free to manage your men and make sure they don't end up as collateral damage. Have Knot get all of you to Ramstein, and then I'm clipping his wings until this is all over."

"You expect him to take orders from me?"

"He used to. He will again because he's now on the Navy's dime. I think he would anyway because he likes you better when you're breathing."

Admiral Jameson ends the call, and I take the moment I have alone to try and work through the big picture. If the admiral's right and this is some revenge plot, I don't understand what all these targets in Europe have to do with anything.

Something's missing here. It has to be. None of this makes any sense. The only thing clear is that we're dealing with a group, not an individual. And this group is big enough and funded enough to pull off a global attack.

I shove the phone back into my pocket while shaking my head. I've never doubted Admiral Jameson before, but his theory about this group's motive seems way off base. He could be wrong, but I'm unwilling to bet Cass's life on it.

The best thing I can do now is help Warden's people find out as much as they can about the people pulling all the strings. To that end, I need to find out what Lawson learned from going through Gilley's things.

Looking up from the blank spot on the ground where I'd been staring, I scan the camp and see Lawson standing outside one of the tents. He inclines his chin to me, indicating he's finished with his search.

"What have you got?" I ask when I reach

him.

"Not a damned thing. Since you got your wife back, I assume you found and dispatched our asshole. It'd be nice if we got his phone."

"We didn't kill him. Cass did. Your boss has his phone and ID. He's probably already contacted Birdie to get started on the asshole's background. If she's as good as I've heard, we'll hear something soon, and maybe we'll finally figure out what we're up against. For now, I hear we've got a plane to catch."

"My team leaders have already contacted me. The helo will scramble as soon as they get word from us that we're ready to move. Phelps and Hosfeld are already on their way to Germany."

I offer the man a chin lift. He's proven himself to be a valuable asset on this mission. "Gather the tow rig for the crawler. As soon as Cass is released, I want to move out. We'll map a good landing zone for the helo and meet them there."

"On it."

Trusting the man to do his job, I turn back toward the hospital tent and return to my wife's side.

BULLETPROOF

JO CHAMBLISS

CHAPTER 15

CASS

The whole tent goes quiet when Tim leaves. Not the comfortable quiet of curling up in a blanket with a good book, but the kind of silence you're met with when people are suspicious of you.

Unaffected by the oppressive tension, Rachel checks to confirm that I'm numb and begins suturing my arm. Rachel glances around the tent, eyeing the conspicuously large number of people that remain.

"Rachel—"

"So, what about this guy by the door?" she interrupts. "He a spook or something?"

I glance at Dillan, who gives the slightest shake of his head. When I look back at Rachel, she winks at me. "He's one of Tim's longtime friends."

My friend then grabs a pair of thumb forceps and leans close to inspect the wound. Whispering, she says, "Be careful what you say in here. As many good people as we have, there are just as many media whores that would love nothing more than to blast your story for a few likes. It's probably best to keep what happened between you, that big guy, Tim, and the state department."

She sits back up, holding the forceps to the light, even though they never actually touched me. "Ah, there. Got it."

Her warning has me scanning the faces in the tent. Several of them are people I've known for years and respect, professionally and otherwise. And, as Rachel said, many more seem to be waiting around out of sheer morbid curiosity over my disappearance and the sudden arrival of two mercenary-type men and my Navy husband.

Regardless of their motivation for loitering, it's clear by the curious stares that everyone here has questions. The most obvious would be concerning what happened to Angela and Kasim.

I know Tim started his search for me here, and I heard him contact Rachel when we were on our way back. During the mad dash back to camp, I asked Tim about finding two bodies. All he said was that my friends were being taken care of. Trusting Tim, I didn't press for details.

But now, I'm wondering what Rachel knows about them. She hasn't asked, so I expect she, at least, assumes they're dead. I bend down to speak to Rachel, not even caring to hide my attempt at secrecy. In a low tone, I begin, "Rachel, he killed them…" My voice breaks off, and I'm unable to say anything else.

"I know. The younger guy with your husband took the helicopter and found them. The bodies of our friends are already on their way home."

Rachel snips the thread of the last stitch and sits upright to study her handiwork. With a nod, she sets down her tools and begins placing a bandage over the sutures. "That'll do it. I'm not worried about the rest of these scratches. All you need now is a bath and a long rest. And maybe a few glasses of wine. What I'm saying is, I believe it's time for you to go find that man of yours and let him take you home."

"I'm sorry, Rachel. I never would have come if I thought I was putting you all in danger."

"Stop that, now. No one here is going to blame you. Just let me know you're okay when all this is over."

"I promise."

Despite the sadness in her eyes, Rachel looks over my shoulder, gives me a wink, and then wraps me up in a tight hug. In my ear, she says, "It's been a pleasure having you with us all these years. You go home and let that man doctor you for a while."

Speaking of. A warm hand touches and spans my lower back. Rachel lets go and steps back so Tim can move to my side. The tightness around my husband's eyes and the grim set to his mouth gives me the idea that this shit is not over, not by a long shot.

Before I can ask what he's learned, one of our staff nurses approaches from behind Rachel, holding a bowl and washcloth. Tim steps into the nurse's path, takes them from her, and turns, placing himself between my knees.

Looking straight into my eyes, he lifts the cloth and begins dabbing at the mud and blood on my face, not caring what anyone thinks of our intimate position.

I study my husband's furrowed brow as he works the warm, wet cloth over my skin, being so tender as he does. Though wholly focused on Tim, I hear Rachel putting away her tools and the snap of her nitrile gloves as she pulls them off. The sound catches Tim's attention, reminding him we're not alone. His gaze leaves my face then, but only for a moment. "Are you all done with Cass?"

"Yes. All she needs now is some ice, rest... and you," Rachel answers.

Tim bows his head slightly to her. "Thanks, Doc. Can we have the room then?"

"Of course," she says with a smile. To the rest of the medical crew, she says, "You heard the man. Everybody out."

Tim returns to cleaning while everyone begins filing out of the tent. "Warden, you stay," he says without looking up.

As doctors, nurses, techs, and support staff file by, I acknowledge their well-wishes and ignore most requests to reach out if I need to talk. Wisely, no one pitches any questions about what happened with the man they knew as Bill.

It isn't long before the room has emptied except for Dillan, Tim, and I. Tim remains quiet as he continues his work on my face. The cloth and bowl of dirty water are set aside when he's done, and then gentle fingers inspect the bruising on my cheek and my split lip.

"I should have listened to you and stayed home," I say with much remorse.

His muscled arms wind around me, pulling me against his hard chest. "There is no blame here. Neither one of us could have imagined this happening. If I'd thought it even remotely possible, I would have tied you to our bed and hidden your phone."

I bark a watery laugh, and Tim pulls back to wipe my tears. Dillan approaches at this point and gently squeezes my shoulder. "I never knew you were so badass. I'm sure this puts you at the top of Trish's tough bitch list, right next to Sadie."

"Thanks, but given the choice, I'd gladly remain on the lower end of the spectrum. I'm not enjoying my stint as a commando."

Having enough of the lighter conversation, Tim takes my right hand, lightly massaging the dirty skin. "Cass, there's a lot more going on here than I realized, a lot of it happening since Warden and I left Virginia. And most of it I don't understand.

"I know your work here is just as important as the work I've always done, but I need you to leave with me right now. No questions asked. I can't explain why, but many lives depend on it. This thing is bigger than the three of us, and we'll need some help to end it."

Sliding off the exam table, I answer without argument. "Help me pack."

Tim pulls me to him once more and breathes, "Thank you."

The tent flap opens and closes, and when I pull out of Tim's embrace, Dillan is gone. With us finally alone, I reach up to pull Tim's face to mine. "I thought I was never going to see you again."

His lips take mine in a gentle kiss, causing little flutters in my middle. "You and I have a lot of living to do yet, Mrs. O'Reilly, and I want to do all of it with you."

I'm led from the medical tent and rushed across the compound in the waning daylight. My stomach rumbles as we pass the busy dining tent, but we don't stop until we reach my private sleeping quarters. Inside, Dillan is already throwing stuff into my bags, and Tim joins in to finish the job.

Neither seems worried about who ends up with a handful of bras and panties. Their sense of urgency tells me their only concern is leaving as soon as possible. What I *thought* would happen was that I would shower, get a bite to eat, and *then* Tim and I would pack up my tent.

That Tim isn't insisting I get out of these bloody, torn-up clothes makes it abundantly clear how dire our situation is.

Less than five minutes have passed when the haphazard packing job is done. We leave my tent and head straight for the big four-wheeled vehicle, where a man dressed like Dillan stands guard with a wicked-looking rifle.

My three bags are tossed in the back, the men's gear is added next, and then everything is strapped down by bungee netting. The men don't hesitate or check in with the camp again once the loading is complete. They jump in and strap down, me right alongside them.

With Dillan's man behind the wheel of the big machine, Tim updates them both on what the admiral said. Dillan occasionally pauses the briefing to yell orders into his phone. I tune them all out and focus on the jungle flying by as the wind whips my hair through the vehicle's roll cage.

Though the vehicle handles the terrain well, the ride is rough at the speed we're racing away from the camp. The only time we slow down is after breaking through the tree line of the jungle to an open plain. Then we stop altogether.

Still operating urgently, the men hop out of the crawler and begin yanking out equipment bags again. For a moment, I fear they're preparing for a coming attack and turn to watch the road to Orus.

No one is seen chasing after us, but I soon hear the familiar sounds of an approaching helicopter.

The helo lands in a stinging cloud of hot air and dust, and a single crewman jumps out and runs to the crawler. The man with us, whose name I learn is Brock Lawson, works with the crewman to secure heavy cables to the ATV while Tim and Dillan are loading our bags onto the chopper's deck.

Everything is moving so fast. My body is still high on adrenaline that, I swear, is pumping in a steady stream, fueled by Tim's and Dillan's mad rush. I'm not used to being so on edge that I'm borderline paranoid. That paranoia has me constantly checking the jungle road, expecting an army of bad guys to emerge at any second and attack our group.

The loading finishes with me still watching that road, and a tug of my hand pulls my attention to our getaway chopper. Running behind Tim, I hop into the seat he indicates and sit still while he straps me down with the complicated harness. A radio headset is secured over my ears, and Tim slides the door closed before sitting on the floor in front of me.

I fight to regulate my breathing as I wait the last few seconds before we lift off, out of reach of anyone on the ground. My eyes are squeezed shut but snap open with a firm grasp on my thigh. Tim's strong grip and subtle smile calm me, and my harsh breathing slows back to normal.

I wrap my hands around his and lean back in my seat. My stomach falls away as the helicopter lifts off, jolting only slightly when there's no slack left in the crawler's tow line. When the machine lifts off the ground, we're finally steered away from the African jungle.

We made it. The breath I held during takeoff comes rushing out, and I slump in my seat. Exhausted and crashing from the adrenaline rush, I lean against the headrest and close my eyes. I'm alive, and I want to go home.

I hold on to Tim's hand for several minutes, listening to the pilot and crew's chatter over the radio. Everyone in my ear sounds business-like as if today is just another day for them. I'm the only one in our little escape party operating on the opposite side of calm.

Since Tim found me, I haven't had time to sift through what happened... until now. And now that I'm racing away from the scene of my nightmare, surrounded by trained warriors, I've got all the time in the world to recall watching two good people be gunned down and discarded in the ditch. If that wasn't enough, I'm reminded I took a man's life.

I withdraw my fingers from Tim's hand, feeling the mud, blood, and filth all over my skin again.

I saved two lives, watched two die, and took a life all in the same day. I am a doctor who dedicated her career to bringing life into this world and swore to do no harm. I killed a man.

The chatter in my ear goes silent, replaced by a soothing, gravelly voice. "Breathe, Cassidy."

Lifting my head, I open my eyes to see Tim wearing a headset on his knees in front of me. He grabs my wringing hands and holds them in his. "Talk to me, Cass."

Tears track down my cheek as I struggle to form the words. "Three people died yesterday, two of them only because they were with me. The other… I killed him. I did it to protect myself, but I killed someone, Tim. How will I ever deliver another baby with the same hands that ended a man's life?"

My face falls forward as more silent tears spill from my eyes. Tim releases my harness and stands to pick me up, taking my seat and sitting me across his lap. With one hand, he pulls my head down to his shoulder. The other hand tucks my arm around his waist.

"Nothing I could say to you is going to help, but you need to hear it anyway," I hear through my radio. "When your life was on the line, you only did what you had to do to survive. You're going to get past this. It won't be today, next week, or even next month, but one day, you'll wake up and not see that bastard's blood on your hands.

"You're right about your friends. They didn't deserve to die like that, but their deaths are not on you. You killed the man responsible for ending their lives too soon. You brought your friends justice and saved countless others that would have been harmed at his hands."

Tim tips my chin up to look directly into my red-rimmed eyes. "You saved me, Cass. By fighting to stay alive, you saved a man who can't see living a single day without the woman he loves. You saved a woman who hopes to have a child of her own one day. You saved our future children."

I hold on tight to my husband, my love, my anchor. Tim was right about his words not helping, even if I believe every word he spoke. Not wanting to think anymore for a while, I burrow deeper against his muscled chest and close my eyes.

The helicopter touches down sometime later, the soft impact jarring me awake on Tim's lap. When the doors open, I notice we're not at the Nairobi airport. We appear to be at a military base or compound.

A black SUV pulls up next to the crawler that had to be dropped before we could land. The man who steps out to greet Dillan is dressed just like him and is another somebody I've never seen before.

The two men shake hands, and a set of keys is passed to Dillan, who then tosses them to Lawson. We all get loaded into the SUV and pull under a hotel portico a short while later.

Lawson runs inside, and Dillan turns around in his seat to face me. "We'll check into some rooms to clean up and rest before we fly out. I can give you two hours, but that's it."

Tim steps out of the truck and walks around to my side, still as uptight as he was in the jungle. Judging by the battle-ready set to Dillan's shoulders, he's just as anxious to leave. That tells me this reprieve was planned for my benefit. If I weren't with them, these guys would be headed straight for the plane.

My door opens, and Tim reaches for my hand. "Look, guys. I know how this works. I've watched Tim have to rush out the door enough to know you don't have time for this. Let's just get going. I'll be fine."

Tim starts to object, but Dillan interrupts him. "Yes, you do need this, but I'm not stopping for you. That man standing before you has many lives depending on him, and I need his head to be on straight for whatever is coming. If he's worried about you collapsing from exhaustion, he won't be able to put his focus where it's needed. That can get people killed."

Dillan tempers his brutal honesty with a small smile. "Besides, I know what it's like to see my family in danger. It does something to a man. Please. Get cleaned up. Get some food in you. Give my best friend a chance to calm his frayed nerves. We're all going to need him before this is over."

I look from Dillan's stern yet caring face to Tim and realize he's right. Tim looks desolate. Without taking my eyes off my husband's worn face, I whisper, "Thank you, Dillan."

Tim and I grab the bags we'll need as Lawson returns and passes two envelopes to Dillan. One of them is handed over to Tim, who leads me inside with Dillan behind us.

The hotel appears to be a top-end establishment for the area, complete with gilded furniture artfully arranged around the lobby, multiple fountains dividing the ample space, and expensive artwork adorning the walls. However, most of the opulence goes unappreciated, with me focusing on the armed security stationed around the lobby instead.

Though I only notice the security measures in place, plenty of the hotel's patrons notice us. And why not? I stick out like a sideshow circus freak with my bloody and torn clothes, bandages, filthy hair, and numerous cuts and bruises. As fast as some people scatter as we walk by, I figure I must smell as bad as I look.

Tim untangles his fingers from mine at the elevator long enough to get us moving but quickly reclaims my hand in his. A short ride later, we stop at the top floor, and I let him lead me down the hall to our door.

I'm ushered inside a room bathed in light from two large picture windows. A filmy white canopy flutters in the breeze generated by the rattan ceiling fan. This place would be straight out of a dream vacation if every soft surface weren't white.

There's practically zero chance this room will survive the level of dirty I'm bringing to the game. Regardless, the shower calls to me, and Tim has just barely gotten the door closed and locked again before I drop my bags and start stripping on my way to the bathroom.

Everything I'm wearing gets thrown in the trash; none of it worth the effort of cleaning that asshole's blood from the fabric. I don't even bother grabbing my soap from my bag before I turn on the water and pull my hair down from the messy bun.

Stepping under the steaming spray, I lift my face and hold still as if the deluge will wash away the remnants of yesterday. It's a futile gesture, I know.

My eyes are still closed, and I still haven't moved from under the spray when fervent hands begin massaging a sweet-smelling shampoo into my long hair. Feeling fragile and near the point of shattering, I let Tim take care of me, washing me from head to toe. He even shaves my legs before tending to his own washing.

Tim rinses himself under the rain head in the middle of the stall since I've yet to move from my spot. When finished, he wraps his muscled arms around me, and a trembling sob emanates from *his* chest. I'd held it together thus far but break down entirely at his show of vulnerability.

With gut-wrenching sobs, my legs give out. Tim swoops me up in his arms and buries his face in my neck, gripping me as though afraid I might slip away.

Through the worst of it, Tim doesn't shush me or try to get me to calm down. He's just as shaken as I am. His voice, heavy with emotion, vibrates my neck. "I was fucking scared, Cass. So damn scared that I wouldn't get to you in time."

"But you did. I never would have survived the long hike back to camp if you hadn't found me."

I wriggle out of his arms to plant my feet and force him to look at me, but he shakes his head. "I wasn't in time because you had to kill a man. You'll carry that with you for the rest of your life."

At that moment, I recognize the shadows in my husband's eyes. Though Tim has never talked about it, I know he killed before. Since he's never been a sniper, any of his kills would have been up close. And all of them would have been necessary to protect or to stay alive. Nevertheless, he still carries that burden to this day.

His sorrow for what I had to do shows that the burden is heavy. There is no making it better. There is only learning to live with it. I lean into his chest, knowing he understands what torment my mind is going through. And I ache for him, knowing he carries the burden of all the lives he took for his country.

Tim holds me a minute longer and then turns off the water. We dry off and walk to the bed to rest for a while, not bothering to dress before climbing between the cool sheets, where I settle into Tim's open arms.

I lie still, tucked in tight to Tim's warm, naked body. Sleep should come quickly, given everything I've been through since yesterday. I'm not still awake because I'm worked up and tense or seeing horrific flashbacks when I close my eyes. I want to stay awake and soak every second of being wrapped up with the man I love.

For a while, I'm content to bask in the comfort his strength provides, but soon, I'm desperate for more, something to chase away the ghastly images from yesterday. "Love me, Tim," I beg.

With a gentle kiss on my lips, he rolls me to my back and sits up between my knees. His hands grip my ankles and begin a slow massage, working up from my calves to my thighs. I moan as he kneads tight muscles.

Nearing my hips, he pushes my legs open and slides his hands over my inner thighs. Tim reaches my center and swipes a thumb through my wetness and around my clit, keeping his gaze locked on mine.

His big digit passes directly over the tight bundle of nerves, sending a jolt through my system. Tim leans over me, pulling his hand from my aching center to swirl his slick thumb around my nipples.

The breeze in the room chills them instantly, pebbling them both into tight peaks. My back arches off the bed, silently begging Tim to touch me again. His stare finally leaves my face when he dips his head to latch onto a taught nipple.

His tongue laps against one sensitive peak while he massages the other. Before long, I'm writhing beneath him, wanting more and not caring if he doesn't give my other breast equal treatment.

I let go of my grip on the sheets and grab my husband's face, pulling him back to my mouth.

As my tongue slides past his lips, his hard length slides into me. I gasp as he stretches me, and Tim begins to thrust ever so slowly. He props himself on his elbows and rests his forehead against mine, never looking away from my eyes. I don't move beneath him, not seeking an orgasm. All I need is this connection, this oneness to chase away the darkness.

As I get lost in his eyes, I become grounded again, centered. I'm alive. I made it. I'm back where I need to be and have a life to live. We have a family to make.

Tim's body goes taught after a few more thrusts, and his eyes flare as he groans through his release. I moan at seeing pleasure wash over him. Fire licks up my insides, igniting the desire for climax. I begin thrusting my hips upward, trying to create whatever friction I can against his softening penis.

Tim figures out what I'm doing and moves off me. Rolling onto his back, he pulls me with him so I'm lying on my back on his stomach. His knees come up between my thighs and spread wide, forcing me open.

The breeze from the fan caresses my skin as Tim does the same, trailing his hand down over my breasts and middle until finding my drenched slit. Coated by my wetness and his seed, Tim's fingers glide effortlessly between my lips, over my swollen clit, and inside me. I squirm atop him as his fingers tease until I'm a wanton mess. Adding to the sensations is his swiftly hardening dick resting between my ass cheeks.

I try to sit up and straddle him, but his firm grip holds me in place while continuing the sweet torture. Before long, a final stroke of his finger rocks me into a powerful orgasm that shakes me to my core. With his lips on my neck, Tim eases me down, continuing his soft caresses to my pulsating clit, and we lie in that position for a while, catching our breath.

Eventually, Tim rolls to his side, settling me in front of him, and covers us up with the sheet. Held tight to his chest, I lie with Tim as we drink in one other for what feels like hours. Eventually, the warmth of his body and the security of being wrapped in his strong arms soothes me to sleep.

The alarm on Tim's watch goes off a while later, bursting our euphoric bubble and notifying us that it's time to get moving again.

I start to roll away, but Tim catches my arms in his hands. He captures my lips in a fiery kiss that ends all too quickly and then lets me go. We clean up quickly and get dressed, making it to the lobby a few minutes early.

Dillan is already there, looking no less intimidating in street clothes than he does decked out in tactical gear. Typical Dillan Knot. He appears to be checking in with someone on his phone, maybe coordinating the next leg of our journey. Hopefully, the journey is no more complicated than a flight home.

Lawson exits the elevator, spots our group, and joins us in the lobby. "You're looking much better, Mrs. O'Reilly."

The handsome blond is all smiles, as though we didn't just come from a nightmare. I shouldn't be surprised. Given that he works for Dillan, he's probably seen much worse on a regular basis. "Thank you. I'm sorry I haven't asked before, but who are you?"

"You know my last name, but you can call me Brock. Former Air Force pilot and NYPD SWAT."

"He works for me," Dillan explains. Then, without further explanation, he orders, "Let's get out of here."

Something about Dillan's urgent insistence catches Tim's notice. "You've spoken to Jameson." *Not a question.*

Dillan nods. "He'd already been in contact with the company. Sadie switched some personnel around so that she could be the one responding. She and Hosfeld are already on their way. They should be there to meet us when we land."

I'm only half following the conversation as we walk outside, but my ears perk up hearing Sadie's and Aaron's names. Besides Birdie, those are the only two of Dillan's employees I've ever met. And I don't understand why they would need to meet us at the airport.

I open my mouth to ask, but Tim holds up a hand to stop me. "Let's wait and lay it all out on the plane."

Yes, we can talk about it on our way home. Moments later, we're seated in the big SUV on our way to the airport and Dillan's private jet. Not long after that, we buckle in the jet's comfortable seats and taxi to the cue for our turn at takeoff. While we're rolling, Tim places his hand on my thigh, drawing my eyes from the view out the window.

The look on his face makes my hair stand on end. A glance at Dillan finds the same ominous expression. Lawson isn't smiling anymore, either.

"What's going on, Tim?" I ask, turning

back to my husband.

"Cass, we're not going back home just yet. Admiral Jameson is sending us to Germany."

"Germany?! I don't understand. Why would he send us to Germany?"

Tim lets go of my leg and leans back in his seat. "Normally, I wouldn't be able to discuss any of this with you, but since you're directly involved, the admiral thinks you should be kept in the loop.

"All of my men have been called out to cover numerous threats to American embassies all over Europe, recalled, and then scattered again. The Pentagon believes a coordinated setup like this is likely a decoy for something. Since mistakes can be made in this type of chaos, Admiral Jameson wants me back on the job and close to them to be a familiar handler during... whatever this is."

I struggle to take in this new information and sudden change of plans. Tim managing his men from Germany makes sense. The flight there would put him in the driver's seat much sooner than waiting for us to get back to Virginia.

What doesn't make sense is Dillan's people meeting us in Germany. Scrutinizing the men's faces again tells me something else is happening here. If it were only about Tim's men, he'd be on his way to Germany, and Dillan would be escorting me home. "There's something you're not telling me. Gilley told me that my kidnapping is related to Bishop's murder, but you never explained how *you* know. Tim, what made you come to Africa?"

My husband slumps in his seat, appearing lost and defeated, a look I've never seen on him before.

CHAPTER 16

TIM

"It's all been a fucking game."

"Game?" Cass says, confused and clearly disgusted.

"Maybe you should start from the beginning," Warden suggests.

I nod in agreement and slump forward onto my elbows. "By now, you know neither Warden nor I believed Bishop fell asleep behind the wheel. We were proven right when an autopsy found a note left on Bishop's body, a note that very few people would understand. Warden and I weren't told about it until the day of Bishop's funeral. That was the reason we were called to the Navy Yard. The note seemed to be directed at us."

"What do you mean, directed at you? What did the note say?"

"The investigation is ongoing. I shouldn't—"

"Come on, man, she's in this shit as deep as you," Warden says, then speaks directly to Cass, "The note said *Knight II takes Bishop*. Knight II was a guy in our SEAL squad, but he didn't kill

Bishop. Steven Knight died seventeen years ago."

My wife turns sympathetic eyes toward me. "So, this is what Trish was talking about. You didn't have to carry this alone, Tim. You could have told me. It wouldn't have changed my mind about our decision."

She reaches across and takes my hand. "You still haven't told me what sent you to Africa."

Staring at the silicone band on her finger, I answer quietly, "Probably about the time you were delivering that baby, another note was found. *Knight II takes the Stone Queen*. That's when we knew your attack in DC wasn't random."

Cass abruptly sits up. "Ok. So, the two being related is no longer news. I'm still unclear about what's next. There has to be more to this, or we'd be on two different planes right now."

I nod at her wise assessment. "That's what has me stumped. Something's missing here, and I could use the extra insight to figure this shit out."

Warden pulls a laptop out of his bag and opens it up when I start explaining what the admiral said. Over the next hour, I break down everything that's happened since Stoddard's death from my perspective. Afterward, I relay everything that Jameson has suspected. Thinking aloud, I mutter, "The one question with zero answer is, why Stoddard? And why reference Steven Knight?"

Cass's brow furrows. "That seems like the

obvious part to me. Revenge against your old squad."

I push up from the seat and sigh. "The admiral said the same thing, but I still don't see someone blaming us for Knight's death, or if they did, waiting seventeen years for retribution."

Knot looks up from his laptop and says, "But what if the reference to Knight is a ruse?"

What if? I sit back down and think for a minute, talking through the possibility. "If that's the case and the admiral's right about me being the target for some asshole's revenge, Cass's kidnapping would make sense. It stops making sense when you add Bishop into the mix. Say someone wanted to torture me by targeting those I care about. I imagine in four weeks, there would've been more attempts. So far, it's only been Bishop and Cass."

"That's not true," Lawson says.

His announcement draws my eyes up sharply, and I glance at Warden in time to see his dark eyes cut over to his man. I get the idea there's more to this story that never came to light. "Dammit, Warden! What happened? And why the hell am I just finding out?"

"You're just finding out because we were already dick-deep trying to rescue your wife when I learned of it."

I'm set to argue when Cass squeezes my hand. I keep my mouth shut to allow them to fill me in. Turning my focus to Lawson, I gesture for him to start talking. "A bomb with a remote triggering device was found on Knot's car after we took off from Norfolk. The same car *you* drove to the airport.

"Me and several others figure that if you hadn't left the base with Knot, this asshole would have taken him out. You can guess what that means."

"That means he's been watching us."

Lawson shakes his head. "No, Commander. It means he's been watching you."

Cass gasps beside me, but I keep pressing the younger man. "What about a note? This asshole leaves love notes all over the place."

Warden sighs, finally ready to fess up. "A note was delivered to the main gate at Little Creek right after the delivery at Knot Corp. We were in the air before it ever came to light. The admiral intercepted the message and kept you in the dark to avoid dividing your focus. The note said, *'Knight II takes Black Rook.'* I guess they wanted you to find out about Cass, flip out trying to get to her, and then I would be taken out by the car bomb.

"What these guys failed to anticipate was that we would work together. He didn't blow up my car with you in it, which means he doesn't want you dead, at least not yet. The admiral is right, Stone. You're the target. This asshole is using Bishop, Cass, and me as collateral damage to hurt you. The admiral kept it to himself because you had to concentrate on getting your wife back and then getting out of Africa."

"Dammit, Warden, this changes things a fuck of a lot."

I jump out of my seat and start pacing again. "Now I understand why Jameson is sending us to Germany," I bark at him.

"What do you mean? Changes what?" Cass asks.

"It means Admiral Jameson was right all along. Europe is a set-up, but not in the way he thinks."

"I don't follow," Cass says.

I stop directly in front of her and take a knee. "This same group of douches that killed Bishop, tried to kill Warden, and kidnapped you are behind the threats to embassies in countries representing SEAL Team Two's territory. That calls out men under my command."

Unable to keep still, I'm again on my feet, talking to myself. "So, I'm the target and Bishop, Warden, Cass, and my men by proxy. That still leaves questions of why, by whom, and why now?"

All other conversation ceases at my muttered musing. "And what the hell does Europe have to do with anything?"

"I have a theory on the why now question," Warden begins. "You made national news because of what happened protecting Mira Canaveri. Maybe that exposure put you on someone's radar."

"That makes sense," I agree. "If this guy or group started watching then, he'd have easily identified the people I'm closest…"

Oh shit. Now *everything* makes sense.

"Tim? What is it?"

Ignoring the question, I pull out my phone to call the Admiral.

"Jameson here."

"Where was third platoon assigned?!"

"They're one of the groups I had to split up. Bennet is in Belarus. Hill is in Estonia. Why? What's going on?"

"This shit in Europe is a setup to make my men vulnerable. They're planning to go after Hill's squad!"

"Where are you getting this from?"

"The attempt on Knot that you should have fucking told me about. Whoever we're dealing with has been watching me for at least two months. Hill's men were with me nearly every day in the hospital and during rehab. Bishop's killer has been trying to take out those closest to me and would know Hill and his men mean a lot more to me than just another SEAL squad."

"Shit, you're right. Dammit! Get to Ämari Air Base. I'll see if I can get you patched in to Hill."

The admiral hangs up, and I lower the phone from my ear. "Where are we going?"

Warden asks.

"Change the flight plan to Estonia. We've got to get to Lieutenant Hill."

Warden gets up to handle the pilots, and I return to pacing the small craft. Fifteen minutes later, the admiral is calling me back. I snatch the phone from my pocket, placing the call on speaker to answer.

"O'Reilly, we're too late. The shit's hit the fan in Tallinn. The ambassador to Estonia has gone missing. His name is Jenkins. His car was found disabled about a mile from his home, and Jenkins wasn't inside. So far, we have nothing to go on, nothing pointing to these assholes. Currently, the SEALs are holed up inside the embassy, as the threat was against the building, not an individual. I've ordered them to remain inside embassy grounds until further notice. How fast can you get there?"

"Four hours," Warden calls out.

"Understood. I'll keep you updated."

The phone goes back into my pocket, and Cass approaches. With her hand on my arm, she says, "Fish and the others are safe inside the embassy. No one can get to them there, right?"

If only it were that easy.

About an hour away from the airfield in Tallinn, my phone starts ringing, and my gut tightens. "O'Reilly here."

"We're out of time, Commander, and I'm no longer calling the shots. The media has been blasting a picture of Jenkins all over the damned news. He's bloody and tied to a chair. We even have a location. The president has ordered your men to go in after him. The order went out straight from the Pentagon. I was only just notified."

"No! It's a trap. You've got to stop them!"

"I tried, Stone. Hill's already gone dark."

Oh. My. God. The quicksand feeling I had during the flight just swallowed me whole.

Sadie Phelps and Aaron Hosfeld wait for us by a transit van when our plane lands at Ämari Air Base in Estonia. Though the Admiral officially contracted their services, they've only been given a location and instructions to provide support. During the flight, Warden updated them on the situation, from Stoddard's death to the ambassador's rescue mission. It's soon yet to have heard about Hill's progress, but that doesn't lessen the strain of waiting and worrying that this whole thing is about to blow up in my face.

"We've secured rooms at the embassy and have already set up a command center," Sadie reports while herding us inside the van.

"Has there been any word about Fish's team?" Cass asks the group.

"Nothing," Sadie reports. "Given our temporary official capacity, we've been liaising between the embassy, police, and Admiral Jameson. We'll know the moment Fish makes contact."

After a tense ride from the air base, the van pulls through the embassy gates. We're dropped off in front of the main building and have just walked into a borrowed conference room when Warden's phone rings. He answers, and the look he shoots my way has my heart falling to the floor.

My phone rings a second later, and I dread hearing what Admiral Jameson has to say. "Local police have responded to an emergency call from an empty warehouse. Inside the abandoned building, they found the body of Ambassador Jenkins. They also found a note and a printed QR code."

At the whispered curses of those around me, I turn to see a large TV screen hooked up to Sadie's laptop. Displayed on the screen is a live stream of Lieutenant Hill and the rest of the Wendigo squad. They appear to be in an underground room, tied up and suspended from the ceiling. A couple of them are hung upside down.

Their bloody faces tell me they've been viciously beaten. Most are unconscious, but some are alert. While watching the feed, three men come into view and deliver vicious blows to those still conscious. *He's doing it to torture me. He wants me to watch.*

I grab the vase off the conference table and hurl it at the nearest wall. Glass shatters, and water and flowers go everywhere. Cass shrieks and shoots a glare my way just before noticing the image on the screen behind me.

Before I think to block her view, she sees the feed. Cass responds immediately, becoming hysterical over the horror happening live. She knows these men, knows their wives and children.

The video is quickly taken down, but it's too late. Cass has already witnessed the bloodbath. "Put it back. We need to analyze their surroundings."

Pulling Cass to me, I press her face to my shoulder and step closer to the conference table where Sadie is set up. "Show me the note."

A second big screen activates, and in the center pops up a picture of a note in the same style as the others. It reads *Backward Pawns*.

Cass turns her head, sees the screen again, and starts clawing at my chest, trying to loosen my grip. One of the bastards has taken to using a metal pole to beat my men. "Oh my god! Oh my god! They're killing them!"

"Cass."

She's inconsolable and ignores my attempts to get her attention. "Fish and Devil have kids! Skin's going to be a father soon! Hawk doesn't know it yet, but Cailyn's pregnant—Judge and Ink haven't even—"

"Cassidy! Stop!" I grasp her face to get her attention, and her tear-filled eyes plead with me. "Please, Tim. They can't die."

I pull my wife's flagging body to me again. Whatever strength she'd been holding onto bled out at the horrific sight of our surrogate family being tortured.

Cass sobs in agony as I stroke my hands over her hair. All my career, I've hidden the darkest parts from her. I never wanted her to know the evil my men and I deal with.

I want to promise her every one of those men will make it home, but truthfully, I'm not sure. If the guy calling the shots gets what he ultimately wants, they won't, and I won't either.

Instead of lying to my wife, I squeeze her tighter against me. That's the only assurance I can offer her right now.

My phone vibrates with an incoming text, and I reluctantly let Cass go. This could be information related to my men, and I need every advantage I can get my hands on.

The message isn't from anyone I know, and it confirms everything I assumed about whoever we're dealing with. They want me.

Check. Your move, Stone.

CASS

Tim's jaw clenches with rage at whatever he's reading on his phone. He doesn't relay the message, but his body language sends the assembled team into overdrive. Although the scene looks and sounds like chaos, everyone in this room is calculated in their moves as they work with various connections to locate Fish's team. For all their efficiency, I don't know how any of them can function after what we just saw.

I'm breaking apart inside after seeing the most horrific scene imaginable play out on a TV screen. I don't watch movies that violent, and what was on screen... what's still on screen... is very much real.

Keeping my eyes diverted, I stoop to pick up the scattered flowers and broken glass. My hands shake the whole time since I can still hear the sick sounds of the beatings and our friends' grunts of pain. Part of me wants to run away from the nightmare Tim's men are going through, but I can't make myself take a step toward the door because of Dillan's request. *I need his head on straight. If he's worried about you, he won't be any good to us.* For that reason alone, I'll stay here, if only for Tim's peace of mind.

At one point, Sadie walks over and lays a hand on my back. "I'm sorry you had to see that. You should know that almost everyone in this room owes their life to those men. I swear we won't give them up without one hell of a fight."

I'm about to reply when Dillan lets loose a string of expletives that would embarrass a fisherman. He's studying a computer screen, apparently still watching the feed from the dungeon where Tim's men are being held. "I want the source of that stream, and I want it right fucking now!"

I don't look to see what set him off, and

thankfully, someone muted the sound so that I no longer have to hear it. With only slightly more restraint, Dillan asks Tim, "I know you got a text from this bastard. What did the message say?"

Tim hesitates and then answers, "He says it's my move. He wants me to come after him."

I'm on my feet instantly, dropping all the broken glass I'd just collected. "No! No! No!" I yell as I run to him and grab his shoulders. "He'll be ready for you. If you try to trade yourself for those men, none of you will make it out of this alive."

Tim pulls my fingers from his biceps and holds my hands out in front of him. Dillan rushes over to the both of us, aiming to put in his own two cents. "You would pull that kind of shit, but it's not happening. I'll concede that the only way to end this is for you to make an appearance, but there's no way in hell I'm letting you go alone. You'll go in with my team or not at all."

The tears streaming down my face are kissed away, and Tim nods. "Get Birdie fed in. We're going to need her help. I'll contact Cle Maxwell from Pantera. She's former CIA."

"I know who she is," Dillan says. "Pull in that Grant woman that Dallas Allred knows."

"I can't do that without alerting Dallas about Ink."

"Fuck!" Dillan swears and shoves a hand over his shaved head. "Shit. All right. Leave her out of it, then. Everyone else get to work! I want to know where these bastards are!"

Tim and Dillan's people scurry around the room, making calls, pulling up maps, and anything else they can do to find the missing SEALs.

I allow my eyes to travel back to the live feed of Fish and his men on one of the big screens. The scene is just as gruesome as before, but at least no one is beating on them right now. Silently assessing them, I have no doubt they're all in serious condition. A couple of them look like they could even be listed as critical. Even if we got to them right now, it's possible some of them won't survive.

With everyone except me working to locate the team of SEALs, I pace the floor, feeling anxious and useless. Not knowing what else I can do to help, I seek out security stationed in the hall and ask about procuring food for the group. The man forwards the request, and I start working on a place to set everything up since the large table is filled with computer and communication equipment.

Half an hour later, a server delivers a cart loaded with cafeteria to-go boxes and drinks and transfers everything to a sideboard I cleared off for use as a buffet. Once everything is in place, I grab several coffee cups and the carafe and carry them to the table. I pour a cup of the steaming brew for Tim, but the acrid scent turns my stomach.

Noticing my repulsed face, Tim asks, "What is it?"

"I don't know. The coffee. It doesn't smell right."

"Don't drink it!" Dillan yells.

He rushes over and takes the cup from my hand as if it's laced with poison. He tentatively lifts the cup to his nose and sniffs. His brow knits together as he studies the cup's contents. "It smells fine."

Dillan then takes a small sip and looks over at Tim. "I can't detect anything wrong."

Tim walks over and pours a cup, taking a sip of it black. "It seems fine to me. What did you see or smell?"

"I... I don't know." I take the cup from him and bring it to my nose. "It just smells bad."

Dillan looks at me pointedly and says, "Trish developed an aversion to coffee when she was pregnant. I couldn't drink it in the house for the whole nine months."

My shocked gaze snaps to Tim, whose eyes are big as saucers as he stares back. We both seem to be struggling to draw in a breath. "Could you be...?" he croaks.

"I don't know. I guess it's possible, but it's only... we just..."

My voice trails off as I count the days since I had the IUD removed. Six weeks. *Shit. Tim doesn't need this right now. Keep his head on straight.* "It doesn't matter right now anyway. You have to focus."

I back away from my stunned husband, reeling over the chance that I could be pregnant. Despite the distance I create between us, Tim doesn't look away from my middle until Dillan grabs his shoulder.

He forces Tim to turn around and face the second big screen, where an image of a woman with strawberry blond hair is looking out over our group.

"Thanks for coming on, Cle."

She waves away his thanks and jumps right in. "I know we're critical, so I won't waste any time. I've had my system running the ID of your wife's kidnapper, Gilley, and found something, but I don't know what to make of it. Does the name Rick Crendall mean anything to you?"

"Son of a bitch," Dillan whispers.

Tim passes a shocked glance to Dillan before he explains. "It should. He's the man responsible for the death of Steven Knight."

"Knight II, right. That makes sense. Well, I'm showing that there's been recent and much contact between Gilley and this Crendall."

The woman outlines the scope of the contact between the two men, but her fingers never stop moving over her keyboard. All of a sudden, she stops and looks up. "Crendall was the reporter that blew a SEAL mission seventeen years ago."

Her fingers pull away from the keyboard, and she looks directly into her camera, coming to the same conclusion I do. "You were there. You and Dillan," I whisper.

Tim gives me a barely perceptible nod and turns back to the screen. "We were there."

Tim talks the woman through a disaster of a mission that saw one man's lust for notoriety cause the death of a doctor and a SEAL. Crendall was the one who created a deep-seated hatred for the press within Dillan and my husband.

During the whole classified report, Cle types furiously on her keyboard as she listens. She must be good at her job, as by the time Tim is finished with the awful story, she's already prepared preliminary findings. "Okay. I've got some news, and you won't like it. Crendall's old cameraman was found dead in his network truck three days ago. Crendall hasn't been seen since."

"Presumed dead?" Dillan asks.

"No. No one reported him as missing either," Cle answers. "He's just gone."

"Could that damned reporter be the one orchestrating all this?" Dillan asks Tim.

"He'd have motive. Not only did he get the shit beat out of him for getting Knight and the doctor killed, but with Jameson's help, I made sure his journalistic career was over. No one would touch him after it came out that he was the reason for the doctor's death."

"Find Crendall," Dillan barks to the room.

"I don't know how, but this son of a bitch is involved."

"Involved, maybe, but the guy's financials are not lush enough to even partially finance this operation," a familiar voice joins in from over the phone speaker.

"Cle, Birdie. Birdie, Cle," Dillan offers gruffly. "If not Crendall, someone out there is helping him by footing this bill. Someone that would share in his hatred for Stone. I want to know who."

The group of war strategists converge over the conference table and phone, but their voices fade away as I stare at the heartbreaking live feed again.

Those men are in trouble. Only one of them looks to be conscious. Ink had been out cold like the other guys, but he's awake now. For his sake, I wish he were still out. Instead of blessed unconsciousness, he's feeling every bruise, cut, and broken bone dished out to him. Thankfully, the bastards that tortured them are still on a break.

The lighting set up by the abusers is enough to see a lot of bloody damage but not enough to diagnose anything more than his outward injuries.

Amazingly, with blood running down his face and one eye swollen shut, Ink is aware of the camera and is staring into its lens, blinking erratically. *Wait a minute. No, not erratic, just in a strange rhythm. Almost like…*

"Everybody shut up!"

Shocked by my outburst, the room goes silent, and everyone turns to look at me. I point to the screen. "Look at Ink's eyes. I think he could be blinking in Morse Code."

"How the hell did we miss that?" Tim asks.

"You didn't miss anything. He only just woke up."

Tim leans over the tangle of computer cables and grabs a notepad from behind Sadie. Ripping off the top page to reveal a clean sheet, he watches the screen and starts writing, translating as he does. "Working with terrorists. Five men. Underground… and he gives coordinates. Jenkins dead. RC given five hours to produce Stone. Working with terrorists. Five men."

Tim looks up from the paper. "He's now just repeating the message."

Dillan nods. "RC, that has to be Crendall. Okay. Sadie, plot the coordinates. Birdie, recon the site. Cle, you stay on this Crendall connection. Aaron, you're on weapons and logistics. Stone, update the Admiral."

My eyes are glued to the screen and the pain on Ink's face. The furious blinking continues for several more seconds but then slows and eventually stops. I'm afraid he's succumbed to his injuries and hold my breath, looking for signs of life.

Though shallow, Ink's chest rises and falls, and I know he's still alive.

I reach up and touch the screen. These men have to get home to their families, and I have to help make sure that happens.

Behind me, it seems the research part of the operation has come to an end, and the team is gearing up to leave.

"I'm going with you," I announce to the group, surprising myself.

"The hell you are," Tim growls.

I hold up my hands in a calming gesture. "Tim, these men need a doctor. Some of them are in such bad shape that simply moving them the wrong way could kill them. You'll need someone to triage on site."

"Bandaid can tell us what to do."

I understand his concern, but we don't have time for this. Those men don't have time for this. A little more harshly than I intend, I back up and point to the screen. "Bandaid. You mean this guy with the dislocated shoulder and head injury who hasn't moved during the entire stream?"

Tim's jaw clenches, and he bites, "Lawson, go get the embassy physician."

"Yeah, Lawson, go get the sixty-something man living out his golden years doing physicals between rounds of golf. I'm sure he's mastered the two-minute SEAL shooting drill like I have. He's sure to have had all the close-quarter sparring training Tim's put me through over the years."

Tim drops his bag and storms toward me. "You're not fucking going, Cassidy!"

I don't back down. I can't. I have to be able to tell Willa, Charli, and the others that I did everything I could to save their men.

"Those assholes have gotten their hands on you twice now."

Standing toe-to-toe with my Navy SEAL husband, I fire back, "And I've freed myself twice, thanks to your training."

"Enough!" he thunders. "I don't want you out there, all right?"

His eyes are full of anger and fear over my willingness to take on such a dangerous mission. Never mind that he was considering trading his life for his men.

Swallowing down my own rage, I pull his hands from my face. "But you need me out there, Tim. Your men need me."

BULLETPROOF

JO CHAMBLISS

CHAPTER 17

CASS

Tim backs up, putting some space between us. Dragging his hands over his head, he begins pacing. My husband is struggling between the need to keep me from danger and acknowledging that some of his men could die if we don't get them the right kind of help quickly.

"We're in!" Birdie shouts over the phone, unaware of the faceoff between husband and wife. "I've got some nearby security cameras with views of three out of four sides of the building. I'll be able to give you real-time updates on anyone coming or going. I'm also sending you a building schematic."

Cle chimes in next with the information that she's been able to gather. "Though the angle isn't great, I've got satellite views, including IR signatures of the building. Based on the lack of activity on the roof and surrounding area, these guys aren't expecting you to act this fast or with this much intel."

On and on, people around us are shouting out status updates, but Tim remains frozen.

"Stone, we need to move," Dillan urges

carefully.

I approach him slowly and place a hand on his arm. "Tim?"

Once hard and unmoving, his eyes soften to reveal his greatest vulnerability. "I can't risk you. I have to know you'll make it out of here, even if I don't."

"I'll be fine because you'll be there watching my back. I can do this. I have to do this."

Tim drops his head, a sign that he's giving in and hates himself for it. He's still angry and scared when he looks up again, but I know I've convinced him. "Fuck! Give her a gun and a vest."

Once I'm outfitted in body armor like the rest of the team, Tim hands me a gun. I tuck two spare magazines in the vest, load the gun, and rack the slide. The pistol goes in my belt, and Lawson hands me a bag of supplies he collected from the embassy clinic.

Tim places a hand on my belly and leans down to whisper in my ear, "Whatever happens out there, you keep your ass alive. If shit goes sideways, don't wait for me. You run. And don't stop running until you get to safety."

He straightens to his full height and turns to the others. "Run through it again."

Birdie's disembodied voice directs our attention to the big screen. "Abandoned office building about twelve miles from your location. Two stories above and an underground floor."

Using a virtual marker, she points out

several key components. "Main entrance on the south wall, secondary entry on the western corner of the north wall. There's cellar access on the eastern side in the alley."

"Good. Cle?"

"No outside movement in the last fifteen minutes. We caught a break. The building must not have any windows left. That, paired with the low angle, allows the IR to see inside a short depth. On the eastern side of the building, I'm picking up a large, stationary group below grade. I'm guessing these are your guys."

"Can you confirm we're dealing with five hostiles?" Dillan asks.

"Negative. However, I am detecting light bleed near the entrance on the northern side, indicating their location."

"We'll make it work. Hosfeld, what are we working with here?"

"We've got Berettas fitted with suppressors and subsonic rounds for a quiet entry. M84s for when we breach, and M4 Carbines for quick disposal. All but Mrs. O'Reilly will have night vision and a thermal scope. I've also got coms and ear protection for everybody. To get us out there, I've confiscated the embassy maintenance van. It's a piece of shit that no one will give a second look. We'll have to use it as an ambulance to cart the guys to an empty parking lot we plan on using as a helipad six blocks away."

"Phelps, how's our setup?"

Dillan's top operative takes the group through infrastructure and access routes in and out of the area, and then her boss gives his update. "I've got a helo coming that's big enough to evac everyone at once, even if the pilots have to knock a fucking building down to make room," Dillan announces.

During the briefing, I stood back, watching the group, amazed and proud of the Warrior I married. Not just Tim, but every man and woman in this room and communicating over the phone who has dedicated their lives to our country's safety and security.

Tim walks over to the screen, which still shows the building, and begins handing out assignments. "Hosfeld, I want you on point. Find a spot to nest and cover our approach. Phelps and I will set up at the cellar entrance. Lawson, you'll join Hosfeld and take the back entrance. Birdie, can you hijack the video feed coming from the cellar?"

"I'm already on it. I've got three minutes of footage and will keep recording. I'll start broadcasting when you arrive, so anyone monitoring the hostages won't know you've arrived unless they walk in on you."

"Good work. Cle, that leaves you. I want you patched into our coms. You're our only eyes and ears here."

"You've got it, Commander. Hyper and

Omen have been monitoring and are patched in as your tactical spotters."

"Commander, we've got your backs. You just get our brothers out of there."

"Thanks, Omen."

Tim turns around slowly and glances my way before focusing on Dillan. "Warden, you'll hole up across the street with Cass. Take down anyone that walks out the front door. When clear, bring Cass in to assess and stabilize the men. You do not leave her side."

He takes a deep breath and scans the ready faces in the room. "Keep your eyes open. Ink indicated we're up against five men, but Crendall's people are not the only ones we'll have to be on the lookout for. Tallinn is the most dangerous city in all of Europe, and we're heading into an area where even the police won't go. Do not let your guard down. Let's move out."

Each person grabs their equipment and a bag of medical supplies, and we file out of the conference room. Walking outside to an older box van, I review all the SEAL shooting drills I've run over the years with Tim. Between the gun training and combat sparring, I'm probably as well-trained as any civilian could be. *Which isn't saying much, considering the group we're going against got the drop on a squad of SEALs.*

What I have to remember is that I'm not going in on the front line. I'm serving as a medic here. I'll only go in once the field is clear. Until then, I'm just protecting myself in an unfamiliar city with a giant of a man keeping me company while I do it. No sweat.

I'm silent during the van ride to the city's warehouse district. The others are occupied giving and receiving updates, but I'm too busy trying not to throw up to follow the conversation.

I've never been this scared before, and I won't even be in on the action. Needing a distraction from my jittery nerves, I concentrate on the passing scenery. It's startling.

The transition from the government-run part of the city to the rundown, crime-controlled region happens much faster than I would have thought possible. Even in Africa, I've never seen a society devolve so sharply in such a short distance.

Upon arrival at our staging point, Tim instructs Cle to scan the area in case our arrival stirred up anything. The rest of us are ordered to hold still until she reports. The drafty old van provides no protection from the chill, and soon, the inside is cold enough that I can see our breath.

I look around at the assembled warriors, each appearing as calm as a glassy pond. On the other hand, I can feel my heart beating in my throat.

Hearing Cle's voice in my earpiece startles me, given that I'm not used to having voices in my head. "No new players or major changes. Zero heat signatures on the building across the street from your target. If Knot and the doc hold there, the hostiles shouldn't be able to detect them."

"Thanks, Cle," Tim says, his voice having lost some of the tightness from earlier.

At Tim's signal, Lawson disables the dome light in the ancient van, and we spill out onto the darkened street. The air is even colder outside. Without the humidity we created in the closed van, the air is so dry that it hurts to breathe.

Out of the blue, Tim grabs the shoulder strap of my body armor, shoves me against the side of the van, and presses his whole body against mine. He captures my lips in a desperate kiss in front of the entire crew. Even through the thick body protection, I feel the slight tremor of his hands. *He's still scared.*

My husband pulls away and locks eyes with me. "You take orders from Warden. You don't move unless he says so."

Tim turns away from me and levels a glare at Dillan while addressing the group. "Let's move out."

Dillan moves back to stand next to me, and the two of us watch while Tim, Aaron, Brock, and Sadie set off toward the warehouse from hell.

Once they've disappeared around the building we're using for cover, Dillan whispers, "Don't worry, Cass. In the field, your husband was always a scary son of a bitch. The assholes holding his men will all be dead before you and I cross the street."

God, I hope he's right. Having never seen the battle side of Tim before, or a real battle for that matter, it's hard to keep calm. I'm one big ball of nerves. At the first bursts of suppressed gunfire, I grab Dillan's arm hard enough to bruise. *What the hell am I doing here?*

TIM

My hands ache to touch Cass one more time before I set off across the street, but if I turn around, I'll lose my nerve and order Warden to take her back to the embassy.

I put one foot in front of the other because I know if I tried to get her out of here, I would be fighting a losing battle. Any effort spent convincing my wife to leave would be wasted, and my men would have only suffered that much longer. For my men, I keep my eyes forward and focus on what's ahead.

Despite Cle reporting that the area is clear, Sadie and I get in position to guard the rear as Hosfeld and Lawson traverse the alley toward our target. Their approach goes unnoticed, cloaked by the darkness afforded to us by the broken streetlights. That, and every creature with a brain has abandoned the area in search of warmth.

At the corner opposite the target building, another thermal check is done for any surprise participants, but Cle reports that the area is still clear. Sadie and I lower into a crouch as Hosfeld crosses the cobbled road and approaches the left side of the building. Barely audible through the radio, he signals his teammate Brock, and Sadie and I remain in place until the two men have joined up.

"Omen, are we clear near the front entrance?" I ask the former Ranger Colonel.

"That's affirmative. All hostiles are in the rear of the building. Two of them appear to have relocated to the basement."

Shit. More bloodshed. "We need to hurry," I tell Sadie.

At her nod, we move as one, crossing the street as silently as our counterparts. Our suppressed weapons ensure we won't have to worry about waiting for the other pair to signal before we can engage. I won't allow these bastards to lay another finger on my men. Worried they're about to do just that, I pick up the pace on my approach to the southeast corner of the building, hoping for easy access.

Ideally, the cellar door will be wide open from when my men were brought in. If not, Cle reported the windows are broken, which should give Sadie and I line of sight to take out the insurgents. Worst case scenario is that we'll have to abandon the cellar entrance and backtrack to the front door.

Upon turning the corner, I have to adjust my NV monocle for the light coming from the cellar. Between my skill as a marksman and what

I've heard about Sadie's abilities, we should drop all unfriendlies quickly.

I scan the ground every few feet to avoid stepping on anything that could give us away. At a distance of twenty feet, I hear the wet sound of impact on bloody skin followed by a broken groan. I see red and forget about stealth.

I shove the NV out of my face and step into full view of the window. Sadie hurries to get into position next to me, but I've already fired through a missing pane.

The asshole holding the metal pipe over Judge's back drops like a rock, and the pole clinks loudly on the concrete floor beside him. Sadie's victim falls with a grunt a second later.

I report our status but know Hosfeld and Lawson won't answer if engaged. "Two in basement down."

"The other gun team is about to reach the main group. Hold your position, Stone," Omen says through my earpiece.

Though I've never had to work with the group of former Army Rangers personally, I know my men have multiple times. Lieutenant Hill's team has a tremendous mutual respect for Chase "Omen" McDaniels and his team from Pantera Security.

I click my radio in response to Omen's order and wait, though it's the hardest thing I've ever had to do. Even from outside, the lights for the livestream cameras showcase the damage done to the eight SEALs trapped in that god-forsaken basement. Every moment they wait for help is one moment too long.

Sixty anxious seconds pass with me watching my men hanging bloody and bruised in various states of consciousness. The second I hear Aaron's voice declare that his three targets are down, I hoof it to the cellar door and pull it open.

Sadie covers me as I descend the stairs, though we already cleared the room from outside the window. I look down the line to find Lieutenant Hill, shrugging off my pack and racing over when I spot him.

His condition, as well as the others, is startling. For all I've seen in my long career, I still cringe at seeing the damage up close. Not even wanting to touch him to feel for a pulse, I bend down close and listen for breathing sounds. *Thank god.* "Fish is alive."

Over the radio, a collection of voices celebrates the good news.

Behind me, Sadie checks in with the rest of the rescue team, ordering the two men upstairs to check the building for explosive devices. *Dammit. That should have been my first thought.* Under normal circumstances, it would have been, but I was too tunnel-visioned in getting to my men.

One by one, I check each man and find them all breathing, though some of them don't sound good. I hate to admit it, but Cass was right. They need her help, and they need it now.

I've just returned to Fish when Hosfeld and Lawson check in. "The rest of the building is clear, but I still don't like the setup," Hosfeld says. "I know Birdie is broadcasting recorded footage, but someone out there watching is going to notice that these dead assholes have stopped going rounds with your guys."

"Then I suggest we move as fast as we can. Warden, you're clear. Get Cass over and call the helo."

Fish is still out when I give the order, so I go to the man who was the last one seen to be conscious. Since he's one of the ones hanging upside down, I kneel near his head. "Fischer. Ink, can you hear me?"

The man opens the one eye that will and offers me a sardonic half-smile. He opens his mouth to speak, and blood dribbles out. "Does this mean I'm not dead?"

"I haven't given you permission to die. How bad are you?"

"Manageable, I think. Cut me down," he says in his soft Aussie accent.

"I've got the rope. You hold him," Sadie orders.

Placing Ink's hands on the side straps of my body armor, I grab a fist full of his belt and pull upward, taking some of his weight. Sadie follows the rope to where it goes over the metal truss above our heads and anchors to a metal bar near the stairs.

After wrapping the excess around her waist, she pulls the loop holding the rope to its anchor and slowly walks forward. Ink grits his teeth as his battered body flexes with the movement, but together, Sadie and I get him down to the hard floor without hurting him further. "I take it... you got my... message."

I reach for my pack and pull out something to put behind his head. "Actually, Cass did. How did you know we would see you?"

"I didn't. I hoped the camera and the beatings were set up for your benefit and thought I'd try."

Ink's face contorts in pain, so I drop the line of questions for now. "You rest a minute. Evac is on its way."

I'm still chewing on Hosfeld's concerns, which have my gut churning. Knowing Cass is on her way, I check in with our eyes in the sky again. "Cle, can you confirm that we're still clear?"

"I'm seeing no activity within a two-block radius, Commander. Nothing outside that range is moving toward your location. It looks like these guys didn't anticipate you finding them so soon, if at all."

Omen's voice breaks in after Cle finishes with her update. "Stand by, Stone. Cle's receiving some new information, but nothing indicating your people are at risk."

"Copy."

Despite Omen's calm assurance, I remain

tense, knowing Cass is about to enter this hell.

"Sorry about that, Commander," Cle says when she comes back online. "I have good news. My connections on the hill are still valid. An emergency medical team from Landstuhl has been dispatched and is en route to Amari Air Base. They're on a hospital plane fitted with a proper operating room. They should land in about half an hour. Your chopper pilot can relay Mrs. O'Reilly's triage report to the trauma team, and they'll be ready to treat your men before they arrive."

I'll be damned. "I don't know how you did it, but thank you."

"Hey, you're not the only one that can pull strings."

"Apparently, I've met my match. As for those strings, I need you to keep pulling. Crendall wasn't here. Go ahead and sign off. I need all your focus on locating him and any others involved."

"On it."

"Omen, you have my thanks again."

"Any time, Commander. Keep us updated on your men. Those pricks have grown on us over the years."

"You got it, Colonel."

The radio click indicates the Pantera team has signed off, and movement to my left draws my attention. I look up at the cellar stairs just in time to see Cassidy walking down them with Warden right behind her.

Her steps falter as she takes in the wounded men hanging from the trusses. Seeing the scene in person is a lot different than watching it on a damn TV screen.

"Oh my god."

BULLETPROOF

JO CHAMBLISS

CHAPTER 18

CASS

This can't be real. I'm stuck in a nightmare, and I can't wake up.

My leading foot moves back up a step as my head and heart struggle to take in the scene. Everything in me is screaming for me to run, to get out of this place.

A big hand rests on my shoulder, holding me steady and in place. "Easy, now," Dillan's velvety voice croons.

I'm in way over my head. Being the only medic here is beside the point. The emotional toll it's taking to see these men in this condition is debilitating. Broken and bloody men have been left hanging from the ceiling, unconscious. Most of them have been stripped of their shirts and boots and left exposed to the frigid winter air. Some of them are so severely beaten that they're nearly unrecognizable.

Tears blur my vision, and I swipe a hand across my eyes. *Come on, Cassidy. Don't wimp out now. These men need your help.*

I take a deep, shaky breath and walk the rest of the way down the stairs. *God, they look so much worse up close and in person.* I regret not dragging the embassy doctor with us just for the extra set of hands.

Handing Dillan my gun, I pull off my coat, radio, and armored vest and then rip off the black gloves borrowed from Sadie. The rest of the team converges on the basement while I strip down, bringing the medical supplies each operative was made to carry.

Holding a flashlight in my teeth, I start going through the bags and pulling out essential medical equipment. Next, I pour alcohol over my arms and hands and pull on some sterile gloves. Now, where to start?

Ink is awake again, already freed from his binds. He's actually sitting up, drinking from a bottle of water. The trained commandos with me are either keeping watch or waiting for orders, so I start giving them.

"Lawson, one of those bags has blankets in it. Get him warm," I say, pointing to Ink.

The man jumps to action, and I turn back to the others. The rest of the SEAL squad is unconscious, luckily for them. "I don't want any of you touching them unless I say so. Until we have some idea of their injuries, moving them could cause more damage, maybe even kill them."

A closer inspection of the guys has me thinking Bandaid is likely in the worst shape. He has a dislocated shoulder, but it's the facial lacerations that have me concerned. His aren't just cuts. One of them is deep and is accompanied by a lot of swelling.

"Aaron, come here. Stand behind Bandaid. Dillan, you too."

With a penlight, I study the cut and bruising on his face, tenderly touching the area and swearing inwardly when the site gives slightly. *Fucking monsters. His cheekbone's fractured.* Manually opening his eyes, I check his pupils and find they aren't equally responsive. I pray he's only concussed and no traumatic brain injury is present.

A check of the rest of his body doesn't reveal any complete breaks. That doesn't mean there aren't any fractures, but he should be safe to move. And he'll need to be moved quickly. "Tim, we need to get him out of here now. Can we get him loaded on the chopper and to the medical team first? He has a zygomaticomaxillary fracture with significant fragment displacement. He needs surgery immediately to ensure his eye isn't in danger."

"We can do that. A round trip for the helo shouldn't take more than six minutes. I'll—What the hell?"

Tim stops talking and stands frozen, staring at his phone. Something is happening, but I can't worry about that right now. Turning away from him, I appoint another assistant to do Tim's job. "Dillan, get me that chopper. Lawson, take

Dillan's place. I'm ready for you and Aaron to get Bandaid down. Be as gentle as possible, and do not touch his face. Sadie, there's a collapsible litter in the biggest bag. Open it up, and then you and Dillan get the van. We've got to get Bandaid out of here right now."

Once Sadie brings over the litter, Tim calls Aaron and Dillan to discuss the new development. Sadie takes over for Aaron, and Bandaid is slowly cut down and laid prone. After stabilizing Bandaid's head, I begin securing the rest of him to the litter. "Ok, you two go get the van while I check out Judge."

An angry outburst from Tim catches everyone's attention, but these injured men are my only concern. "Brock! Sadie! Move!"

The two speed off on my command, and I move down the line to Judge, who has a lot of blood pooled beneath him. The amount indicates a deep laceration but not enough to suggest an open artery. Starting at his neck, I inspect his uniform for the location of the cut.

My touch startles him, and his shocked gaze locks on me when his eyes open. "Wha — Cass?"

His eyes swim like he's drunk, but I know he's not. Still, with him conscious, I stand back up to check his eyes and find them equal and reactive. "You're safe now, Judge. I'm just checking you for injuries before we take you down. Where are you hurt?"

"I... I don't..."

Judge's voice fades as though he's forgotten what he was going to say. Though a fair amount of blood is on the floor beneath him, it's not enough to cause his confusion. That has to mean he's bleeding internally, so I quickly check the rest of him. I find that the source of the bleeding is his left thigh. I cut away the fabric of his pants and find a laceration in a large, discolored area. *Shit. Broken femur with internal bleeding.* He needs surgery now.

I look up and yell at the three men talking strategy, not caring in the least about what they're discussing. "One of you get over here!"

Tim and Dillan both jog across the room, and I point to the bag I carried in. "I need the biggest splint you can find. Judge needs to go on that first chopper with Bandaid. He needs immediate surgery to set a broken femur that's bleeding internally."

The two men help me apply the splint before lowering the man onto another litter. Sadie and Brock have just returned, and I point to the two men who appear to be in the most danger. "They need to go now. The rest can wait till the chopper returns."

Dillan and his three operatives grab the end of a litter and start up the steps as I scribble down notes for the medical team. I run up the stairs to hand the notes to Brock, who has jumped in behind the wheel. "Get them there as fast as possible, but do not bounce them around."

Tim runs up the stairs behind me and grabs Aaron. "We're going too. We've got a chance to stop this guy, and I'm not wasting it." Turning back to me, he says, "Sadie and Warden will stay here with you, and Lawson will be back as soon as we transfer to the helo."

I turn to reenter the cellar, but stop to face my husband and give him an order of my own. "Be careful, Tim."

Back in the basement, my bloody gloves are pulled off, and fresh ones are pulled from a box in the equipment bag. With none of the remaining men showing indications of life-threatening injuries, I move to the closest patient and get back to work.

Fish has bruising around his neck as though he was choked, not to the point of death, but as a means of torture. Still, I examine him thoroughly, starting with his pulse and respiration. His heart is fine, and his breathing is normal.

When palpations find no complete fractures, I instruct Dillan and Sadie to take him down, laying him on a sterile medical drape. Next, I break a vial of smelling salts and pass them under his nose. "Be ready to hold him down if he lashes out, but don't hurt him any more than he already is."

Fish's eyes flutter open, and he stares at me as though hallucinating. He tries to speak, and his voice comes out sounding damaged. "Cass? How?"

"Later. Can you tell me where you are?"

"Hell," he answers without hesitation.

His wit at a time like this makes me smile. "What city is that in?"

"Tallinn."

"Good. I know you were choked. Are you hurt anywhere else?"

"Ribs."

"Okay. Sit tight. We're going to get you out of here."

"The others?"

"Bandaid and Judge are being airlifted to the air base where a surgical team is staged. I'm checking on the rest of you now."

Though I would have advised against it, he sits up and looks over the four men left hanging and Ink lying on the floor unconscious again.

By the time I've moved on to Skin, Brock is jogging down the stairs again. "The chopper should have returned by the time I return with another load."

"Go ahead and take Fish and Ink. It'll save us time down the road."

Fish refuses to leave at first, but I convince him that his staying behind will only slow us down later. Sadie and Brock help the two men onto their feet and lead them up the stairs. That leaves Dillan and me to work on the remaining four until my orderlies return.

Skin seems to have suffered a concussion and some significant bruising. Wrench has a lump on the back of his head and appears to be mildly concussed. Along with his other injuries, Wrench had a tooth knocked loose with one punch and pierced his cheek with a second blow.

By the time I finish with Wrench, Sadie and Brock are returning to gather the next two men and leave Dillan and me to care for the last two SEALs.

Hawk is one of the men that was suspended upside down. I'm almost certain he has a broken rib or two, though nothing seems to be displaced. He also shows choking bruises on his neck. Devil has woken up by the time I reach him but doesn't speak. He's shirtless, and after what I've seen of the rest of the men, the bruising and welts on his body outnumber all the others by a wide margin. I don't think a single part of his body escaped abuse.

Most shocking about Devil's appearance is the tear rolling down his clenched jaw. The man must be in a tremendous amount of pain.

Since he's conscious, I don't wait but have Dillan go ahead and lower him to the ground. The man crumples like a rag doll, and it takes all my strength to keep him from crashing onto the filthy concrete floor.

With me supporting all Devil's weight now, Dillan rushes over to help me lower him safely to the litter. Devil grunts through the pain as we shift his body, and fresh tears squeeze from his eyes after he's finally flat on his back.

"Devil, look at me."

Those tormented eyes open, and my heart breaks for what I see in them. "You're going to make it back to your kids. I swear it. I need to know if you could have a head injury. I don't feel any lumps."

"My... head is fine."

His eyes are clear and focused, so I have no reason to doubt his word. I would prefer to let the medical team treat Devil's pain, but moving him will be excruciating. I would rather risk the medication than take a chance that he injures himself further during transport.

Decision made, I pull the vial and syringe out of my bag. "Devil, I'm going to give you something for pain, then we're getting you home."

Devil closes his eyes, which I know is a sign of trust. I draw the medicine and pick the arm with the fewest bruises. Within seconds, I get the satisfaction of watching Devil's battered body slowly relax.

Glad that I could provide at least some relief to my last patient, I stand to start packing away the supplies while I wait for our turn to evacuate.

I've just stuffed my stethoscope into a side pocket of my bag when a gunshot rings out.

Dillan grunts and collapses to the floor, landing right next to Hawk.

"Dillan!"

I dive to the floor beside the big man, placing one hand on his side and one against his cheek. He doesn't rouse, so I get up to move around him. The hand on his side comes away with bloody fingertips, so I roll him onto his stomach. *Oh, please, no.* The bullet hit just below his body armor.

I have three injured men on my hands, one dying, and a shooter between us and safety. I have no idea where Dillan put my gun, and my radio is piled up with my coat and other gear.

My only option is to defend our position. However, I have absolutely no hope of getting any of us out of here alive if I'm dealing with more than one asshole with a gun.

With Dillan bleeding out beside me, I risk dislodging the bullet in him to reach for his gun, knowing I'm the only protection these three men have. I aim the gun at the cellar entrance to cover our group. Several seconds pass, but no one approaches. *What the hell are you waiting for?*

A glance at Dillan reveals a growing pool of blood beneath him. *Dammit.*

If the shooter isn't going to rush me, maybe Sadie and Brock will make it back before he makes his next move. That means I have one chance to save Dillan.

I drop the gun and dig through my

medical bag for scissors and a hemostatic bandage. Luck is on my side, and I find them quickly. I've just finished cutting away Dillan's shirt when someone grabs my hair.

My body is yanked backward, away from Dillan, and I spin around on the floor to kick out at my attacker. Two of my kicks make solid contact, but my upper body is lifted and slammed on the hard floor, jarring my head. Before I can recover, I take a brutal kick to my hip. The combination of both blows has me seeing black spots, leaving me temporarily out of the fight. With no defense against this new threat, I figure we're all about to die any second now.

Wrong.

The guy grabs my arm, violently yanking me off the floor. He looks to be Western Caucasian, but without hearing his voice, I'm only guessing. One thing I'm sure of is that he's responsible for Bishop's death and for my friends being tortured. I'm equally sure that I'm done with his bullshit.

"I have no idea what you're after, but if you think I'm going to help you get it, you can go fuck yourself."

Though I'm presenting a brave face, I'm hoping and praying Sadie and Brock will be back soon and catch this bastard. All I have to do is remain calm, keep his attention away from the injured men, and stall for all I'm worth.

The man sneers in response to my bravado

and drags me toward the interior staircase. *Oh, hell no. I am not doing this a third time.*

Seriously hoping that Sadie and Lawson are close and can hear me through Dillan's radio, I start screaming my head off. I'm also dropping my weight after each step he takes, trying to throw the asshole off balance. By the time we've reached the dark stairs, the man is beginning to regret taking me.

I fight and claw with every ounce of my strength to keep him from going any farther. Unfortunately, my plan works too well. The man stops completely, throwing me against the wall and handrail.

The impact is jarring, with my back absorbing the contact with the metal bar. The impact shoots lightning down my legs, but still, I keep fighting until he gets his hands around my neck. The guy has lost control of his temper and seems no longer interested in letting me live.

Remembering all the times I've practiced this hold with Tim, I weave my hands through his arms and execute a spin, breaking his grip. Then, I'm taking off, limping up the stairs, knowing If I can make it to the main floor, I have two verified exit points.

I've made it up two steps before the guy grabs my left ankle, pulling my feet out from under me. I smack my head on the edge of the stair tread, and for a moment, all I know is pain. I take one brittle breath, then I'm rolled over onto my back on the stairs and backhanded across the mouth. The furious strike dashes my cheek against my teeth, cutting the inside, and my head, again, bounces off the concrete steps behind me.

My whole body goes limp. Thinking he's made his point, the man grabs a fist full of my hair again. I feel the stitches on my gunshot wound rip as he jerks me upright. Instead of moving again, he aims his gun at the three men below. "I've already had enough of your shit. Start cooperating and move it, or I blow them away."

Though my desire to fight and escape is strong, there's no way I can choose myself over three men with wives and children. My body goes slack, and the man must realize I'm giving in. He spins me around and resumes shoving me up the stairs.

The *American* asshole attacker wins... For now.

The building's main floor isn't as dark as the basement, having several broken windows to let in the moonlight. The soft glow is just enough to illuminate the bodies of the men killed by Dillan's people earlier. I feel no remorse over the bloody scene or that their lives were ended, not after seeing firsthand the damage they inflicted on Tim's men. I also have no intention of ending up like them.

Walking past the bodies, I notice a knife lying just beyond a dead man's fingers. My kidnapper's focus is on the door ahead, and he either hasn't noticed or doesn't care about the bodies of his associates. This means he also hasn't noticed the blade. Lurching out of his grasp, I make a show of tripping, landing on the knife.

I brace myself for a kick that doesn't come, but my arm is nearly pulled out of the socket when I'm yanked back up to my feet again. After much abuse, my shoulder is throbbing, but the pain is worth it because I've risen with the seven-inch blade hidden against my side. Now, I just have to wait for the right time to make my move.

This has to be done outside. If I strike at him now, my escape route would be too predictable, increasing my chances of being shot. Outside, I'll at least be able to make myself into a more difficult target to hit.

Five more feet, and I'm stepping through the door opening, still held in a vice-like grip. The door opened onto a covered loading dock with stairs leading down to street level. A pickup truck is parked on the street just beyond the sidewalk at the bottom of the stairs. *I now wish Cle had stayed with us instead of pulling away to search for Crendall.*

Figuring the truck is where we're headed, I surmise my only chance to make a solid strike is when my feet are planted firmly on the concrete walk.

Just as I reach the last stair tread, a loud pinging sound comes from somewhere around the back of the truck. My captor hears it and becomes noticeably distracted. *Now, Cass. Make your move!* I feign tripping again, but as I set to lunge, a low voice rumbles from the stairs behind us. "Let her go."

Oh no! The asshole swings around at the growled command, taking me with him. Devil stands at the top of the loading dock, gripping one of the awning poles. He's half-naked, barely able to stand, and is holding Dillan's gun in a shaking hand. Even with the lethally trained SEAL aiming a loaded gun at him, the man holding me laughs and pulls me in front of him. "You won't fire shaking like that. You wouldn't risk her life."

He raises his own gun to aim at Devil, slightly loosening his hold on me.

"NO!"

Instead of pulling away to escape, I'm moving closer to save Devil's life. I strike up with the knife in a tight arc, slicing down on the man's arm as a shot goes off. I can't tell how much damage I inflicted or how much his aim was deflected. Spinning back around, I watch helplessly as Devil falls, meaning my effort wasn't enough. He lands face down on the steps as the asshole that shot him howls and reaches for my throat. "You bitch!"

I'm slammed against the side of the truck twice before his fist slams against my face and then to my middle. My knees buckle, but before I can crumple to the ground, Crendall opens the door and shoves me inside. I can't even fight back

when my hands and feet are zip-tied.
    Not again.

CHAPTER 19

TIM

Two men jump out of the helicopter holding guns as we approach in the embassy maintenance van. Though these men were expecting us, this is a shit part of town, and they're smart for not taking chances. I step out of the van with my hands up, glad I thought to pull my dog tags out of my shirt for easy visibility.

"Commander Timothy O'Reilly. SEAL Team Two."

Recognizing the name, the men stand down, and I motion them over. "We've got wounded!"

The men holster their weapons and run toward us as Lawson opens the back doors. Brock remains at the wheel to guard against someone boosting the van while we're not looking. Aaron hops out, and he and I grab the litter holding Bandaid. The SEAL doctor hasn't stirred, and I pray he's not dying on me.

Dismissing the possibility, I focus on what needs to be done right now. We need to get Judge and Bandaid loaded, and I need to get support back to Cass. Speaking to the helo crew, I say,

"You two, take the litter from my men. Phelps, you and Lawson get back to the others. We'll send the helo back as soon as we've offloaded."

The exchange is careful but quick, and Sadie jumps back in the van a second later. The tires screech, heading back toward Cass and the others while the four of us secure the litters in the helo. Hosfeld and I are in the process of strapping in when the skids lift off the ground.

The noise level inside the fuselage doesn't allow for communicating without headsets, and given the brevity of the trip, none are provided. Hosfeld and I will have to wait until we land before working through our next move.

The helo is on the ground again a short three minutes after takeoff, and we're rushed by a team of men and women sporting medical scrubs. The man in charge of the group accepts the notes handed to him by Aaron and promptly turns his attention to where it's needed. Not wasting another second, the doctors race the gurneys to the waiting hospital plane.

The helo's engine ramps up again and lifts off, returning to ground zero. I watch it until the deafening sound fades away, and the paramilitary operative and I are left standing alone on the tarmac. Ever the efficient operator, Aaron jumps right in. "What did the message say?" he asks.

"The guy says he had people watching the airfield and knows I'm in the country. He'll accept a trade, me for my men. I've got two hours to respond, and then he'll send further instructions."

"How would he even have known you'd be here? Does the Navy have a leak?"

"No. This guy's been watching. He knew I would figure out his notes and go wherever Fish was sent. As soon as Fish's team was seen in Estonia, all he had to do was wait for me to show."

"What are the chances he still has eyes on this field? He'd have seen us just now."

"Not likely. They'd know I wouldn't get back on a plane without my men. Since we met no resistance at the warehouse, they still don't know we found it."

"Unless this is all part of the setup."

"This whole damn thing has been one giant fucking setup, and I want it to end. We're taking these bastards down tonight. I'm going to check in with Cle. You go find us a ride."

Hosfeld nods and jogs off in search of some wheels, and I dial Cle Maxwell again. "There's been a development, Cle. I received contact from someone who knows I'm in the country. They're offering to let me trade myself for my men, meaning he doesn't know we've got them already."

Cle offers me her own update, which isn't much. The helo returns a short while later, pausing my briefing with Cle, and the medics offload four more men who are whisked away to the hospital plane.

The helo's engine ramps up to take off again, and I move away from the noise to get back to Cle. As I do, my phone alerts with an incoming call, but I ignore it. With Cass seeing to the men, finding and stopping this guy has become my top priority. "Cle, I think—"

"O'Reilly!"

Aaron jumps out of a Humvee and shoves his phone in my face. His expression is dim. Ignoring Cle momentarily, I bring the phone to my ear and bark, "What is it?"

"Commander, Knot is down. Brock and I just got back and found him on the basement floor, unconscious. He's been shot. Hawk is still out but doesn't look to have any gunshot wounds. Sir, Cass and Devil are gone."

My heart seizes in my chest, feeling like it might split apart at any second. *I made the wrong move.*

Though I'm finding it hard to breathe, I put one foot in front of the other toward the military truck. "They couldn't have gone far. Find them!"

"Sir, if I don't get Knot to the air base, we'll lose him. It may be too late already."

I grip the door and roof of the truck, duck my head, and swear loudly. Decide between my wife and my best friend. I don't think I can do it.

"Sir," Aaron begins. "Let them put Knot

on the chopper. Even if we wait for the bird to return and fly us back, we'll still get there faster than driving."

Grunting my assent, I tell Sadie through clenched teeth, "Get Knot and Hawk to the chopper. As soon as they land on base, we'll be on our way back to you."

Ten minutes. I'm standing around waiting with my thumb up my ass for ten minutes while god-knows-what is happening to Cass. While I pace the tarmac, Aaron runs to the hospital plane to inform them of Knot's impending arrival and his condition.

For the rest of the time, he paces the helipad alongside me. The evac pilots must have informed the medical crew they were close, as two stretchers are rolled out to meet the helo.

Warden is too still and too pale when the doors open. "I'm sorry, my friend." I lay a hand on Warden's shoulder as he's transferred to the gurney and strapped down, but then I'm climbing inside the helo and slamming the door.

The three-minute return ride over the dark and dangerous city seems to take hours with a million horrible endings playing out in my head. This guy, this group is finally getting what they wanted. Bishop is dead, Dillan's skirting too close to that line, and now, they have my wife. I've never been a pessimist, but up against this much of a unit, I can't imagine a scenario where any of us make it out of this alive.

Regardless of the outcome, as long as I'm breathing, I'll be raining hell down on these bastards for what they've done. I just have to find them. They took Cass for the purpose of getting to me. Whatever their plan, I'm sure it involves watching my wife die before my own life is ended.

One thing's for damn sure. I won't make it easy for them.

Aaron smacks my arm, getting my attention just before the helo touches down. I open the door and jump off the deck, running full tilt to the waiting van. Lawson is behind the wheel and peels off toward the abandoned building as Sadie sits quietly. Fury darkens her features, as does fear over Warden's condition.

A short minute later, we skid to a stop just in front of the cellar entrance of our original target, and all four of us explode from the van toward the stairs.

The night is still dark, the air just as bitterly cold as when we first arrived. However, none of it can be felt through the burning, rancid rage coursing through my veins. I've faced thousands of enemies in my career and taken many lives, but I've never felt a hunger to kill until now.

I'm the first to reach the bottom of the cellar stairs, still lit by that damned light ring. Just beyond the bottom step, I find a large pool of blood, indicating where Knot fell. There's also a trail of blood and a shuffled set of barefoot prints leading away from the sterile paper mat Murphy must have been lying on. I point them out to my borrowed team and set the group in motion. "Sadie, you and Lawson go back out the cellar doors and backtrack around the front. Aaron and I will follow this trail.

Patching my phone into the team coms, I call Cle again. Somehow, she's already been updated on our new situation, even though I cut her off earlier. "I'm still here, Commander," Cle says through my earpiece. "I'm pulling your location back up to look for them. I need sixty seconds."

"Do what you have to, but I'm not waiting."

"Sir, I'm... sorry."

"Don't, Cle. I made the call to pull you from surveillance to find Crendall. It was my wrong decision."

Following the blood drops, I take the interior set of stairs three at a time. The shuffled footsteps in the dust continue in a trail leading to the back of the building through the wide-open rear door. Stepping through the opening, I quickly scan the platform and beyond, aided by the light from the full moon.

"Shit."

Devil is lying face down on the stairs, unmoving, and Cass is nowhere to be found.

CASS

My head is pounding. That means I'm still

alive. Being alive means feeling the ache left by every kick, punch, contact with the concrete, jerk of my arm, and rip of my stitches.

But I… Am… Alive.

And now, it's time to plan. Even though my eyes are closed, a bright glow through my lids tells me I'm in a well-lit room. I don't know if it was from my injuries that I conked out or if I was drugged. I don't feel groggy, and my heart isn't racing. That means I gave in to the blows to my head and let sleep take me under.

I should have fought harder to stay awake. As it is, I have no guess as to how long it's been or how far I was taken from that building. The best thing I can do now is study my surroundings while maintaining the sleeping ruse.

The sounds I hear are muffled, meaning there must be at least a wall between me and any activity. Trusting my assessment, I lift my head off the hard floor and open one eye to look around. The image is slightly blurry, but inches from my face, I recognize my captor lying beside me, eyes wide open and wearing a sickening grin. Dammit, now he knows I'm awake.

A wave of unease washes over me, and I lay my head back down, trying to wish away the nausea, blurred vision, and confusion. Any moment now, the next phase of my hell will begin, and I haven't yet figured out what happened while I was blacked out.

I work hard to keep my breathing slow

and calm, focusing on taking stock of my body. Overall, I feel sore from being manhandled but also relieved to note that I'm still fully dressed.

Confused that the man lying next to me hasn't responded to my wakefulness, I open both eyes and discover why. The leering grin he's wearing isn't what I thought. It finally registers that he's not smiling at all. His throat has been slit from ear to ear. Now that he's not behind me or tossing me around, I get my first good look at him.

Holy shit! I know who this man is. And if he weren't dead already, I would have volunteered to kill him myself. It turns out this bastard is… or was… that prick reporter, Richard Crendall. I'd seen him on the news and knew of his involvement in the death of a doctor nearly twenty years ago. Only a few hours ago, I learned it was Tim's team that was compromised by Crendall's selfish ambition.

Looking away from Crendall's mutilated neck, I study everything else in my immediate vicinity. That's when I notice I'm lying in a pool of Crendall's blood. I roll over to get out of it, but it's useless. My left side is already soaked in crimson.

Being coated in a dead man's blood freaks me out, and I scurry out of the sticky, wet puddle. The abrupt movement makes my head swim, and I end up lying flat on my back, staring at the concrete ceiling.

The room stops spinning after I take a few deep breaths, but I have to squint my eyes at the bare bulb above me in the ten-by-ten room. Once my eyes adjust to the light, I resume my study of the cell-like space where I'm being kept. The walls are made of cinderblocks, and the ceiling is cast concrete like the floor. The only way in or out is a heavy steel door in the middle of the wall closest to me.

A lack of arterial spray on any of the walls means my former captor wasn't killed here, but merely his body stashed. *So, why kill him, and who has me now?*

Once more, I ignore the pain in my body and summon the energy to roll over to my stomach. My hands are bound, but with much effort, I push up into a sitting position. That's when I notice I'm no longer alone.

A man of Arab descent sits in a chair in the now-open doorway. "How do you do, Mrs. O'Reilly?" he asks.

Though the man seems to know who I am, nothing about him seems familiar to me. I study his impassive face and deceptively casual body language. The man watches me carefully but appears to have no weapons to defend himself should I attack. That tells me he has plenty of muscle just beyond my line of sight, willing to jump in if necessary.

Knowing that talking will hurt my busted lip and cut cheek, I ask my new jailer, "Who are you?"

The man shrugs nonchalantly. "I am a man seeking revenge."

No emotion whatsoever. Gesturing to the dead man beside me, I ask, "Who was this man to you?"

A ghost of a smile plays on his lips. "A pawn."

Pawn... The notes. They were all chess-themed. There's no way this is a coincidence. "Crendall wasn't the one sending the messages. You were."

The man nods.

"If the two of you were working together, why did you kill him? Was kidnapping me not part of your plan?"

The Arab man stands and picks at a spot of rust on the steel door, appearing bored with the conversation. Instead of answering my questions, he asks me one. "How much do you know about your husband's military missions?"

"Nothing. He couldn't discuss them with me. Even if he could, he wouldn't have, and I wouldn't have asked."

A dark, disbelieving stare is leveled back at me, and my new captor's head tilts in faux interest. "Not curious? What a rarity you must be among nosy Western women," he adds sarcastically.

"Living with what he had to do for his country was hard enough on him. I wanted to be his refuge, not someone who forced him to relive his pain."

The man scoffs. "Your man knows nothing of pain."

"And you know nothing about my husband, what he's done to protect innocents from people like you."

Gesturing to the body on the floor, I add, "My husband knows what it's like for people like him to interfere with a mission for selfish gain and get two good men killed."

The Arab man spares a disgusted look at the dead man before raising an eyebrow at me. "I thought you didn't know about your husband's work."

Now, it's my turn to scoff. "Tim didn't have to tell me about Crendall. This disgraced reporter was all over the news for what he'd done. Even though it's been seventeen years, I'll never forget his face. He may as well have killed that doctor himself."

"Ah, yes. I can see how this man's crimes would have offended you personally, *Dr. O'Reilly*."

I shrug off his knowledge of my occupation. "So, you hired decent researchers. Where you should have spent your money was on better mercenaries. Then, maybe you would have gotten to me sooner. To that end, I'll ask again: Who is this man to you, and why am I here?"

The Arab man leans back in the metal folding chair as though we're having a lovely Sunday afternoon chat. "This man was foolish enough to approach me seventeen years ago with a proposal. At the time, I was enjoying the... employ of a certain doctor who was not pleased with his commission."

"You're talking about the doctor that was killed."

Again, a nod. "Crendall wanted to make a deal with me for access to the doctor. I learned, rather quickly, that his motivation was not as altruistic as your work but that he wanted to be the only American journalist to have seen and spoken to the doctor. Not that I was interested in either case, but an associate of mine convinced me that Crendall could be useful. I did not trust the man, so I offered him my own deal instead. I knew your government would eventually come for the doctor. I told the reporter that he was to inform me of the rescue team's arrival, and in exchange, he would be allowed to document the slaughter of the American operatives. Since carnage sells better than happy endings, he agreed if only for the boost it would mean for his career."

"So, the whole thing was a setup to kill Americans?"

"No, but since they were coming, I planned to use the opportunity to inspire my brothers who had been scattered by the alliance between the West and the Jews."

From what I remember of the news reports, only the two Americans were lost, whereas all the jihadists were killed. I don't understand how anything from that day could have inspired anyone on either side.

I also don't understand why I'm conversing with a man who put a lot of effort into kidnapping me and is likely planning to kill both Tim and me. Nevertheless, I can't seem to let this go until I understand the big picture. "None of what you say makes sense. There was no slaughter of American forces that day. The SEAL team killed all your men. It seems Crendall betrayed you, so why was he working for you now?"

"It was not for betrayal that Crendall deviated from the plan but impatience. Sheer stupidity on his part ruined what would have been his big break. His charge was to remain at a certain boundary to film the team's demise, but he entered the camp hoping to obtain better footage. The actions of his incompetent cameraman saved the soldiers' lives."

"Don't let Tim hear you call his men soldiers," I warn on reflex before getting back on track. "You seem to have glossed over the fact that Crendall got all your men killed."

He dismisses my comment with a wave of his hand. "Martyrs for the cause. Each one volunteered to die with your husband to spread our message."

"I think I get it now. You were going to blow the whole camp, your men included, but Crendall's cameraman wrecked the plan and your man's concentration when he turned on his light."

"Very good. The man holding the doctor was supposed to set off the explosion when the operatives reached his position. The camera light made him panic, and our efforts were for naught. Sadly, Crendall left the country before I could intercept him.

"Imagine my surprise when he showed up in my country many years later and requested an audience with me. Only because of my curiosity did I entertain his offer instead of killing him outright. It came as no surprise that Crendall blamed your husband for ruining his career. When the mighty Timothy O'Reilly surfaced in the news recently, Crendall thought to hand him to me on a silver platter so we could both have our revenge.

"I had no faith in the failed reporter's ability to produce the illustrious SEAL commander. It was by the slimmest of margins that I decided to let Crendall live in case he might have success. Astonishingly, his attempts have delivered you to me, and your husband will soon follow. The added advantage of having video footage of the torture of American Navy SEALs will ignite those whose faith in our cause has wavered."

You bastard.

"If you got what you wanted, why am I here? I am a woman. You will gain no respect from your men by killing me."

"True. Like the others, you are merely a pawn, but you will bring me my prize. Before I'm finished, those in my world will see the best that the United States military has to offer brought to his knees, begging for mercy."

"You must enjoy hearing yourself talk. Otherwise, why would you be telling me all this?"

The man's answering smile chills my blood. I expect some threat or a taunt about my future role in all this, but the man walks out of the room, locking me in with the corpse and my thoughts. And all my thoughts are of Tim and needing to get the hell out of here.

Knowing it's pointless, I quickly search my pockets, finding them predictably empty. I'm surrounded by four block walls and a concrete floor and ceiling. The heavy steel door opens to the outside, so even if I had a knife or hammer and chisel, I couldn't access the hinges to remove the pins.

Completely out of options, I scoot backward to lean against the wall instead of getting up to sit in the chair left behind by the terrorist mastermind.

Looks like I won't be rescuing myself this time.

CHAPTER 20

TIM

Flying down the stairs, I drop beside Murphy's head and check for a pulse. His skin is cold to the touch, but I hope it's because he's half-dressed in near-arctic air. I reach under his neck and offer a silent plea as I press two fingers against his carotid.

Still alive. Thank god. I call out to my current field partner as he runs through the door. "Aaron, help me."

The two of us get Devil rolled over as carefully as possible in consideration of his numerous injuries from earlier. Devil's pained wheeze is heartbreaking, but it proves he's not dying.

Besides new scrapes and bruises from his collapse on the stairs, there's a gunshot wound in the area just above the clavicle on his left side. He's not bleeding as much as I would expect, which I attribute to the cold.

"Murphy. Devil! Look at me."

His eyes flutter open, but it's taking him a lot of effort to focus. "Devil, where is Cass?"

"He took her," Devil croaks.

"What can you tell me?"

"One man. White. Blue truck."

This must be Crendall. "How long?"

"Don't know. I couldn't stop them."

But he damn sure tried. "No, that was my job, and I fucked it up. This is not on you, man."

Knowing he must be freezing, I peel off my coat and wrap it around him.

"What now?" Aaron asks.

Pounding footsteps approach as Sadie and Brock round the far corner of the building. "Now these two get Devil to that hospital. After that, I give Crendall what he wants."

"Watch," Devil gasps.

"Watch for what?" Sadie asks, bending down to hear his weakened voice.

The man shakes his head. "Knot's watch. I took it off him and threw it in the back of the asshole's truck before he shot me."

The rest of us look up from the wounded SEAL to one another in sort of stunned awe. Devil knew he couldn't keep Crendall from taking Cass, so he risked his life to make sure I'd at least have a chance to find her.

"Devil, I…" my words choke out.

"Go. Find Cass," he rasps.

"Thank you."

Standing up, I grab Sadie's arm as I rise. "Sadie, contact the air base and have them send transport for Murphy. I want you and Lawson to stay here with him. Aaron and I are going after

Cass."

Lawson tosses me the van keys, and Aaron pulls out his phone as he runs around the building with me hot on his heels. "Birdie, I need you to track Knot's watch and send the feed to my phone!"

I don't hear whatever she asks of the man, but he barks back, "Do it!"

We reach the van, and I jam the key in the ignition as soon as my ass hits the seat. Guided by Birdie, Aaron barks out driving directions, leading us out of the city while I work to keep my shit together. We've been going for about half an hour when my phone buzzes in my pocket.

I toss the device to Aaron, who answers the call on speaker. "What?!" he yells.

It's Cle's voice that comes over the line. "Commander."

Knowing she's keeping in touch with the medical team, I ask, "Cle, what is Knot's condition, and how are the rest of my guys?"

"Knot is critical, and the medical team doesn't have enough hands. They had to put off Bandaid's surgery to try and stabilize Knot. They ordered the plane to take off for Landstuhl shortly after the helo delivered Knot and Hawk to the airfield. I won't know anything else for a while."

"What have you got on the asshole that took Cass?"

"I don't have anything yet, but *you've* got

company coming. I deployed back-up to ground zero just after you left in the helo. Devil made it on the plane before takeoff, and Knot's other people are not too far behind you. They're bringing the four of your men that could stand on their own feet."

"Those idiots," I mumble, shaking my head.

Despite my words, I'd take four of my men in any condition over an army of others.

"Do you know where Crendall is?"

"Europe is as far as I can narrow it down."

"Keep looking. This is him. I know it. I just don't know who he's working with or how he's managed such a broad reach."

"Working for is a more likely scenario. Birdie was right about Crendall not having the financial backing for such an operation. If it is Crendall that took Cass, he's not calling the shots," she reports.

"Thanks, Cle. Stay on in case I need you."

"Yes, sir."

With Cle's report over, Aaron resumes giving verbal cues to go with his directional pointing. Our cross-city trek takes us to an industrial park at the Port of Muuga. It's about zero-two hundred when we drive through the open gates at the mouth of the port. I stop the van long enough to turn off the lights and proceed into the park slowly, using only the moonlight to see. As a precaution, Aaron alternates between his night vision and infrared scopes to scan the area for lookouts and traps.

A half-mile from the location of Warden's watch, I stop the van and kill the engine. The source of the homing signal indicates the truck is parked next to a hangar-type building near the harbor.

Hosfeld switches to his long-range NV scope and scans the hangar and neighboring buildings. He zeroes in on something and grabs his IR once again. "Got him. Dark truck. Engine's still warm."

The former marine raider passes me the scope, and I get my first good look at our target area. "He's not alone. I've got heat signatures from three other vehicles parked at the same building."

"Call Sadie, have her come in dark and stage here," I tell Aaron. Activating my radio, I call out to my only ground support, "Cle, what am I up against?"

Her voice comes through my earpiece loud and clear. "The SBIRS satellite isn't returning any signatures besides the vehicle engines. The IR can't penetrate the building shell. There's no way to know if or how many are inside."

Shit. "All right. Keep your eyes open, and let us know if you spot any movement."

"Yes, sir."

"Aaron, how far out is Sadie?"

"Twelve minutes."

Twelve minutes. Long enough to kill. Sufficient time to violate. Not long enough to come up with a Bulletproof plan to get my wife out. I'm at the end of my frayed nerves, the point where I lose my shit. That hasn't happened in a very long time. Seventeen years, to be exact.

Time slows to a torturous crawl, and I feel a shift in my focus. *I'm not going to let him do this again.* My eyes drift closed, and I do what I do best: work through all the ways things can go sideways. I treat this like any other mission.

The difference here is, though we always look to ensure each man comes home after doing his job, above all else, I have to make sure Cass makes it out.

Maybe Cass and our baby. Thinking again of the possibility of Cass being pregnant derails my attempt at calm logic. *With nine minutes until backup arrives and us flying completely blind, how the fuck am I supposed to do this?*

I fight to pull myself back in form and find that the only way to do so is by including Aaron in my thought process as a sounding board.

"The bastard that took Cass has to figure I know by now that she's gone. He'll also know that I won't be sitting on my ass. Based on the message he sent earlier, I've got a little over an hour left before I'm supposed to receive his instructions. My advantages are that I already know where he is, and, being early, he won't be ready for me."

"Why not shake him up a little?" Aaron suggests. "Who knows. He might let something slip."

Liking his idea, I pull out my phone, open the messaging app, and reply to the summons. *I want my wife, asshole.*

I keep the phone out, expecting a fast response, but I don't get one. While waiting for Crendall's reply, I get a notification of an incoming message from someone else, but I don't recognize the number.

An uneasy feeling settles in my gut, leading me to check the message.

The man that took your wife is dead. I have assumed control over her fate. Don't worry. You'll see her soon.

"Fuck!"

"What is it?" Hosfeld asks.

I turn the phone screen around to show him the message. He swears, and I slip out of the van's rear doors, needing to move. "Cle!"

"I'm here, Commander."

"We either have a new player or a change at the top. I'm sending you a number. See if you can learn anything about the owner."

With the players changing faster than we can keep up, my mind is splintering apart. I have lost my capacity for rational thought and have no desire to wait on my improvised team.

Aaron joins me at the back of the van and stops me before I take my first step toward the building.

With a hand on my chest and a menacing growl, he warns, "I will not let you fuck this up. Do you hear me? I will fucking knock your ass out and leave you tied up in the back of this damned van if I have to. That woman needs every chance we can give her if she's going to live to see the sunrise."

"Do you think I don't know that?!" I yell. "What if it was someone you loved? What if it was Sadie, huh? I know all about how Fish had to fight to keep you from jumping the gun and fucking things up in the Philippines, so don't preach to me."

"Stone."

A new voice over the radio cuts through the bloodlust thrumming in my ears. "Stone, I know better than anybody what it is to be in your shoes. You know it's true because your team was there to watch me break down," Hyper's calm voice says. He must have rejoined his wife in this new operation.

"I'm not going to try and talk you down, but I want you to take me through everything going on inside your head."

Aaron's hand is still on my chest, and I know he heard everything Hyper said.

"I'm… not exactly stable," I tell them both.

"Don't care. Talk me through it," Hyper demands.

"They're going to kill her if they haven't

already."

His reply is instant. "They'll keep her alive at least until you show up. What else?"

"I'm not leaving without her."

Again, no hesitation. "So don't. How do you make it happen?"

Only one thing comes to mind. "I make it so…"

Son of a bitch. I've just noticed that Aaron's hand is no longer on me, and I'm not facing the target anymore. "You're a sneaky bastard," I tell Hyper.

"Welcome back," he says.

"You manipulate Omen like this?"

"Not that I would ever admit to it. Now that your head's on straight again, you've got work to do."

"Yes, sir."

As if on cue, a base truck pulls up behind the embassy maintenance van. Sadie and Brock file out, followed by Fish, Wrench, Hawk, and Ink, who move slowly compared to the paramilitary operatives. I glare at the lieutenant, my objection stinging my lips at the irresponsibility of bringing compromised men to this fight. However, Fish's words halt the reprimand before it's delivered.

"Save it," he says, holding his hand up. "As long as we can walk, we'll help you get Cass back."

To show that I yield, I offer him my hand.

"Officially, I should hand your ass to you. Unofficially, I'm glad you're here."

"Always," he says, accepting my hand.

After acknowledging the other SEALs, everyone gathers around and looks to me for direction. Though I'm technically in command here, I don't have the luxury of intel or surveillance to set strategy or even position people for the best tactical advantage. Additionally, Warden's team isn't used to taking orders from someone other than Sadie or Warden himself, and the SEALs are operating at sixty percent at best.

Even so, I discern from the group of warriors an unfaltering determination. That, I can work with.

I take a moment to look each of them in the eye before saying anything. "I have no idea what's waiting inside that building. All I know is that my whole world is in there. While I'm grateful you're here to back me up, you need to understand something. I will not leave here without Cassidy. If they kill my wife before I can get to her, clear your asses out because I'll personally escort every last one of those bastards to hell."

Wisely, no one argues, so I continue with specifics. "Sadie, you and Aaron circle the building and look for a view inside. Lawson and I will check the vans for anything useful."

Wrench perks up and glances at the scope

held in Aaron's hand. "Van? Give me your scope," he says to Aaron. "Our shit was thrown into an old GMC van before we were gassed and our skulls were cracked."

The automobile expert takes the offered scope, lines it up, and focuses on the cars outside our target. "I'll be damned. That's them. If those guys haven't cleared our stuff out, we can get to it and be a hell of a lot more useful."

"Change of plans then. Wrench, I trust you can get in if it's locked?"

"No problem. Somebody, give me a knife."

Lawson hands one over, and Wrench grins. "Fuck yeah. I can get in."

"Then, let's move out."

Ink, being the least wounded among my men, teams up with the PMCs toward the left side of the building. The rest of us split off to hug the buildings lining the opposite side of the street. Considering my guys are injured, we make good time, but Warden's people still beat us there.

I press my back to the wall opposite the hangar and order the other team, "Make your way around. See if you can get a layout of the inside. Let me know if you spot Cass."

I receive an answering click and hold my position until I confirm zero activity around the vans. Besides the other team, I don't detect any heat signatures during an IR scan. "All right, Wrench. You're up."

He moves out front and leads the rest of us

across the dimly lit street. Wrench inspects both vans and gets to work on the rear doors of the one farthest from the building's main entrance. In less than two minutes, he has one of the back glass panels removed and the cargo doors opened.

We all press in and get a good look at the eight SEAL packs piled up in the back.

"Jackpot."

Wrench reaches inside to grab the closest pack, but I stop him with a hand on his arm. I'm sure I have the look of a crazed man when I say, "Delano, I wasn't fucking around earlier. I want you to load me up with enough explosives to level this building. I also want a dead man switch with a timer override and the ability to deactivate. I meant what I said. If Cass doesn't come out with me, no one comes out."

Wrench lays a hand on my forearm, and in his eyes, I see an unwavering respect, something that had been lost from his eyes at one time. He nods and says, "You're both going home with us, but I'll do what you want."

Each man retrieves his gear and quickly inventories what's there. Their guns and radios are accounted for, the assholes inside having not plundered the packs yet—another point for us in the luck column.

Once the team is wired in and geared up, I check in with Sadie. "What have you found, Phelps?"

"The windows are ten feet off the ground.

I used a pole camera to take some stills of the inside. I'm sending them to you now."

The four of us circle as I pull out my phone. The first picture confirms the building to be a hangar but for seaplanes. I hadn't realized how close the building was to the water's edge, but the plain hoist shows we're right on it.

The second picture shows an angled view of the inside front wall. This view shows four men seated around a table playing cards. Their clothes and skin tone indicate we're dealing with men of Arab descent. One more man, an older one, sits off to himself, checking a phone. I don't see Cass anywhere.

The final image shows the east wall, which features what appears to be a secure storage room constructed of reinforced CMU block with a poured concrete ceiling. That must be where they've got her stashed.

Going back through the pictures again, I clock the locations of all exits. Besides the main entrance in front, there's one to the left of the hangar doors and one in the middle of the western side wall.

"Cass has to be locked in the block room. She'll be safe from gunfire as long as she's in there. We'll need to strike hard and fast so they don't have time to pull her from the room."

"That's assuming she's in there alone," Sadie points out through the radio.

I don't like the possibility and what it

could mean for Cass. *Don't think about it. Your job, your only job, is to get her out.* I shake my head to clear it and say, "You're right. Hawk, you're the best shot. Take your rifle and set up somewhere near the launch ramp. I want you watching that storage room door. If anyone comes out other than Cass or approaches that door, you take them down."

Hawk nods, and I continue passing out assignments. "Sadie, where are you now?"

"We're positioned near the west entrance. Hawk will have to walk right by us."

"Okay. I want you monitoring the inside with your camera until Hawk is in place. Lawson and Hosfeld, be ready at the door. If it's locked, Ink can pick it. I'll send his tools and a radio for him with Hawk."

I hand my phone to Fish and issue the last of the orders. "I'm going in alone, but I want all of you ready to run at a moment's notice. If I say the word "wolf," rush in and fire with extreme prejudice. If I say "stone," fall back, and I mean fall back as far and fast as you can, or you'll be going to hell with the rest of us."

Now, I turn to Wrench. "I'm ready. Set me up."

The explosives expert, who'd been working while I spoke, drapes a strap to which a bomb has been attached around my neck. He then hands me the wired remote, pointing out the various functions.

"To arm the device, hold this button down for three seconds. Once you do that and squeeze the trigger, releasing the trigger will detonate the bomb in two seconds. To disarm, keep the trigger depressed and push the arming button. Hold them both for three seconds. Two beeps will signify a successful disarmament."

"What about a timer?"

"There is no timer. I'm not letting you play chicken with your life. I have a wireless remote. *When* your ass walks out of that building, I'll hand it to you should you still feel like blowing shit up."

"Good enough. Hawk, are you in position?"

He answers with a single radio click. "Aaron?"

"Ink picked the lock. We're ready."

It occurs to me to tell my men it's been a pleasure serving with them, but once again, Fish stops me. "You're not dying today, O'Reilly, so keep your mouth shut."

I don't agree or disagree with him. I offer a solemn nod and walk toward the front door. Just before reaching for the handle, I take a deep breath and let it out slowly. *I'm coming, Cass.*

BULLETPROOF

JO CHAMBLISS

CHAPTER 21

TIM

Over the three seconds it takes to arm the device, I flash back to several of my favorite moments with Cass from the last ten years. The flush of her cheeks after dashing through the rain in her wedding gown, her swearing sleepily the first time we met, and the way she shivers when I kiss the skin behind her right ear.

I'm not ready to lose her and refuse to live without her.

Imaging life without Cass fuels me with the last bit of determination needed to squeeze the trigger, activating the dead man switch. If she's gone from this world, all I have to do is let go to be with her again.

Now, I'm ready. The squeak of the aluminum and glass doors announces my arrival, and I rush inside the lobby, holding the device trigger out in front of me. The bomb, with all its flashing lights and yellow wires, stands out against the black of my borrowed uniform, ensuring any and all will recognize its existence and what it means.

Everyone inside reacts as expected to my

sudden entry, shoving away from the card table and holding up their weapons. "Stop!" I command. "Drop your weapons, or every one of you is a dead man."

I progress about fifteen feet inside the building and stop ten feet from the card table. The four younger men are on their feet and holding their weapons with twitchy fingers.

The older guy on his phone remains calmly seated and orders his men, in Arabic, to stand down. They lower their weapons to the table, and I further order them in their language to step back.

"Commander O'Reilly, you're early," the older man says. "I did not intend to invite you here until tomorrow night. I underestimated you."

"Clearly. Where's my wife?"

"She is here. And though her current accommodations would keep her safe from a stray bullet, I don't think she would survive a blast."

The man's confident demeanor pisses me off, but I have to keep my head. "I want to see her."

"That would be unwise. If we bring Dr. O'Reilly out, we introduce her to a potentially deadly situation, I think."

My chin lifts in challenge. "If you don't prove to me in the next thirty seconds that my wife is still alive, you and I will both die."

The man's smug face transforms into one of disgust. "You would end your life over a whore."

I chuckle darkly. "I would end yours over a speck of dirt."

"Very well." He commands one of his men in Arabic, "Rafi, collect the woman."

Also in Arabic, I warn Rafi, "If you touch her, you're dead where you stand."

I draw my pistol and aim, but only for show, knowing Hawk is the real threat to Rafi. The man walks over and opens the door slowly. Though I'm focusing on the men around the table, the entrance to the little room is well within my peripheral vision. Sighting motionless legs on the floor has my finger loosening its grip on the remote's trigger.

"Hold, Commander. That's not her," Hawk's calm voice says in my ear.

My finger tightens on the trigger again, but the thug at the block room door tenses. The man doesn't immediately see Cass and sticks his head inside the dark space. A metallic clang echoes in the hangar, and the man crumples to the ground like a ragdoll.

Cassidy steps out of the room, holding a metal folding chair in front of her like a shield. "Cass, get back!"

Responding to my voice, Cass whips her head around, and her eyes widen when she spots me. "Tim!"

"Get back inside and shut the door!"

Cass scrambles to obey my panicked order as I watch the men in the room. I listen to her struggle to move the large man blocking the door, holding my breath until the latch of the handle clicks into place.

"Satisfied?" the assumed leader asks.

Ignoring his question and playing my hunch, I begin my own interrogation, wishing Judge was here to analyze the leader's responses. "Who is Crendall to you?"

"An annoyance. One that, thankfully, I no longer have to endure. Crendall was a self-serving attention seeker. At one point, I thought him useful, but I wasted a camp full of my men thanks to his incompetence. Although, before his end, he helped rectify that."

Wasted a camp of his men… Understanding dawns as pieces begin to fall into place in my mind. *Crendall tailed us to the camp to rescue the doctor. He knew. He fucking knew all along.*

The cameraman didn't fuck up. He got cold feet and saved our lives. That explains *why* he was murdered, if not when. Maybe Crendall made an offer for this second attempt, and the cameraman refused. It all makes sense now. "My team was supposed to get slaughtered that night."

The Arab leader agrees. "You are a hard man to kill, Stone O'Reilly. And so is your wife."

A sinister laugh bubbles forth, and the

men behind the table share nervous looks. "You know, that wasn't my first nickname in the service."

The uneasy glances continue as though they're dealing with a madman. They are. Even the leader is shifting in his seat now.

"During basic training and for a while after, people avoided me because I was as likely to rip them to shreds as say hello. Over the years, the men I served with came to believe that I'd mellowed out, that I was steady as a rock."

My voice is menacing when I add, "The truth is, I'm still that first man. Ruthless, cunning, and bloodthirsty. So I guess maybe you should call me Wolf."

CASS

I pace the room in the darkness like a caged tiger. Tim is here, and he has a bomb strapped to his chest. Trapped in this room, I'm helpless to do anything for him. The only weapons in my arsenal are the metal folding chair, now sporting a head-sized dent, courtesy of the unconscious man lying outside the door, and a loose lightbulb.

Speaking of... now that the darkness is no longer an asset, I set up the chair where I think the fixture is and climb up to screw the bulb back in. Finding the right spot takes a second, but a moment later, the room is bathed in a blinding light again.

I shield my eyes until they've adjusted and

climb down again, readying my flimsy shield near the door. Looking around my prison, I shiver at seeing the drying pool of blood, knowing I'm still wearing a good bit of it.

The next excruciating moments are spent pacing the small confines of the room, hating that, beyond muffled voices, I can't make out what's going on outside that door.

My mind has no trouble, however, comprehending what it saw just a few minutes ago or replaying it in my head repeatedly. *Tim found me. Tim's out there facing off against four men with a damned bomb strapped to his chest.*

I'm simultaneously relieved, totally freaked out, and frustrated because there isn't a damned thing I can do to help him. Even if he hadn't ordered me back into this room, my only play would have been throwing the chair at somebody, which wouldn't have accomplished anything.

All I can do to help my husband is stay here and not become a distraction. Tim has a plan. I know it. He wouldn't have come in here without one. I stop pacing and get down on all fours to place my ear near the bottom of the door. I can make out voices from this position, but they're not speaking English, not even Tim.

I stand back up, not wanting to be caught off guard when something does finally happen. Suddenly, before I'm mentally prepared, I hear Tim yell, and I start to open the door and rush to his side. A bullet strikes the wall next to the door frame, the impact creating an explosion of block fragments shooting out in all directions. I pull the handle closed again to keep from becoming a casualty in the war that's breaking out beyond the safety of this room. After that first shot, gunfire erupts all over the building, and my heart clenches in my chest.

I could be losing him out there.

The staccato of gunfire seems to go on forever, with occasional shots pinging off the steel door. I sink back down to the floor and cover my ears, resigned and waiting for my inevitable end. When the door to my prison finally opens, I don't even look up to meet my death.

Instead of a bullet, I'm met with a familiar voice. "Come on, Cass. Let's get out of here."

Hawk? My face snaps up in shocked disbelief. "Hawk, what are you doing here? You're supposed to be on a hospital plane."

He reaches for my hand and smiles. "We weren't leaving you. I hope I didn't scare you too bad with that shot. I did it to chase you back inside where you'd be safe."

I'm pulled to my feet and follow Hawk out the door, not quite believing what I'm seeing. The man I knocked out with the chair is still unconscious and hog-tied on the floor. Three Arab men are dead, and the man who spoke to me is tied to a metal support on the wall.

A continued scan of the room finds that

Dillan's people and four SEALs came with Tim. Fish is on the phone, Ink stands with Sadie, Aaron, and Lawson next to the captive, and Wrench carefully removes the bomb from Tim's neck. I step in their direction, but Hawk grabs my hand, holding me in place.

"Just another minute. Wrench built that bomb, but he still needs to be careful removing it."

"I don't understand. Why is Tim wearing it at all?"

Hawk's eyes burn into mine for a long moment before he looks over at Tim and takes a deep breath. "If you didn't walk out with him, he wasn't planning on walking out at all."

Realizing what Hawk is telling me, I turn away from his profile, back to Tim, and find him staring at me. Our gazes lock onto one another and remain there while Wrench finishes disarming the device. As soon as the bomb is lifted off Tim's shoulders, Hawk releases me, and I run and dive into my husband's arms.

Tim catches me, wrapping my legs around his waist and holding me against his chest in a vice-like grip. After a moment, he pulls back just enough to pull my mouth to his.

I don't care that we're both wearing the blood of our friends and enemies. I'm just glad that we're both alive.

We're alive, but what about the others? I reluctantly pull my lips from Tim's. "Crendall shot Dillan and Devil. Are they still alive?"

Tim drops his forehead to mine. "Devil was lucky. His wound was mostly superficial. I don't know anything about Warden's condition."

Tim tilts his head as though listening intently to someone. A few moments pass with him in this state, and he sighs in relief. "Thanks, Cle."

He's still wearing his radio. "What does she say?"

"Cle reports that Warden is still considered critical but is stable. It looks like he's going to make it."

At the news, I tighten my arms around Tim's neck again. A taunting laugh from the terrorist mastermind has Tim turning around and my feet sliding from around his waist. The older Arab man is defeated, tied to a support post with his arms secured around the pole behind him.

"You American men are all so predictable and pathetic." He gestures to Dillan's people with his chin. "You let a woman lead you into battle. You're not men. And the rest of you, you'd start a war; you'd fight and die to earn the passing glance of a whore. That makes you weak and easy to control. The man might have been wrong about everything else, but on this, Crendall was right."

As the man continues to spew his venom, I shrug off Tim's restraining hand and take a few steps in the bastard's direction. When I'm eye to eye with him, he smiles. A rage-fueled right hook breaks his nose, wiping that smug grin off his face.

Not wanting to waste another second on this asshole, I turn back to Tim, but it's Sadie who catches our attention. "Commander, get your men back to base. We'll handle things here and be right behind you."

Aaron, Sadie, and Brock move to stand in front of the man with the broken nose, and no one argues or questions the group's plans or the fact that I see Brock holding Wrench's bomb behind his back.

Tim tips his chin to the operatives, turns to me, and grabs the hand that didn't just smash a guy's face in. He draws it to his mouth and brushes his lips over my knuckles. "Let's go home."

At the main entrance to the hangar, four armed and battered SEALs stand waiting. They walk outside ahead of us, Fish's limp catching my eye as much as Ink's eye being swollen shut does.

The sky is still black, and the air still painfully cold when we step outside. It's quiet. Eerily quiet. Anywhere else, I would have expected the chaos to have drawn a crowd of curious onlookers, even in an industrial area. Not here. I guess living in a place as dangerous as Tallinn, people would be more interested in protecting themselves than risking their lives to have a story to tell.

Tim leads our group away from the

harbor, the SEALs falling in step beside us. We move slowly in the darkness in consideration of the injured men. I have no idea where we're going, but as long as it's away from here, I don't care.

We've walked maybe a quarter of a mile up a dark street with the occasional streetlight illuminating our path. We've been quiet up to this point, but Fish breaks the silence when he asks, "What do you think they're doing back there?"

Tim's eyes remain forward as he answers, "I don't know, and for once, I don't care. Whatever they're doing, they didn't want us to see, and I'm perfectly ok with that."

Satisfied with Tim's answer and likely agreeing with it, the men go quiet again. I scan up and down the line of warfighters, stunned that they could be so calm. Being a civilian and unused to this kind of action, I'm hyped up and feel like running laps to burn off this excess energy. Tim must notice as he keeps a firm grip on my hand.

We walk a few yards more, and a massive explosion lights up the night behind us. My head whips around at the sound, though Tim ensures my feet never stop moving. Glass shatters, and flames lick the sky, but the group of SEALs acts as though they don't even notice.

Two seconds after the blast, a rush of wind meets the group, but no one slows down. The men keep marching forward as a building burns down behind them, a building with, I'm guessing, five bodies in it.

CHAPTER 22

CASS

Our group continues down the dark street until reaching a mismatched pair of vehicles parked about half a mile away from the burning building. I recognize one as the embassy van we used to rescue Tim's men. The six of us climb inside and drive back toward the city without anyone breathing a word about the explosion.

Half an hour later, security ushers us through the embassy gate, and we continue until we parked next to the building where we did all our planning. We exit the van, and Tim pulls me toward the entrance.

Tension bleeds from Tim's every pore, and he doesn't stop moving until we're inside the suite adjacent to the conference room we used earlier. The door is shut and locked, and I'm picked up and placed on the kitchen counter.

Tim moves to stand at the sink, bending forward to rest his hands on the marble top and breathing heavily. I sit still, giving him a moment to decompress. He's just had his world rocked for the fifth time in the span of two months.

Gradually, his shoulders relax, though his

head stays bowed. I hop down from the counter when Tim still hasn't moved a minute later. I grab his arms, forcing him to face me. Only then does he finally look me in the eye, and his eyes are haunted.

I push up on my toes and brush my lips against his. A new emotion washes over his face in equal parts with the fear still there. Passion. Tim wraps a hand around my neck one second before his lips crash onto mine.

The hunger and rage in his kiss take my breath away until I notice the tremble in his hands. Then, his anguish makes itself known. My courageous and mighty husband falls to his knees, wrapping his arms around me and pressing his face to my middle.

His powerful body shakes, crushed by the weight of his fear from nearly losing me in Africa and from the meat grinder we just went through. Seeing him like this, I can't hold back my sobs and bend to hold him just as tight.

When the worst of the tremors subside, I sink to the floor between his knees and take Tim's face in my hands. There are no words I could say to ease his agony. However, I can remind him that we won and are still alive when the ones who tried to destroy us are not.

I unclip his body armor and shove it off him. Next, I move on to his utility belt, which falls to the floor when I release the latch. I pull his shirt from his pants, and Tim lifts his arms for me to take it off completely. It's added to the growing pile of equipment, and then I bend and kiss my way up his stomach.

My tears drop onto Tim's chest as I skim my lips along his collar. My emotions overwhelm me for a moment, and I drop my head to his shoulder. Using the barest of touches, I run my fingers down the chain of my husband's dog tags.

A warm hand lifts to my lower back, pressing us tightly together. Another hand finds the back of my head, holding me in place. Tim's smooth, warm skin grounds me, bringing me back from the edge, and then I'm wrestling out of his grip.

My exploration of his solid body resumes, my lips teasing their way back down and across his chest. I reach a nipple, flicking it a few times with my tongue. Tim sighs and then shudders when I do the same thing on his other side, and that's all it takes to snap him out of his zombie-like state.

Impatient hands lift me to my knees and grab at my clothes, first untucking and then pulling off my shirt. My bra is gone two seconds later. Tim's forceful movements make my breasts jiggle in front of his face, and he groans.

He throws an arm around my waist and stands up while bending me over. Even as Tim walks us into the attached bedroom, his head is bent to suck a nipple into his mouth.

The backs of my legs contact the mattress,

and I try to work out how to get us both naked. We're both bare from the waist up but are similarly dressed in cargo pants and boots. The only difference is that mine are safari-appropriate, and Tim's are tactical black. In both cases, they're not quick or easy to remove.

Tim sets me on my feet, and I reach down to unlace my boots. That isn't what my husband had in mind, apparently. He buries his hand in my hair, fisting tightly to hold me in place while he plunders my mouth. Not wasting any time, I reach for his fly and free his rock-hard cock. *Now, all I've got to do is get rid of our damned boots.*

Tim isn't interested in waiting. Showing even more impatience than I've displayed, he opens my belt, yanking it free from the loops. His next move is to wrench my pants and panties down in one violent motion.

My pants are left around my knees, not leaving much room to work with. I reach out to take hold of his shaft but end up with a handful of air instead. I'm spun around, and Tim drops to sit on the edge of the bed, pulling me down onto his lap and impaling me on his engorged dick.

My legs are bound in a useless tangle, so he uses his strong arms to piston me up and down as he pleases. And, oh god, does it please.

His movements are so out of control that I can only hold onto his wrists as he jackhammers me up and down. My hands keep losing their grip, and without warning, Tim picks me up and turns, throwing me on the bed on my back. My pants are pulled down to the tops of my boots, and he jumps on top of me.

My feet are still trapped together, but I can open my hips just wide enough for him to fit. Tim shoves into me again and again, still with his pants around his hips. The tough fabric is abrasive against the sensitive skin of my inner thighs, but I don't care. I might regret it later, but right now, all I feel is him moving inside me.

Tim holds his upper body off my chest so his gaze can burn into me, and he speaks for the first time since arriving at the embassy. "You risked your life to care for my men, and someone took you because of it. I'm so damned angry and proud of you at the same time. You're the most infuriating, brave, and selfless woman I've ever known. I won't put you in a cage, but you're done putting your life on the line for others. My heart can't take it anymore. Do I make myself clear?"

The glorious, punishing thrusts never slowed while handing down his ruling. Tim's timing isn't fair, but I'm too lost in the moment to care. Three-years-ago-me would object to his attitude and demands, but today-me has had enough of this shit. I figure I've put in my time and have paid dearly for it. From now on, I'll do what I can from the safety of home.

"Yes, sir," I moan.

Tim halts his thrusting and pulls back to give me a sideways, skeptical look. "No bullshit?"

I shake my head and grab his belt to pull him all the way inside me again. "No bullshit, but I have a few demands of my own. Well, one, actually. I'd better never see nor hear of you strapping another live bomb to your chest again, or I will beat the shit out of you."

Tim grins, finally rid of the haunted look. The smile highlights the lines around his eyes that make him look so distinguished and so mine. "Yes, ma'am. Anything else?"

"Yes. As you were."

My husband lowers his head and licks the seam of my lips while resuming his brutal claim of my body. Tim intensifies the assault on my senses by snaking a hand around me and down to my ass. Lifting that hip slightly has the hard ridge of his erection hitting just the right spot to send me sailing into oblivion. I call out hoarsely through my climax, and Tim drops my hip, doubling his efforts to reach his release.

I feel it, the moment he comes. Tim goes stiff in my arms and groans my name through clenched teeth. Tim drops his forehead to mine and breathes heavily during his fall back to Earth.

He rolls us to the side and draws me to him, resting my head over his pounding heart. "I love you, Cassidy O'Reilly. Don't ever make me walk through this world without you."

"I won't," I promise in a whisper, not even caring that I don't wield that kind of control over my life.

TIM

The cabin lights in Warden's jet are dim, but I don't need light to see that even after all these years and these three hellish days, Cass is still a beautiful treasure and the best thing in my life. She's filthy, covered in blood, and bruised all over, but she's alive.

Cass rests on my lap, tucked against my chest, fast asleep. It's a wonder that we're not all passed out, but some of us just can't shut down. Since I'm one of them, it would have made more sense for Cass to nap in her own plush leather seat, but I needed to have her this close, to be touching her.

We're about an hour into our flight to Landstuhl with an hour and a half to go. I can't see my watch, but I figure it's just before zero four hundred.

Our departure from Amari Air Base was swift. Every person in our group was anxious to get to Germany to check on our people. By the time Cass and I reemerged from the suite at the embassy, Warden's crew had packed up and loaded all their equipment. My men rested with large cups of coffee and even larger ice packs.

Not long after the jet took off and reached cruising altitude, I opened my arms, and Cass came to me willingly. She was exhausted, and I soothed her to sleep, stroking my fingers up and down her arms and back. Now, she's breathing softly against my neck with one of my arms around her waist and the other draped over her thighs. Damn, but she feels good.

I press my nose into her hair, breathing her in, and press a kiss there. Then I lean back to rest against the seat, thinking this has to be the most relaxed I've been since Bishop was killed.

Across the walkway, Sadie, usually always on the move, sits still as a statue, staring out the small window beside her seat. Though she hasn't said much since taking off, her closed expression means she has a lot on her mind. Warden has placed a lot of trust on her shoulders over the years. She's his top operative and the most capable team leader in all of Knot Corp.

With Warden's condition being a big question mark, she's undoubtedly wondering about her future. Regardless of what happens to Warden, I doubt the paramilitary side of Knot Corp is in danger of shutting down, but if Knot can't come back, who knows what the company's future will look like?

I'm holding out hope for the man, though. Dillan Knot is my best friend, and I'm not ready to give him up yet. Besides, I'm looking forward to dishing out a little payback for all his ass-kicking after I was shot to hell and back. There's no way he's getting out of what he's got coming.

Behind Sadie, Aaron watches over the whole group, though he seems to spare a few more glances for his female teammate than his male peer. I know all of Knot's people respect the force that is Sadie Phelps, but I sense a little more than mutual respect coming from former Marine Raider Aaron Hosfeld.

After hearing the reports from Sadie's rescue mission in the Philippines and since joining up with them in Estonia, I've noticed how Aaron looks at her. That man would give his life so that not a hair on Sadie's head comes to harm. He seems confident that Sadie doesn't know how he feels. He has no idea that Warden does.

My focus shifts to the younger of the three operatives. Brock Lawson and I have been through a lot together in a very short time, but I haven't learned a thing about the man except that he's solid. He would have made a good SEAL. For all I know, he was a SEAL, just not on Team Two.

I make a mental note to get to know the man once we land in Germany and have had a chance to catch our breath and check in with our injured.

The plane must fly through a cloud as the craft shimmies briefly. Cass shifts, and her left hand works under my shirt. Within seconds, her breathing evens out again, her occasional soft snore reminding me that she's safe and in my arms.

I glance down to where her hand lies against my stomach. Her skin, usually soft and smooth, is scuffed and scratched from her second fight and escape from Gilley in Africa. Cass was kidnapped and beaten twice in two days, not to mention shot.

God, I'm having to refer to her kidnaps by number now. And for each one, I swear, I lost about ten years of my life.

So much has happened since leaving that god-forsaken jungle. It's hard to believe it's been less than forty-eight hours since we left Nairobi. Considering all my wife has been through, I'm amazed she could walk onto this plane under her own strength.

Throughout this harrowing ordeal, I've learned how incredibly resilient my wife is, far beyond what I realized or gave her credit for. In all my years as an active SEAL, she had to watch me march off hundreds of times without a guarantee that I would come back. Cass never once complained, never let on that she was scared about me leaving.

I've only spent three short days on the other side of the coin and lost my mind. Now that I've experienced firsthand what it was like for her all these years, I attribute the success of our marriage to Cassidy O'Reilly's indomitable spirit.

Since we're both walking away from this nightmare alive, I vow to myself that I'll spend the rest of my life making it up to her. My career is important to me, but not more important than my wife. None of my medals or rank would matter if I'd lost her. Nothing at all would matter.

I know I'm not to blame for her life being in danger, but if I could, I'd go back in time and leave the Navy if it meant erasing what happened. If I had any idea that my job would put her at risk in the future, I'd resign today. She's earned it and would be worth it.

When I do retire, I know the men I'd like to see carry the torch forward. My eyes draw upward, landing on the sleeping faces of my men. Men that I've fought with, fought for. Men who have become friends and family. Men that I love as though they were my brothers... or sons.

Men who will one day take my place and be responsible for the safety of our country and our children's future.

I lift my hand from Cass's hip to rest on her belly. She's carrying my baby. I don't know how I know it, but I know it as surely as I know my name. I'm simultaneously elated and terrified about becoming a father.

My greatest fear is that my child will one day face the demons I've been fighting back my whole life. *And that's why you'll keep doing your job.*

As if my worry is affecting her, Cass stirs and wraps her arm tighter around my waist, burrowing deeper into my side.

I brush a stray hair behind her ear and glance again at the men and woman on the plane. Lieutenant Hill is now awake. He's surveying the three sleeping SEALs and probably worrying about the badly injured men being treated in Germany. He and I share that same worry.

Their lives and livelihoods are most

important, but unlike most other squads, I know these men would be devastated if tonight's attack ended their time on this team. They're a family; none want to be knocked out of active duty and leave their guys vulnerable.

That's a worry for another day, and I don't want to borrow trouble. All we should be focusing on now is getting to our teammates and doing what needs to be done to get everyone home safe to their families.

Not me, though. I'm holding my family in my arms.

Comforted by the warmth of Cass's body, I close my eyes for the rest of the flight, hoping for good news when we land.

EPILOGUE

CASS

Sexy, wet kisses on my neck draw me out of a comfortable sleep long before I'm ready. I groan into the darkness, half in invitation, half in protest, but I don't get my way in either case. Tim lifts me off his lap and plants me in the next seat over, buckling my belt when all I do is close my eyes again.

Lights come on in the cabin, making me groan again. This time, I open my eyes and search out a window. The view outside is of darkness. *How long is this damned night going to last?* I swear I've lived three lifetimes since the sun went down. *And three people nearly lost their lives. One might still.* That thought wakes me right up and reminds me where we're going.

The jet glides down, landing perfectly at yet another airport in another country. At least since Estonia is in the European Union, we don't have to worry about customs. We have a lot of *extra* going on in this plane.

The sleek, comfortable jet taxies to the far side of the grounds to a row of small craft hangars. Until now, I hadn't stopped to appreciate the ease with which we've made our mad dashes around the world since leaving Africa. And until now, I'd never thought much about the prestige afforded to CEO Dillan Knot.

This trip has opened my eyes. Even more so when the jet door opens, and we're met on the tarmac by two armored SUVs. And these aren't hired trucks. The drivers greeting Sadie and Aaron are more of Dillan's people.

Within seconds of landing in the darkness of early morning, our whole group is being rushed across the city to Landstuhl Hospital in Rhineland-Palatinate, a US military and coalition medical facility.

We're all starving and badly in need of showers and clean clothes, but only the thought of getting to our friends seems to hold anyone's interest. Sitting next to Tim in the middle seat of the SUV, I ask, "What do we know about Dillan's condition?"

"The only update we've gotten is that he survived the flight and surgery. Trish was called sometime during the night and is on her way."

The ride to the military hospital is brief, and we're let out at the main entrance to go inside and find our friends. Despite the late or early hour, depending on how you look at it, our group is greeted by three banged-up and bandaged SEALs.

Devil and Skin stand when we walk in, albeit slowly and with much effort on Devil's part. I don't know how Devil managed to get on his feet at all. He's wearing a boot on his left foot, a cast on his right arm, and his left arm is in a sling.

Skin looks a little better, but to a passerby, the two black eyes, sling, and various lacerations and contusions would still be shocking. Judge looks the best of the three despite receiving the most severe injury. He's currently seated in a wheelchair, something I'm sure is only temporary while the anesthesia wears off. His femur would have been surgically repaired, and though very sore, he should be good to go without walking assistance.

I bite my tongue against scolding them for not being somewhere they can rest. Fish and the others, however, gently shove them back into their chairs, Skin a waiting room seat, and Devil, his wheelchair. "How's Bandaid?" I ask the group.

"He's awake," Devil answers. "Or he was. There was no damage to his eye, though I think something happened to his head."

Oh god, no. "What?! What happened?"

Judge smiles. "I think someone swapped his brain for Skin's. After waking up, the first thing out of his mouth was, '*Charli's going to have to find somewhere else to sit for a while.*' It was a little garbled, but that was the gist of it."

My brief panic fades, and a laugh bubbles out of me. The others react similarly, though trying to cover their laughter with coughs. I slump back against Tim, thankful Bandaid will be okay.

Skin stands back up and announces, "Come on, we'll take you back. There's decent coffee and something to eat."

In a waiting room off the ICU, our group spreads out, sipping hot coffee and munching on fruits and pastries Dillan's people arranged at some point. In a short time, I've torn through two muffins and two cups of juice and now sit with my head leaning against Tim's shoulder.

The sun is just rising in the sky, and I'm nodding off when a doctor walks into the waiting room. He's an older man and walks right up to my husband as if he knows him.

"Commander, I have good news for you. You're going to be stuck with the jackhammer a while longer."

"Jackhammer?" I ask.

The older doctor reaches up to rub his chin and laughs. "I patched Knot up a few times while he was in the service. Let's just say a man like that leaves an impression. I'd also say the descriptor fits."

"Yeah, I guess it does."

The doctor shifts his focus to Sadie as if they're also familiar. "I can't let you back yet since I've still got him in the ICU recovery. Go get some sleep and come back later today. You can see him then."

The doctor gestures to Judge, Skin, and Devil. "And take these guys with you. They could use some sleep too but won't listen to me."

Fish stands and grabs the handles of Devil's wheelchair, and the man doesn't argue. Hawk moves behind Judge's chair, and Tim tugs my hand toward the exit.

Half an hour later, I'm standing under a stream of hot water in temporary quarters on the military base. Clean clothes and a clean bed wait for me, but I'm not enthused about burrowing under the covers, mostly because Tim deposited me here and left with a kiss but no explanation.

I shouldn't be surprised. He's still working, which means a lot of debriefings for the official nature of his mission. An ambassador was killed. There will be a lot of questions asked, and not just by the military. Politicians will be involved this time, but I'm not worried about any blame falling on Tim or his men.

Of course, there's also the fallout from the explosion, for which this group did not hang around. I wonder how Sadie's crew will explain that. I imagine valuable evidence was destroyed in the blast.

Ultimately, it's not my place to worry about such things. There might not be anything to worry about anyway. I know Sadie. She's smart and wouldn't do anything to jeopardize Knot Corp., a company that's a significant part of her life.

What I do worry about is the ambassador's family. They did nothing to deserve the grief that's coming. The diplomat and maybe husband, father, or grandfather was caught up in this sick revenge game and killed without remorse. That shouldn't have happened.

The fatalities that give me no pause were of that damned reporter, the man who orchestrated all this, and all the assholes with him. Had I been given the opportunity, I probably would have volunteered to detonate that bomb myself. So would Tim. I figure that's why Sadie and the others sent us away.

I'm not worried in any case. Questions, I can deal with. Sore muscles, I can handle. Encouraging Trish when she arrives, in my wheelhouse. I can handle anything that's coming because Tim and I survived. Now that it's all over, I want, more than anything, for Tim to be here with me, but he's not.

I'm no wilting flower that needs a man to hold her hand, but this wasn't just a mission I was waiting for him to come home from. This was a nightmare we experienced together that nearly saw us torn apart several times. My emotions are all over the place, and I've just survived the fight of my life versus the darkness that Tim has been warring against his whole career.

Squeezing some conditioner in my hand, I work the cream through my hair and sigh. I concede that regardless of my involvement, military persuasion requires official debriefs and follow-up. From day one with Tim, I've known what I was signing up for being in a relationship with a career military man. For the most part, I've always been patient and forgiving when the Navy called Tim away, and I will be now.

I hope he's able to come back to me soon.

My head ducks under the spray one last time, rinsing off the conditioner and any remnants of soap from my body. Finally, and fully clean, I reach to turn the water off and squeeze the excess water from my long hair.

My towel is draped over the shower curtain rod, which I grab and wrap around me while still cocooned in the warmth of the shower stall.

I pull the curtain back to step out of the tub and jump when I spot Tim sitting on the closed lid of the toilet, elbows resting on his knees.

He's still dressed from the fight and looking down at a bag in his hands. "Tim?"

He looks up with weary eyes, and I'm worried he's here with bad news. *Please don't be that Dillan took a surprise turn.*

"What is it? What's wrong?"

Tim reaches into the bag and pulls out a pregnancy test kit.

TWO DAYS LATER

TIM

Icy wind pierces my coat with each step that carries me up the brick walkway. Though this mission is one I happily volunteered for, it has taken me from my pregnant wife, who I left bundled up warm in a hotel in Frederick, Maryland.

While I wish Warden could be here with me, this mission was too important to wait for his ass to heal. I reach for the doorbell, knowing I'm expected, and thundering steps rush to open the door. The ornate panel is thrown open, and Jackson yells, "Stone!"

Jackson Stoddard launches himself at me. After a long hug, I pull back to study the face of the boy, realizing he's more man than kid now. His grandparents appear through the doorway, welcoming me into their home.

They were the first call I made after landing in Norfolk. I didn't want to update Jackson over the phone, so I worked out this visit with them. I settle in the comfortable living room with Jackson and his grandfather as Lucy's mother volunteers to get coffee.

Just now realizing someone's missing, Jackson asks, "Where's Warden?"

"He's… in Germany."

Pausing to take a deep breath, I dive right in. "Jackson, you were right. Your father was murdered."

The young man doesn't speak. The only audible sound in the room is the click of his throat. His grandfather reaches over to place a hand on his shoulder. I can't tell him everything, but he'll learn enough today to have closure. "The men responsible are dead."

"Who was it?" he demands.

"Someone that hurt a lot of people a long time ago."

Jackson accepts the information but struggles as if he doesn't know what to do with it. His eyes are a mix of anger, relief, grief, and a little what-the-hell-do-I-do-now? Eyes glittering with tears, he asks. "Why my dad? And don't shut me out. I know *you* know."

"It wasn't just your dad. These people planned to kill Warden and me as well."

At his wide eyes, I add, "Warden was shot. He's in the hospital."

"Is he going to be ok?"

"I hope so."

"He will be," the boy declares. Jackson squares his shoulders, and I glimpse the strength and determination that will shape the man he's becoming. He's never looked more like his father than he does now.

"My dad's sea burial will wait until Warden can be there. That's the way he would want it."

"Yes, sir."

Bishop would be so damn proud.

TEN MONTHS LATER

Little Cora sleeps on my chest while I lie on a lounge chair under a big umbrella. Right next to me, Warden is kicked back on another lounger, drinking a beer, not interested in participating in the flurry of activity going on around us.

Today is the Fourth of July, and our big, blended family is hanging out together on a base beach in Norfolk to watch the fireworks later in the day.

Several Wendigo men, Aaron Hosfeld, and Brock Lawson are playing football with Warden's son. Devil and his son are fishing from the end of the sea wall away from the swimmers.

Wrench stands in the water beside Everly, holding his six-month-old son. Bandaid hovers near Charli, who looks like she's about to pop. Mira hangs out in the water with Dallas, Willa, Rory, and the other Wendigo wives while Skin watches over his wife and newborn daughter. Fish's adopted daughter, Ari, builds sandcastles with her little brother and Devil's daughter.

Cass and Trish are also in the water but only occasionally join in the conversation with the other women. They get along great, but those two are preoccupied. Fairly often, their eyes travel our way. Cass, because this is our first social gathering since Cora was born, and Trish, because she's keeping a close eye on Warden.

Roaring laughter from the football game calls my attention from my beautiful wife in time to see Warden's teenage son execute a fierce tackle on Lawson. Warden laughs but winces, still sore from his most recent surgery.

"Shit, that hurts," he grumbles as he reaches back to rub the spot.

"That kid of yours is going to be one hell of a cornerback. I bet he'll have the pick of any D1 school he wants."

"Yeah. I'm just glad I'll be around to see it."

I reach over and squeeze my friend's shoulder. "Me too, asshole. Me too."

Even after surviving the gunshot that almost paralyzed him, Warden developed complications from an infection. We almost lost him a second time because of it. He was in the hospital and a rehab center for months. Because of the infection, the doctors had to put off the multiple corrective surgeries needed to fix the damage from the bullet.

This most recent surgery is supposed to be the last one. That was two weeks ago, and like Cass, this is Warden's first big excursion out.

He's still heavily involved in his company, just not in person. And though Warden likely won't be capable of field work again, he'll eventually get back to the point where he can recover some of the strength he's lost.

I'm especially glad for that. I still owe him for all that ass-kicking he gave me after I was shot. For now, I'll leave him alone.

"It'll get better," I tell my old friend.

"I guess you would know," he replies.

Trish looks up from the water again,

something she does a lot after almost losing her husband in Estonia. Cora shifts in her sleep, and I bend to kiss her downy head. A slight tug in my chest reminds me of the bullets that tore through me little more than a year ago. "Yeah, I guess I do."

The two of us go quiet again, watching the men and women we've worked and fought so closely with for so much of our lives.

"You know," Warden muses. "We've both come pretty close to making widows out of our wives in the past year. When are we going to give up this fight and just be husbands and fathers?"

I look out over my men, their families, and my sleeping daughter. "I guess when someone comes along that can protect them better than us."

"Yeah, that's what I thought."

Warden's phone rings, making Cora jump. He looks down at his screen and shakes his head. "So much for thinking I'd have a day off."

I stand up with Cora to give the defense CEO some privacy and walk down to join my wife, grabbing Cora's sun hat on the way down.

The water feels good. Almost as good as Cass's hand sliding up my back when I've reached her in the knee-deep water. Having given birth just four weeks ago, that's as far as she can go into the ocean.

"Give me that baby," Trish demands as she inches closer. The Caribbean-born woman squeals and coos when Cora opens her eyes. "You have a touch of baby fever," Cass teases.

"Please. My kids are all in that broody teenager phase. I can enjoy a baby without wanting to go through all that again."

She touches her nose to Cora's and says in baby talk, "Isn't that right, Precious?"

With my hands now free, I snake them across and around Cass's soft waist, turning us so my back is to our crew. Cass drops her forehead to my shoulder, and I murmur against her ear. "And what about you, mama? Are you ready to make another one?"

Cass laughs. "She's not even a month old yet."

"So I should wait and ask again next week?"

She pulls back, smacks my arm, and gives me a sly smile. "How about this? The birth control shot I'm getting on Monday will wear off in three months. Then it all comes down to whether you've still got it or not."

I grab her hand on my chest and pin it behind her back. My mouth goes to her neck, nibbling and teasing my way up to her ear. I'm about to whisper what it is I've still got when Trish's shrill laughter erupts behind me.

"I'm sorry, baby girl. Those don't work anymore. Your mama's do, though."

Releasing Cass, I pull her upright as Trish reaches us. "This baby's hungry and attempting to work a dry system."

Sure enough, Cora is rooting around Trish's chest. Cass takes our daughter and heads for the beach, and I can't take my eyes off them.

"Being a dad looks good on you, Tim," Trish says, patting me on the back before searching out her husband again.

"Yeah."

Though my reply was simple, my feelings are anything but.

I fell in love with Cass the first time I saw her. I never thought anything else would ever come close to how that felt. That all changed when my daughter was born.

Trish and I stare up at the beach in silence, me watching Cass as she sets up a breastfeeding cover and Trish watching her husband. Sadie, Brock, and Aaron approach Warden, pulling my eyes from Cass and Cora, and beside me, Trish sighs. "Well, it lasted longer than I thought."

Her words need no explanation. I'm well versed in this life we've chosen. I'm just glad we're all still around to live it.

THE END

Thank you for coming on this journey with me. If you haven't had enough adventure yet, check out the next series featuring Knot, Sadie, Aaron, Brock, and a host of other private military contractors.

To connect with Jo, check out her socials
www.jochambliss.com
Instagram @authorjochambliss
Tiktok @jochambliss
Facebook @jochamblissbooks
Facebook fan group, Jo's Blissaholics

Jo Chambliss Books

Ranger Mine series (read in order)
Remember Me - Omen & Sam
Forget Me - Squid & Erin
Lose Me - Shark & Ava
Find Me - Hyper & Cle

Waterproof Navy SEALs
(can be read in any order)
Shatterproof - Fish & Willa
Flameproof - Devil & Rory
Crashproof - Bandaid & Charli
Blastproof - Wrench & Everly
Soundproof - Hawk & Cailyn
Fadeproof - Ink & Dallas
Escapeproof - Judge & Iyla
Foolproof - Skin & Mira
Bulletproof - O'Reilly & Cass

Knot PMCs
Knot Guilty
Knot Innocent
Coming Soon… Fail Me Knot

ACKNOWLEDGEMENTS

Rose, thank you for these years that you've put into this new dream of mine. I would not have made it this far without you. I wish you the best in your retirement, but don't think for one minute that this is goodbye.

To my new editor, Audrey, thanks for taking on the role of Jo wrangler. I hope I haven't scared you away with this first project.

JO CHAMBLISS

ABOUT THE AUTHOR

Jo is a big nerd who is married to an even bigger nerd and has two great nerdy kids. ~~And a recent addition of an elitist cat who is convinced he's better than all of them.~~ A kitten has been added to the mix and has humbled the first cat somewhat.

When she's not designing custom house plans, Jo is dreaming up battles and loves that can provide a temporary escape from this world's insanity.

BULLETPROOF

Getting shot several times can teach a man a lot
himself... if he survives.

Commander Timothy "Stone" O'Reilly did survive a
wants more from this life than a successful care
happy marriage to the beautiful Dr. Cassidy O'Re
wants a family. Nearly losing Tim has made Cass f
same way, so the two decide it's time to make a ba

With Tim recovered enough to return to his men, li
good and about to get better with the thou
becoming a father. That is until a close friend and
SEAL teammate ends up dead under suspicious conc

No one knows why Bishop was targeted until the
decides to play a game with the two remaining me
of the long-time trio, Commander O'Reilly and CEC
"Warden" Knot.

Invoking the name of a SEAL that died seventeen
ago, Bishop's killer uses his vast reach to cast all o
world into chaos before making his final move.

Tim is the target on a chess board full of power
determined to destroy him. And if the enemy can't
Stone O'Reilly, they'll gladly start picking off th
important people in the commander's life.

No one is safe.

jochambliss.com

ISBN 978-1-0881-0
9 781088 105276